The Least

" Insomuch as Ye Have Done it Unto One of

The Least

of These My Brethren, Ye Have Done it Unto Me."
Matthew 25:40

Coleen Mattingly Bay

Blue Pine Press LLC

Blue Pine Press LLC
894 S 300 W
Brigham City, Utah 84302

ISBN: 978-1-387-42211-1

To my family.
Please forgive me if I ever made you feel like one of the least—
because you're the most important part of my life.
I love you.

Acknowledgements

I'd be ungrateful if I didn't give special thanks to my critique group, Elizabeth, Jason, and Julia, and my beta readers, Annette and Angela, for their excellent suggestions. It must have been very boring after the first read, yet you persisted.

Thank you from the bottom of my heart to my husband, Dave, who patiently taught me how to use the computer, and formatted repeatedly for me.

Chapter One

Jennifer shifted the last paper from her desk to the file of corrected papers and straightened the desks and chairs as she walked toward the door to go home. She stopped and looked at Jay Borky's desk. Unlike all the others, Jay's chair rested neatly tucked under his desk. He had missed school today, and remembering the trauma that had caused Jay to miss school three months ago, Jennifer felt uneasiness consume her.

She looked up his address and decided to make a personal visit to his home. When she got out of the car at the address, her heart pounded as she lightly ran her fingers along the plastic yellow "Police line—Do Not Cross" ribbon wrapped across the entrance to the dark and blackened house.

Feeling frantic to know what had happened, she rang the bell of the next-door neighbor. There was a sign by the door that read: **Johnson Family est. 1965**.

"I am Jay Borky's second grade teacher," she explained. "He wasn't at school today and I was concerned. May I ask what happened at the Borky home?"

Mr. Johnson looked down at his shoes and gravely said, "You'd better come in, this will take some explaining."

From the look on his face, she expected him to tell her the whole family had died in a fire.

"Were you aware Mr. Borky committed suicide three months ago?" he asked.

"Yes. I've been concerned about Jay."

"Jay was a good boy—quite mature for his age." Mr. Johnson continued, "I don't know if he understood all about his father's death, but he had to know something was terribly wrong because his mother spent a lot of time out on the front porch drinking and screaming at the kids if she wasn't passed out cold. Quite a few times the children came over to our house and we fed them."

"Was?" Jennifer repeated asking for clarification.

"Was what?"

"You said Jay *was* a good boy."

There was a long silence. The wife picked up the conversation. "Last night after the children went to sleep, Mrs. Borky poured gasoline on them and lit the children on fire."

"Oh, heaven help me!" Jennifer whispered. Her throat constricted, her stomach lurched, and she feared she would faint. *How could a mother do such a horrible thing?* She longed to take Jay into her arms and hold him. She wanted to look once more into his large deep-brown eyes that gleamed with inquisitiveness. Choking the words out, she asked, "Did any of the children survive?"

"Two of them left on stretchers with white sheets over their faces. The other two left in an ambulance with paramedics working on them. We don't know which two were dead or which two were alive. The police wouldn't let anyone near the place, and they handcuffed Mrs. Borky and hauled her off in the police car."

"I'm sorry to have taken so much of your time," Jennifer apologized between gasps for air—the tightness in her chest hardly allowed her to breathe. "But I want you to know I appreciate you giving me the information." Jennifer left and rushed to her car. She pulled the car around the corner and finding it difficult to see through her tears, she pulled to the side of the road. She didn't attempt to control her heaving sobs.

Drained of all strength, Jennifer's tears ran dry as she sat in her car until dark. Her mind would not rest; she had to know if Jay was still alive. Where was he? What could she do to comfort him? After running every scenario through her mind, she realized the most likely place a burned child would be was the University Burn Center. She drove to the hospital. When she arrived, she got directions to the burn center and went directly to the fourth floor nurse's desk. She asked the nurse if they had a seven-year-old child named Jay Borky admitted last night.

The nurse's eyes darted up the hall to her right and then to her left and her upper lip twitched as she told Jennifer she couldn't give out any information.

"He's one of my students and I'm concerned about his welfare," Jennifer offered.

"I'm sorry. We may not discuss our patients with anyone because of the gag—I mean the HIPAA law."

The slip of tongue did not go unnoticed by Jennifer. *So there was a gag order in effect.* Jennifer reviewed this in her mind when a tall handsome man, wearing a white coat, came to the desk and asked the nurse if the two children in room 412 had had any family come to check on them.

The nurse's eyes darted toward Jennifer, then back to the tall man bearing 'Phil Henson, Resident Doctor' on his name tag. "*One* person inquired about them, but *no* family."

"D.C.F.S. wants to know if anybody comes to check on them. They would like the name, address, and phone number of anyone coming in. Can you put a note on their chart stating that?"

"Would that be *anyone*, Doctor, or just family?"

"They only asked for family."

<<<

After giving it some consideration, Jennifer had an idea. She placed a call to the Division of Child and Family Services in the Salt Lake City area and got an answering machine. They gave out an emergency phone number, which turned out to be the police department for after hours. She could wait until they were open in the morning, or leave a message on the answering machine. She still wasn't positive Jay was one of the two survivors, so she decided to wait until morning to call back.

Feeling the need to do *something*, but knowing she was helpless to change the situation, she opted to buy some balloons and a stuffed animal; then she attached them to a card and delivered them herself to the front desk in the lobby. If they took the balloon bouquet and agreed to deliver them to Jay Borky, she would assume he was one of their patients. She reasoned they would tell her if he was not a patient at this hospital. Then she would need a plan B.

The woman sitting behind the desk accepted the gift without comment or incident, leaving Jennifer to wonder if her plan would really work.

Chapter Two

Jennifer walked into her apartment after eleven o'clock at night. The message light on her telephone flashed. Exhausted, hungry, and with a pounding headache, she wanted nothing more than sleep. She decided the message could wait until morning.

She poured a glass of milk, buttered a leftover roll, and took three Ibuprofens. After kicking off her shoes, she dropped onto her bed. When the roll and milk were gone, she slid to her knees at the side of her bed and begged God to heal Jay and his brother or sister. Thoughts of Jay and his surviving sibling consumed her mind so much; she couldn't concentrate.

About midnight, she woke up at the side of her bed and could not feel either of her legs. The bed was still wet from her tears. Shifting sideways to allow blood flow back into her legs, she felt the burning pain as feeling returned. When she could move her legs, she stood and changed into her pajamas.

As she was ready to collapse into bed, she remembered she'd had an appointment at the McCune Mansion. "Oh my gosh!" she said aloud. She ran to the kitchen to hear the message on the answering machine realizing her fiancé, Braxton, must have been frantically trying to get in touch with her.

There were three messages. The first message came at seven in the evening: "Jennifer, I don't know where you are. We have an appointment at eight o'clock at the McCune. Did you forget? Call me!" He sounded concerned. The second message came only fifteen minutes later: "Jennifer, we're going to miss our appointment—why won't you answer your phone or your cell?" He sounded irritated. The third message came at ten-thirty: "Jennifer, I'm going crazy with worry. Please call me. By the way, I found a new Mercedes for us today—I can't wait for you to see it."

She fumbled through her purse to find her cell phone. She had five missed calls. There was only one message: "Are you stepping out on me? It's obvious you're trying to avoid me. I understand you not answering your apartment phone because you're not there—I know because I had your landlord check your apartment. But knowing you have your cell phone with you and you still won't answer, I'm assuming you don't want to talk to me."

Jennifer looked at the clock. It was a little past midnight. He deserved an explanation, but at this hour? From the sound of his voice, she wasn't sure he wanted it whether he deserved it or not. She knew she wouldn't be able to sleep until she had talked to him so she dialed his cell phone.

"What do you want?" he answered.

"Braxton, I'm so sorry. I had an emergency come up with one of my students and I got so involved in dealing with that problem, I totally forgot about our appointment."

"You called me now—obviously your finger isn't broken—why couldn't you call me then?"

"Honestly, I didn't even think about it."

"Yeah well, I need you to transfer $75,000 into our checking account to pay for the Mercedes."

"Did you hear what I said? I had an *emergency* come up with one of my students."

"Well, an emergency with your student shouldn't be more important than me!" The phone went dead.

A new flood of tears erupted. She stared into the darkness for hours before finally drifting off to sleep.

She overslept in the morning. Wondering if she had dreamed this nightmare, or if it was reality, it took several minutes to clear the cobwebs from her mind. Then it all came back to her. Yesterday morning she woke up in a world where everything was beautiful; then it had all imploded.

She numbly climbed out of bed, showered and brushed her hair up into a ponytail. When she was dressed, she grabbed a frozen breakfast burrito and popped it into the microwave. On the way to work, she ate her burrito, knowing that if she drove a little faster than the speed limit; she might make it to work on time. As luck would have it, she hurried too fast and a policeman pulled her over in a school zone.

He didn't even get to her car before her tears overflowed once again. *Will I ever run out of tears?*

"In a hurry, lady?" he asked.

Unable to speak, she handed him her driver's license and the vehicle registration without answering him.

He looked at her driver's license and called her by name. "Jennifer, I'm just a police officer trying to protect the innocent children going to school here. I promise you, I'm not going to shoot you or anything."

The words "innocent children" made her think of Jay and she burst into louder sobs.

"Jennifer, you don't appear to be in any condition to be driving. Is there someone I can call to come and take you home?"

She shook her head. "I have to get to work," she managed to choke out.

"Where do you work?" he asked.

"Frandsen Elementary School," she attempted to get control of her emotions. Talking to the officer seemed to help. "I have a class of twenty-three... no, I guess only twenty-two now," she realized, and then finished her sentence in a broken voice, "second-graders."

"Well, then, I'm sure you know how critical it is that drivers maintain a reduced speed when going through a school zone."

"Yes sir. I must have missed seeing the school zone sign."

"Look, I'm supposed to have a zero tolerance for school zone speeding. It's an automatic speeding ticket—I have no choice. If you'll wait a few minutes, I'll be right back."

Jennifer tapped her fingers on the steering wheel watching the clock in her car as the minutes passed. She pulled her cell phone out to call work and explain that she would be there a few minutes late. Before she pressed any numbers, the phone rang in her hand. It was Braxton. She answered the call. "Hello?"

"Oh, hi. I didn't expect you to answer. I thought you'd be at work."

"I'm on my way. If you thought I was at work and wouldn't answer my phone, why did you call?"

"Well, I called to leave you a message. I was pretty much a jerk last night and I thought I'd tell you I'm sorry."

The police officer handed Jennifer a speeding ticket and her driver's license and registration through the window. He gave her a few simple directions and told her to please watch for signs and drive carefully.

"Thank you," she answered the officer as he turned and walked away.

"Who the heck are you talking to?" Braxton asked. "Why are you with some guy when you're supposed to be at work?" his voice grew angry.

Jennifer tried to keep her cool. "It was a policeman. I just got a speeding ticket; that's why I'm not at work yet. Look, I need to get to work. Can we talk later?"

"I'll think about it," Braxton said with a huff.

Jennifer wasn't sure if he had hung up on her or not because she flipped her phone closed on him. She was in no mood to put up with a man that was acting like a five-year-old.

She dialed the school's phone number and explained her tardiness. She sighed with relief when the secretary said the principal was in her classroom and had things under control.

<<<

When the children were out for their first recess, Jennifer ran to the office and placed a call to the Division of Child and Family Services. She made the call in front of the school secretary so she could overhear her conversation and know what had happened to Jay.

Using a feigned air of confidence to fish for information, she said, "I'm calling about Jay Borky, the little boy at 590 West 1200 South that was taken to the burn center at the University of Utah yesterday. I am Jennifer Heaps. Jay Borky is a student in my second-grade class at Frandsen Elementary School. I wanted to know how serious his injuries are and if there's anything I can do to help him?"

"I'm sorry, Ms. Heaps. We cannot give out any information. Anything of that nature would be completely confidential for security reasons."

"Oh," Jennifer sighed, "I hadn't even considered the security issues. I was so concerned about Jay—I was desperate to know if he was going to live and how badly he was burned. Would you mind giving my name and phone number to his caseworker in case he needs something? I would be happy to undergo a background security check if necessary. I want to see that Jay gets the best care he can have."

The social worker agreed to give the message to a caseworker.

Jennifer explained the details of the Borky family's misfortune to the principal.

"I heard something about that on the news last night, but I didn't hear them mention any names," he said.

After the last child left the classroom at the end of the day, Jennifer called Braxton. Not sure what would come of her call, she knew she couldn't sit back and do nothing.

"What do you want?" He answered his phone in a tone indicating she was interrupting something.

"Are you too busy to talk?" she asked.

"I guess not," he answered irritably. "Did you get the money transferred into our account?"

"I was hoping we could get together and talk things over."

"Sure. Why don't you fix dinner and then let me know when it's ready and I'll come over to your place."

Too tired to argue but also too tired to make dinner, she said, "How about Chinese takeout instead?"

"It depends, where are you going to buy it? I don't like the Buffet place. Their takeout is nasty."

"Did I say *I* was buying?" she asked.

"Well, *you're* the one who suggested it."

"Look, Braxton, I suggested Chinese takeout because I'm in no mood to fix dinner. I'm not in much of a mood to *buy* dinner either. If I have to provide you with dinner, you'll get a peanut-butter and jelly sandwich."

"Have it your way. I'll be over there in about thirty minutes." The phone went dead.

Does that mean he's going to buy the Chinese takeout or are we having peanut-butter and jelly sandwiches? Not sure what to expect, she wearily drove home.

Forty-five minutes later, he knocked on her apartment door. He was empty-handed when he walked in.

"So I guess we're having peanut-butter and jelly sandwiches for dinner?" she verified.

"If that's all you're going to feed me, I guess it is. I thought you might at least fry a pork chop or heat up a frozen pizza, or something. Isn't that what women are supposed to do? I thought it was a woman's job to feed her man."

Jennifer's jaw dropped as she stood staring at him. Had he always been so self-absorbed? *Have I been too taken with romance to see it? Is this the same person who sent me flowers, wrote romantic notes, fixed my car, and held me close to him while we planned all the ways we would spend my fortune together?* In the past twenty-four hours, she had felt his impatience with her emergency because it inconvenienced him. She witnessed his jealousy when he heard another man's voice over the phone—*doesn't he trust my integrity at all?* She received the wrath of his temper when she missed their appointment and he hadn't even waited to find out why she missed the appointment before he got mad. Come to think of it, even after she explained to him that she'd had an emergency, he never even cared enough to ask her what had happened—like he didn't care enough about her being too tired to fix dinner tonight. Everything was all about him!

She slipped the diamond ring off her finger, pushed it into his palm, and asked him to leave.

10

"Wha-what's this for?" he stammered in a voice two octaves higher than normal. "What did I say? Look, I didn't mean to upset you."

"Braxton, I have *no* desire to marry you. You'll have to find somebody else to take care of your needs. I'm not going to be your banker! Now if you'll please leave. I am tired, hungry, need a hot shower, and I really don't have time to waste giving you my long list of 'whys'," the words tumbled out of her mouth before she had time to think them through.

Looking at Jennifer first and then at the ring in his hand, he grimaced and his face turned red. "What about the new Mercedes I just bought us? How do you expect me to pay for that?"

"You'll have to earn your own money, I guess. Now please... just leave!"

He shoved the ring into his pocket and muttered, "We'll see about that!" and then he stomped out of her apartment.

Jennifer closed the door and dead-bolted it before she leaned her back against it, slid down to the floor and cried.

Chapter Three

As soon as school was out, Jennifer went to the bank and closed the joint account Braxton had insisted they start. She chastised herself for not waiting until they were married to mingle their finances. She had given him two thousand dollars to open the account, but there was only five dollars left, which they handed to her in cash.

Each day she looked at Jay's empty chair and longed to know how he was. She still could get no information from anyone about his condition. Each week she delivered a new balloon bouquet to the hospital volunteer desk and the person on duty accepted it with the promise to deliver it to Jay Borky. She felt hopeful that he must have survived.

The months passed ever so slowly. Summer came and went. A new school year began bringing new students with it. A sturdy girl, who refused to do anything she was assigned, now sat in Jay's chair.

As Thanksgiving neared, Jennifer felt as low as she had when both of her parents were killed in the plane crash. She ate a TV Chicken dinner alone on Thanksgiving Day remembering how her parents had always made a list of all the things they were grateful for. Out of habit, she picked up a piece of paper and a pencil to make her list. When she could think of absolutely nothing to be grateful for, she tossed the pencil down, put her head on her folded arms and cried. Her heart had been broken and her beloved Jay was still in the hospital. He had turned eight years old in July. She had taken a birthday balloon bouquet with another stuffed animal that week. She pondered the severity of his burns; *they must be terrible or he would have been released months ago. What would he do? Where would he go? How could a young child get along in this world with no parents and such memories of abuse?* Her thoughts tortured her mind every day.

She was familiar with these feelings of loneliness. Suddenly it occurred to her that it had been this same frame of mind that had driven her right into a promise of companionship with Braxton.

At the end of the day she came up with only one thing she was grateful for. She wrote on her paper: *I'm grateful I didn't marry Braxton.* Memories of when they cuddled close while riding the Tilt-a-Whirl at Lagoon filtered through her mind and she couldn't suppress a smile. She reluctantly followed her declaration with a question mark.

The following day was traditionally the day she put up her Christmas tree, but this year she lacked motivation. She sat around the apartment and read a new novel. Perhaps if she got lost in a world of fiction, she could forget her own problems.

She finished the novel in the late afternoon, but her own reality closed in around her causing her to feel she might suffocate. She knew the source of her feelings... depression. Determined to resist Satan's power; she turned to prayer for divine help. "Please, Heavenly Father, bless me with the Spirit of Christmas. Surely there is something I could do to get out of this black abyss of hopelessness."

"Serve others," was the only answer the Spirit spoke.

But how? It was black Friday—a time to shop for Christmas— only she had no one to buy a gift for except the students in her school class. The school had rules about gift-giving to the students. It had to be homemade or under one dollar. Not much excitement there. Since Jay was no longer her student, she wondered if she could do something for him.

Suddenly she had an idea that felt right.

On Monday, she had each of the students that had been in Jay's second-grade class last year draw a picture for Jay. She asked each of them to sign their name at the bottom of the picture. Monday evening she took a new balloon bouquet along with the student's drawings to the hospital. Included in the pictures was a digital photograph of his old classmates and Jennifer all waving to Jay.

14

She had absolutely no idea how badly he was injured in the fire. Could he see? Did he still have all of his mental faculties, or his physical body parts? How much of Jay was left?

Chapter Four

Driving a new Mercedes around felt more exhilarating than Braxton could describe. He knew he couldn't afford the payments, but his desire to have the car outweighed his logic to return it, so he called the dealership and told them he had decided to finance it rather than pay cash. He asked them to arrange the financing and then let him know when to come in and sign the paperwork.

Braxton had written out a check for the initial deposit from the joint account he and Jennifer opened. He managed to convince her to open the account with two thousand dollars so they could get two free sets of luggage the bank offered as a teaser for new accounts. He envisioned using them to travel the world on her money.

Braxton was having a difficult time adjusting to the fact that his lifestyle would be ratcheted down to the level of his measly wages… or would it?

He scavenged through his apartment looking for the information he'd gotten from Jennifer when they opened the joint account. He found it in the middle of a stack of papers he'd been meaning to file but hadn't quite managed to do. Good thing too—he might have thrown this away if he'd cleaned before now. But now here it was—his ticket to a gold mine!

His mouth turned up into a sinister grin. Jennifer had humiliated him by breaking off their engagement, but revenge felt sweet right now as he considered what he could do with the Social Security number staring back at him from the paper he held in his hand. It was like seeing dollar signs roll up one at a time across the windows of a slot machine until all the windows matched.

He sat in front of his computer and did a search for credit card applications. If he got enough credit cards and maxed them all out, he might get to keep the Mercedes.

Chapter Five

On the first of December, Jay's caseworker, Lucy, consulted with the medical staff concerning Jay's recovery. Their report was that he had been stoic since his sister Emily had been placed for adoption. The medical staff knew he had to be experiencing some emotion, but he had not cried—nor had he smiled. When Jay saw the picture of his school class, tears trickled down onto his elastic pressure mask and he grinned. Seeing his response, Dr. Henson advised Lucy that he would have a better chance of recovering if he had someone like the attentive schoolteacher visit him and cheer him up.

Lucy searched her records for Jennifer's name and phone number. She pressed the numbers on her phone and picked up a pencil to doodle on her note pad as she talked.

"He has suffered third degree burns over sixty percent of his body—it's a miracle he's even alive," Lucy explained. Then she asked, "Would you be willing to come and visit him?"

"Of course I will," Jennifer quickly answered.

"Jay's sister, Emily, who also survived, has been sent to a foster home where adoption is in process. Her burns were not as severe. Jay's alone and disfigured. His chances for adoption are not good. We feel he'd be eligible to go into foster care within a few weeks, but when prospective foster parents are shown pictures of Jay, they're not interested. We'd like to show *you* pictures *before* you visit Jay, as well. It'll be important for you to be prepared to see a different little boy than what you remember. If you show any signs of disgust or shock when you see him, you may do more harm psychologically than help."

<<<

Lucy was consulting with Kimberly, the guardian at litem appointed as Jay's representative in court, when Jennifer arrived. Introductions were made and Lucy did not waste any time. She laid out ten colored pictures of Jay on the desk top and watched to see Jennifer's reaction. Jennifer did not move. She stared at the pictures as tears ran down her cheeks. The pictures revealed a boy with no fingers except for two little stumps on his right hand. He had no nose or mouth—only holes. There was no hair on his head. He had no ears.

"How is he able to eat?" she asked.

"He can't. He is fed through a feeding tube directly into his stomach," Lucy said.

"Can he talk?"

"Yes. It's like listening to a small child who is learning to talk. His words don't come out exactly right, but after you have been around him a while, you'll understand what he's saying."

"Can he hear?"

"Yes. He's able to hear quite well."

"Can he see?"

"He can see now—he wasn't able to initially because his eyes were burned. The doctors grafted some special skin over his eyes to protect them while they healed and they were kept bandaged for several weeks."

"Does it hurt to touch him?"

"His hands, face, and arms are still tender. They probably will be for years. Normally he has an elastic mask over his face to protect his tender skin and to reduce scar tissue. These pictures were taken while the mask was removed so we could show you the extent of his injuries. Jay has not been allowed to look at himself in a mirror yet. Especially after he showed signs of depression recently, the doctors decided he wasn't ready to climb that mountain yet. He's had three skin grafts so far and as you can see, he'll need to go through years of reconstructive surgeries. Each surgery will bring with it pain and more tenderness. Our concern right now is to help him develop a will to live. He was brave until his sister left the hospital two months ago. After that, he seemed to give up.

"Then your class pictures and photograph arrived and Dr. Henson thought he saw a glimmer of hope again," said Kimberly.

20

"That's why the medical staff contacted us and asked us to contact you. Under normal circumstances, we don't give out this information, but in this case, where the life and well-being of the child are involved, we felt it was in Jay's best interest.

"Just a word of warning, you are not allowed to be alone with Jay. A security guard from the hospital will be assigned to stay with you during your visits, so you'll need to arrange any visits ahead of time—is that clear?"

"I understand," Jennifer replied. *How will Jay feel about me seeing him?*

Chapter Six

Jennifer's heart was pounding with anticipation. She prepared a small nativity diorama to set up on Jay's nightstand or a table. She bought a narrow three-foot Christmas tree and decorated it with lights and wired ornaments on it. She purchased a small lighted star to go on the top. She added to her purchases a bright silver tinsel garland to hang around Jay's door or any place in the room she could make it fit. She was going to deck the halls inside his gloomy little hospital room.

She packed her car with the Christmas decorations and headed to the hospital anxious to see Jay. Her stomach was queasy and she wondered what it would be like when she actually looked at Jay and not a photograph.

Jennifer was met at the nurse's desk by a security guard, a doctor, and two nurses. They were waiting for her. "I have some things to bring in from my car," she said. "Would it be better to bring them in now or wait until after I first meet with Jay?"

"What are you bringing in?" the doctor asked.

"I brought some Christmas decorations to set up in his room. They're pretty small, but I thought they might cheer him up."

The doctor smiled. "By all means, bring them in now. This will give you something to do while you visit."

Jennifer walked from the elevator juggling two oversized shopping bags.

The security guard opened Jay's door and poked his head inside. "You have company," he announced, and then stepped back, holding the door for Jennifer.

She took a deep breath, steeled her nerves, plastered on a smile, and cheerily walked into the room. "Hello, Jay. Remember me? I came to decorate your room for Christmas—is that okay?"

He looks better with the mask on.

"Hi, Teacher." She actually recognized what he had said. She looked around his room and saw twenty-four familiar Mylar balloons taped to two walls and twenty-two pictures drawn by his classmates taped to the third wall. The most recent Mylar balloon still floated in the air at the foot of his bed.

A tear trickled down her cheek. She turned away from Jay so he couldn't see it and quickly wiped it away. Sitting in the chair next to his bed she said, "I've missed you at school, you know."

"I've been in the hospital," he offered as if she hadn't been able to figure it out. She had a little difficulty understanding exactly what he was saying, but she could piece most of it together. She noticed that he couldn't bring the top and the bottom of his mouth together, so some of his consonants were difficult to decipher.

"You'll need to study hard to make up for the time you've spent here. All of your other friends that sent these pictures are in the third grade now."

"Does that mean you aren't my teacher any more?" he asked.

"I guess it does," she answered.

"Then I don't want to go back to school!"

She smiled but said nothing.

Timidly, Jay said, "Teacher, can I ask you a question?"

"Sure, that's what teachers are for isn't it?"

"Teacher, when will my fingers grow back again?"

Jennifer swallowed hard. "Oh, Jay," she fought back the tears, "your fingers will *never* grow back. You're going to have to learn how to write another way now."

"But how, Teacher? I can't hold a pencil."

Jennifer didn't know how to answer him. She nervously got up from the chair and began to set up the Christmas decorations around the room. "I don't know, Jay. Have you asked the doctor about this?"

"No."

"Well, I guess we're going to have to ask him."

"Will I always have to eat through a tube too?"

"You know, Jay, I have no idea. These are all good questions to ask your doctor."

24

"I like the *Thithmath* tree." His *Christmas* sounded like a series of t-h blends.

"Oh good—I hoped you would like it." She fussed with the tinsel to get it hung over the door without falling down and preventing the door from closing all the way. She assembled the nativity diorama with shaking hands. She had no idea what his religious background, but she felt if ever a child needed something to hold on to, this was the time. She doubted he was a member of the Church of Jesus Christ of Latter-day Saints. She sat back down in the chair next to his bed and told him the story of the birth of Jesus.

He was silent for a long time after she finished. Breaking the silence, he asked, "Teacher, how come Jesus loves everybody but me?"

Jennifer wondered if the diorama had been a mistake. Thinking quickly, she answered, "Jay, I think right now Jesus loves you *more* than He loves everyone else."

"Then how come He doesn't make me better?"

Jennifer heard the security guard choke up. She swallowed a large lump in her own throat. She thought long and hard. If she burst into tears now, Jay would surely sense defeat. She had to give him courage. He needed something to hang onto—a reason to fight. She ventured out in faith, "Jay, I have a hunch Jesus wants you to grow up and become a teacher someday. He wants you to teach other people who have been injured or burned like you have. He must think you know how to help them feel better. If He made you all better right now, who would believe you when you told them about your burns? Then how could you teach if nobody believed what you told them?"

"Do you really think He wants me to be a teacher?"

"I really do—which means you're going to have to study hard to catch up so you don't have to stay in the second grade."

Jennifer bent forward to hug Jay, but she asked him for permission first. She didn't want to embarrass him, or worse, to cause him pain. It was the strangest thing Jennifer had ever seen.

The hole without lips where Jay's mouth was supposed to be, turned into a half-moon and actually looked like a grin.

"Yeah," he answered. "I guess."

<<<

Jennifer searched her purse for her car keys. They were not in her bag. She returned to the hospital and explained her situation to the nurse at the desk. "I must have dropped them in Jay's room. Is it possible for me to go look for them?"

Dr. Henson was busy behind the nurse's desk and spoke up, "I'll accompany you to his room." Jennifer couldn't believe her eyes when he rose from the chair he had been sitting in. He towered into the air far above her.

Not intending to be unnoticed but entering Jay's room quietly, Jennifer saw Jay sitting in his bed with his eyes closed and his head bowed. She stopped suddenly to listen and Dr. Henson bumped into her, nearly knocking her over. Holding her finger up to her lips to signal for him not to speak, they both stood in silence.

"God, this is me—Jay Borky. I didn't know you knew me, but Miss Heaps said you want me to be a teacher, so I guess you must know me. I don't have any family since my sister got adopted. Since *you* know me, would it be okay if I called you my Father in Heaven? Then I could at least have a dad. My dad killed himself—oh, I guess you already know that. Well, anyway, if you wouldn't mind, I'd really like to be a teacher, but right now I'm just a little kid. Could you help me learn to be a teacher? I'd be a really good boy and try to learn real hard. I know you probably have lots more important things to do, but if you could find somebody to help me, it would sure be swell."

Jennifer quickly ran out of the room, choking with unbidden tears.

Dr. Henson called out, "Nurse, bring Ms. Heaps a chair, please."

Jennifer shook her head from side to side indicating she didn't need a chair. "I need air," she choked out.

"Nurse, forget the chair, bring Ms. Heaps an oxygen mask."

26

Jennifer could not resist the urge to laugh amidst her tears. "I guess what I really need is my car keys," she finally said in an audible voice.

"I'll go see if I can find them for you," Dr. Henson said and ducked his head slightly as he entered Jay's room.

Moments later, he returned with a familiar looking set of keys. "Would these be yours?"

"Yes. Thank you very much. And thank you for taking the time to cheer me up."

"My pleasure, I assure you," Dr. Henson replied.

Chapter Seven

Grateful for the time she spent with Jay, she set up appointments to visit him the two following Saturday afternoons. She set up her third visit for Christmas day. Only a few weeks ago she had felt nothing but despair and loneliness. Now she was celebrating Christmas with Jay. She realized the Lord had answered her plea for the true Spirit of Christmas to enter her heart.

Security was sparse at the hospital on Christmas day, so Dr. Henson attended her during the visit. She discussed Christmas traditions in many lands and shared bright pictures of different children from countries all over the world with Jay. Then she read the story of the *Little Match Girl* by Hans Christian Andersen. She had read the story four times at home before coming in an effort to desensitize herself to the tears she always shed when reading the story. She needn't have worried. Her tears would have been right at home with Jay's and Dr. Henson's.

"Teacher, how come I didn't die like my brothers did when my mom burned us?"

"I'm sure Heavenly Father has a greater purpose for you in this life and if you had died with your brothers, you would never get the chance to teach other burned people how to feel better."

"Teacher, can I call you 'Mom'?"

"Oh Jay," she could hardly speak. "You already have a mom. But you could call me Jennifer, and I will always be your friend— would that be all right?"

"Okay. I guess. Jennifer, will you still come and see me now Christmas is over?"

"Of course I will. Did you think I was only coming because it was Christmas?"

"I didn't know for sure. But if you're going to always be my friend, you'll always have to come and visit me."

She smiled now. "Well, I think when you get out of the hospital you won't want me to visit you quite so much."

"You mean I won't live here until I die?"

Jennifer was startled by his comment.

Dr. Henson spoke up, "You're about to get out of here in a few weeks, Jay."

A look of terror came into his eyes. "Where will I go? Will I have to go back to my house with my mamma?"

Jennifer calmed his fears. "No, Jay. You won't ever live with your mother again. She will never be given another chance to hurt you. You will stay here until Lucy can find you a family to live with that will love you and take care of you."

"Hey," Jay perked up. "Could I come and live with you?" he asked Jennifer.

"I'm afraid that's not possible. You see, you need a *family* to live with. I live all alone—I'm not a *family*."

"Didn't you get married last summer?"

"No. Things didn't work out. I'm not married."

"Oh," Jay said disappointedly. "I thought maybe *you* could take care of me."

"Sorry, Buddy. I'm not much of a family. You need a *real* family."

Chapter Eight

Monday morning during Christmas break, Jennifer's phone rang. Doctor Henson was calling from the hospital. "Jennifer, we think Jay is strong enough to see his face in a mirror without his mask on. We would like you to be here with him when that happens. Is there a chance you could come to the hospital sometime in the next two days?"

"You set the time—I'll be there."

"Would this afternoon around one o'clock work?"

"I'll be there," Jennifer assured him.

There was a team consisting of two physicians, a psychiatrist, and a nurse all loitering in the hall waiting for Jennifer's arrival. When she walked in, Dr. Henson picked up a hand mirror off the desk and waved it at the group signaling the time for the unveiling had arrived. Jennifer said a silent prayer as she walked down the hallway toward Jay's hospital room. She had seen pictures of him without his mask, but this was the real thing—and it was going to happen for Jay at the same moment.

Jay appeared surprised when they walked into his room.

Jennifer began by saying, "Well, Jay, this would be a really good time to ask Dr. Henson how you're going to learn to write without any fingers."

Jay said nothing. He looked at Dr. Henson waiting for the answer.

"I'm the resident surgeon here," Dr. Henson said. "The attending physician, Dr. Killpack, will have to answer that for you.

Dr. Killpack answered immediately. "There are machines you will be able to talk to and they will type what you say so you won't need to use your hands to write. You will use your voice."

"Cool!" Jay responded. "Will it spell right for me too?"

"Most of the time," Dr. Killpack answered. "You may have to correct it until it learns how to spell properly."

"You mean I have to teach a *machine* how to spell?" Jay asked.

31

"Yes—that's pretty much how it works," the Doctor said.

Dr. Henson spoke up, "I hate to interrupt the Star Wars spell, but we'd like to take your mask off for a while today. We think it's time we showed you how you look now."

"You mean after all my grafts?" Jay asked.

"Yes. I don't think you will recognize yourself in the mirror," Dr. Killpack said.

"Do I look like somebody else now?"

"No. I don't think you look like anybody else," Dr. Henson answered.

Jennifer knew the mind of an eight-year-old. He was expecting miracles. He would never be prepared for what he was about to see.

"Even with grafts, your fingers still haven't grown back—your face will never be the same either," she said.

Dr. Henson bent over and carefully lifted off the mask. "There, now that didn't hurt did it?" he asked Jay.

Jennifer sat on the side of the bed next to Jay.

Dr. Henson held the mirror in front of Jay's face and Jay let out a horrifying shriek. He stared at his reflection for a long time and tears rolled down his cheeks. Finally he bellowed, "I look like a freak!"

Jennifer could not stop the tears from rolling down her own cheeks. She pulled Jay into her embrace and held him close from behind so she wouldn't hurt his tender facial skin. He wriggled out of her arms and turned to face her.

"*That's* why you don't want me isn't it? You don't want to have a freak live with you!"

Anguish pierced through Jennifer's heart. The urge to run from this scene was so great it took all the willpower she had to remember this wasn't about *her* wounded ego. This was all about Jay. She decided this was no time to deny his grotesque features. He had seen his face and it would be futile to gloss over it. She determined honesty was the best policy and the only way she would be able to maintain Jay's trust.

32

"That's not true! I've *always* wanted a *freak* for a friend," she said.

Dr. Killpack and Dr. Henson both gasped. The psychiatrist, Dr. Green, seemed relaxed and his mouth turned up into a slight grin.

Jay's little mouth slowly turned up into a half moon and he somehow managed to laugh and cry at the same time.

<<<

Jennifer felt drained and beaten when she reached home. With school starting up again on Monday, she knew she needed to take down her Christmas tree and get her apartment cleaned up. She pulled the holiday storage boxes out of the closet and proceeded to pack ornaments away for another year.

"That's why you don't want me isn't it? You don't want to have a freak live with you!" Jay's words echoed in her mind. Tears coursed down her cheeks. Her heart ached for Jay and she wanted him to succeed more than anything. She wondered what would become of him and where he would go when he left the hospital. It broke her heart that not *one* family wanted him because of his appearance. If only they had known him before the burns or had seen his handsome dark hair and his innocent features.

Her mind drifted back to the afternoon of the fire drill. When everyone had returned to the classroom, the air was filled with chattering and excitement among the students. She noticed Jay sitting in the reading corner, quietly perusing an advanced grade-level book. She had asked him if his assignment was finished. His large brown eyes gleamed with pride as he told her his paper had been turned in, and when she corrected it, each problem had been solved perfectly. After school that day, he had asked her if he could get some more math worksheets to take home—just for fun. If only someone could appreciate his zest for learning and his great intellect. If only they could recognize his thoughtful gentle nature…*if only.*

The following morning, Jennifer called the hospital to see if she could visit Jay again. The nurse said there was no longer a need to be accompanied by someone. Dr. Green, the psychiatrist, had determined she was not a threat to Jay's safety. Jennifer thought it humorous that anyone could even entertain the idea she might be a threat to anything bigger than a flea, but she did appreciate the confidence being placed in her.

"Does this mean I no longer need to make an appointment?" she asked.

"Yes. You can come and go anytime," the nurse answered.

Before she left home, she decided to give Lucy a call at D.C.F.S. to see if there were any new developments in Jay's possible placement. She would love to have something positive to share with Jay. When she got Lucy on the phone, Lucy's voice reflected hope.

"I understand you did a great job in handling Jay's unveiling process."

"Yeah, I called him a *freak*!" Jennifer said dejectedly.

"According to Dr. Green, you said exactly what he needed to hear. Jennifer, have you ever considered being a foster parent?"

"I'm not married. *I* am not a family—I'm just me—all alone."

"Yes, I believe Dr. Henson mentioned something about that in our last consultation with the hospital staff. As a general rule, we do prefer to have couples as foster parents, but there are no absolute laws restricting single people. At this point, because of your relationship with Jay, everyone involved feels you would be an excellent choice. You already have a trusting relationship with him. You are the only person in his life right now that even cares about him other than Dr. Henson who seems to have developed a real soft spot for Jay. After all these months, you have consistently displayed your commitment to Jay's welfare. Our only concern in the situation would be your ability to provide for his care. We know you teach school during the day and Jay would demand a lot of daytime hours for physical therapy, doctors' visits—not to mention the time he would need to spend in the hospital for reconstructive surgeries. This child is going to consume a tremendous amount of time and sacrifice. Because the state has taken custody of him, all of his medical expenses would be

34

covered by Medicaid until he's eighteen years old. You wouldn't have any financial burdens in that respect, but your job could be in jeopardy. That was our biggest concern."

Jennifer's head was spinning with circuit overload. She didn't know what to say. She had enough money in her inheritance she could afford to not work for quite some time—years, in fact. The airlines had paid her handsomely when her parents died. She had put all thoughts of the money out of her mind since her breakup with Braxton. Realizing he had used her for her money, she had decided to keep her wealth a secret. She'd almost forgotten she had it. Her plans were to save it for her future marriage, but thoughts of helping Jay seemed to make even more sense. If she *never* married, she would at least have *someone* in her life. She longed to have an eternal companion and children of her own. Having Jay in her life could *complicate* her opportunities to marry. *What opportunities*? She laughed aloud. Since she gave Braxton his ring back, she hadn't even tried to meet anyone.

"What's so funny?" Lucy had been waiting in silence on the phone for Jennifer's response.

"Absolutely nothing—actually it's pitiful. Hey, look, Lucy, can I give this some thought? There's a lot to consider here."

"Yes, there is. I know I've probably overwhelmed you with this, Jennifer. We are in a difficult situation with Jay. But we also realize if taking Jay sinks your ship, it will drown Jay along with you. We don't want that for either of you."

<<<

Jennifer passed the nurses' desk with a tingling feeling of freedom. She no longer needed to check in and wait for someone to accompany her. She remembered eight months ago when she couldn't even get anyone to tell her for sure Jay was alive or a patient at the University Hospital. Now allowed into the inner sanctum, she was part of Jay's world. Then she realized Jay had become *her entire* world! She had spent time at school involving other teachers and children in projects to serve Jay. He filled her time and thoughts at home. She had spent each week anxiously waiting for her visit with him. She read children's books all week trying to find the right one to share with him on the Saturday visits. She combed her social studies manual to choose the most interesting highlights to share with him. She hadn't realized until this moment, how much her life had improved in joy and fulfillment since the day she prayed for the Christmas Spirit to enter her life. "Thank you, Lord," she whispered as she pushed the door open to Jay's room.

She was surprised to walk in and find Dr. Henson sitting at Jay's bedside massaging his hands and stretching them backward. Since all of her previous visits were pre-arranged and accompanied, she realized other visits had been put on hold while she was here.

"Hello," Dr. Henson greeted her. "We were doing a little stretching therapy on Jay's wrists."

Caught completely off guard and out of her element, Jennifer asked, "Exactly what field of medicine are you going into?"

"I'm a plastic surgeon. I specialize in treating trauma patients. I decided to go into this line of medicine to help giraffes like me who are traumatized when they hit their heads going through doorways," he said with a smile. "I'm in my last year of residency here and this unit has been a perfect fit for me."

"Do you have a lot of patients here like Jay?"

"This is only a twelve-bed unit, but throughout a year, they average about 300 patients. Fortunately, not all of them are as serious as Jay. Quite honestly, most patients like Jay don't survive long enough for me to do much. One patient like him would keep a doctor like me in business for a lifetime."

A lifetime—would that be how long she would be taking care of Jay if she accepted the challenge from Lucy? "Dr. Henson, could I speak with you for a moment after you're finished here with Jay?"

"Sure. I'd say Jay's had about enough pain for now. What do you think, Jay?"

"I'd like to stop," Jay admitted.

Jennifer promised Jay she'd be right back as she and Dr. Henson left his room for a quick visit. Dr. Henson motioned her to follow him into a private consultation room down the hall. After she walked into the room, he closed the door and took a seat facing her. "What can I help you with?" he asked.

"You mentioned Jay's condition could keep you busy for a lifetime. What exactly do you see is in the future for him? Will he be dependent on caretakers *all* his life?"

"Jay will need to make some adaptations to his unusual physical limitations. He will never have full use of his hands, but that doesn't mean he can't live a normal life—well, normal in many ways. He will always be deformed even after we reconstruct his nose, ears, and lips. But by the time he is twenty-five or so, he should be able to take care of himself, hold down a job, and live a pretty useful life—even marry and have children if he chooses to. There are always people who can overlook his deformities—you certainly have."

"It's easy for *me* to overlook them because I knew him as the brightest and most inquisitive student I ever had. I always worried about him because I could see his potential, but was aware he didn't get any encouragement from home. After his father committed suicide, I watched him decline socially. I loved him before he was burned and disfigured and I guess I'll always see him as the Jay I knew then."

"It's feasible he could find a wife who would accept him as well. Jay has many redeeming qualities that override his disabilities. Does that answer your question?"

"Yes. I feel much better. Quite honestly, after seeing Jay as a gifted healthy second-grader and then seeing him in the condition he's in now, well, I was pretty discouraged. As a matter-of-fact, I think I have experienced almost a feeling of hopelessness for him."

"Oh, no. You needn't feel that way. He's actually past the worst of his trauma now. The next big step will be getting him settled into a safe, secure, loving environment where he can progress emotionally."

"Dr. Henson," Jennifer hedged, "do you think someone like *me* could provide Jay with what he needs to develop to his full potential?"

"Jennifer, I can't explain what it is about that little boy, but he has wormed his way into my heart. I try not to get emotionally attached to my patients, but I've not been able to prevent it with Jay. Months before you started visiting him, I knew his chances for adoption weren't good. It was also possible he'd be ready to leave the hospital before August, when I'd finish my residency here. I considered dropping out of the program to care for him myself.

"Then you came into the picture. I watched how the two of you interacted. How much you loved him. You restored my faith in the human race. Since the moment I saw you with Jay, I felt that you could capably raise him. Are you considering it?"

"Lucy, his caseworker, talked to me this morning about it. I didn't think it was possible for a single person to take in foster children. Now I know that's not the case, and if you really think I could benefit Jay, I'm sure I will agree to do it."

"Do you have someone who could help you get Jay to all of his medical appointments—there will be many, you know?"

"No. I have no living relatives to help me, and not even the hope of a future spouse in the wings."

"How would you support yourself?" he asked.

"My expenses are few. Between the foster care pay and private tutoring, I'm sure we could manage," she said not divulging the whole truth.

"May I be the first to wish you well? I do hope you will allow me to be more than a physician to Jay. He means a great deal to me."

"I have no problem with that."

<<<

"Jay, I have some questions to ask you," Jennifer began. "How would you feel if you didn't get to live with a family?"

"You mean I have to stay here in the hospital?"

"No, I mean you would be living with one person, not a whole family." Jay hesitated to answer longer than Jennifer was comfortable with. Finally she broke into a smile and clarified, "What if the one person you lived with was me?"

"Will Lucy let me?" he asked raising his voice in hope.

"She talked to me this morning and said it would be okay."

"All right!" he answered exuberantly. "When can I get out of here?"

"I'm not sure, but probably right after the school year ends in June." She was trying to organize a schedule in her own mind, without knowing for sure what the doctors were thinking.

Chapter Nine

Time and circumstances seemed to whirl around Jennifer. Once she had agreed to take Jay, she had to meet certain state requirements for D.C.F.S. She was required to undergo a background check. *No problem there.* She was required to take a six-class course on foster parenting. She finished by the first of April. It was necessary to provide a private bedroom for the foster child. She had been living in a one-bedroom apartment. She now faced a dilemma. Should she get a larger apartment or should she bite the bullet and become a homeowner? She was feeling more like a family woman the longer she anticipated Jay's arrival. The tricky part in all of this was timing. Jay might be ready to leave the hospital before the school year ended. She was anxious for him to progress and wanted to give him her undivided attention, but she also felt an obligation to finish out this school year for her current students.

By now she was stopping by the hospital every evening after school. When she found Dr. Henson again in Jay's room, it appeared they were actually playing some kind of guessing game.

"I guess it's not all work and no play around here."

"This is our reward after the pain."

"I see. Well, how is our little man today?" she asked cheerfully.

"That is a matter I would like to discuss with you," the doctor answered quite seriously. "Jay, would you mind waiting a little longer to visit with Jennifer? I have something I need to talk to her about."

"Will you take long?" Jay asked.

"I don't think so. But then I've never been known to be short," the doctor said making light of his height.

"Ohh-kay," he said with a sigh.

In the conference room again, Dr. Henson asked Jennifer if she was ready to have Jay come home.

"I still have one critical decision to make. I have to move out of my single-bedroom apartment, and I'm really undecided about getting a condominium, a larger apartment, or a house. I'm leaning more toward a house. What do you think?"

"I think what you really need to consider is, which one would create the most pleasant environment for your happiness and therefore Jay's emotional recovery."

"Okay, Doctor, why don't you give me a prescription, and I'll see if our local real estate agent can fill it for me?"

Dr. Henson pulled out his prescription pad and scribbled something on it, tore it off, and handed it to Jennifer. Without looking at it she said, "I never could read doctors' handwriting—just tell me what it says."

"You didn't even try to read it, Teacher! I want you to note I have excellent penmanship!"

She looked down at the prescription slip and easily read: *Breakfast at Denny's Saturday morning 8:00 a.m. sharp!*

"Excuse me? The penmanship *is* good, but the content lacks clarity."

"Meet me at Denny's Saturday morning at eight o'clock for breakfast and then before I have to show up for my shift at the hospital, we can go house hunting. As we look at the houses, I'll be able to point out the positives and the negatives for Jay. If I don't actually see them, I can't give you constructive advice. Do you have a real estate agent in mind, or would you like to use mine?"

Jennifer's heart was skipping beats every other second. Was he *flirting* with her? Was this a *date*? She was so speechless she stammered, "Which Denny's was that?"

"I asked if you had a real estate agent, or if mine would do?"

"I guess yours would be fine."

"Great! And the Denny's is on Fifth South between Second and Third West."

<<<

Jennifer's mind floated back to her conversation with Dr. Henson the rest of the week. He was such a nice man.

She remembered how Braxton had been such a disappointment to her. Dr. Henson was nothing like him. He was much taller, had dark brown hair and blue eyes. Such a striking combination she thought dreamily. He had almost an innocent boyish look about him and yet was more self-assured and thrived on selflessly taking care of Jay. The contrast was startling. Now he was offering to help *her* look for a house. She realized for the first time, that after Braxton, she had built a defensive wall around herself. Although she tried to put Dr. Henson out of her mind, she couldn't deny how much she was anticipating Saturday morning.

<<<

"It's beginning to look a lot like Christmas," Braxton sang to himself as credit cards began to show up in the mail in Jennifer's name. Most had a credit limit of ten thousand dollars—some had more... a lot more.

With the arrival of each new card, he called the activation number and then sent in the request for the maximum cash advance on each card.

When checks for thousands of dollars were deposited into his account, his ego inflated equal to the bank balance.

He went online and made reservations for a ten-day cruise to the Caribbean, charging it all on Jennifer's credit cards. He'd make good use of that luggage yet.

Next he went to all the websites of his favorite clothing stores and purchased an entire wardrobe, with extra beach clothes for the cruise, using the same card.

He wrote a check out to pay for the Mercedes. "Screw the bank! They won't be repossessing the car now," he muttered.

Chapter Ten

Jennifer ordered the same thing Dr. Henson did which turned out to be a large breakfast. *Obviously he isn't worried about gaining weight.* "Dr. Henson, how much time do I have before Jay comes home from the hospital?" she asked.

"Jennifer, please call me Phil—and the truth is, he could probably go home tomorrow, but right now he doesn't have a home to go to, until you have a room for him."

"Doctor—umm, I mean Phil, how long can he stay at the hospital if I don't find something right away? I mean, I plan to get *something*, but I don't know how soon I could leave school and get moved."

"The staff was hoping to release him sooner than later, but we weren't sure how long it would take you to get ready for him. That's why I wanted to speak with you about it the other day at the hospital."

So this was just business on behalf of Jay—she felt deflated.

"After I talked with you on Thursday, we had a meeting with our staff and the folks from D.C.F.S. We came up with a compromise that I think may work well. Jay could be moved into a rehabilitation center until you're settled and ready for him to come home. He'd get really good care and therapy there. It would mean another adjustment period for him, but the state isn't willing to pay the high costs of the burn unit any longer, since Jay really doesn't need to be there."

"I had no idea he was ready to leave the burn unit. I should have moved weeks ago."

"Actually, I'd rather see you take your time and make the right move, than to move someplace and then have to move again if it didn't work well for you.

"I've briefed my real estate agent about your situation. He said he'd see what he could find in your price range."

"What price range did you give him?" She had calculated that if she didn't go back to teaching until Jay was thirty years old, and was hopefully able to care for himself, her living expenses would use up some of her inheritance, but if the returns on her investments were good, she would only dip into the interest and not the principal. She wanted Jay to have a good home. She knew the location and the neighborhood would be critical.

"I knew you wouldn't be making a lot as a foster parent, and I don't know how much you anticipate making as a tutor, but I guessed you could afford something in the one hundred-thousand to one hundred-fifty-thousand dollar range. Does that sound about right?"

"We'll see," she mused.

"Well, I might as well tell you now, I have received an offer to join the staff of a clinic in Cottonwood Heights—very fitting for a tall man, don't you think? So, I'm looking for a house for myself as well. I've asked the agent to also take us to some more expensive properties so I might look for a house for me too. He'll be showing us properties in the south end of the Salt Lake valley. I'm assuming location is not an issue for you since you will be tutoring from your residence. I guess I should have consulted with you a little more about it. But if you don't see anything you like today, you could look in another area later."

"I'm ashamed to say, I've been taking care of one requirement after another, and I haven't even given the whole idea much thought. But, yes, I guess it's true—I could tutor out of my residence no matter where I lived. But taking that into consideration, I would probably feel more comfortable working out of a house than an apartment or condo."

"My thoughts exactly. I told the real estate agent to show you a couple of nice condominiums, but mostly, I think he's planning to show us single-family dwellings."

Us. Jennifer longingly thought how inclusive that word sounded.

The agent met them at nine o'clock in front of the restaurant. They left their vehicles in the parking lot and Phil opened the front door of the Agent's SUV to help Jennifer in. Then he got in the back seat.

After the first two condominiums, Jennifer realized she had been living in a hovel, comparatively. Phil discouraged her from choosing them because of the many flights of stairs. "Too much trouble to get in and out," he commented. "Jay has a slight limp. He will need continual skin grafts on his legs until he stops growing taller. He would be better off if he didn't have to climb stairs all the time. Besides, I'd hit my head on the ceilings when I came to visit."

There was no place for a child to play in any of these. Jay would be confined indoors.

The further away from the center of the city they got, the nicer the homes were for the price. As they walked through one of the homes, Jennifer suddenly realized she might now be faced with yard work! "How much does lawn care cost a month?" she asked.

The agent answered, "Depends on the yard. Little ones—a hundred dollars a month. Big ones—three hundred dollars a month. Also depends on how picky you are. Adequate job—in the hundred dollar range. Outstanding job—up to five hundred dollars a month."

Phil laughed and squeezed her around the waist from the side. "You worry about the darndest things. All we have to do is get a riding lawn mower and eventually we'll teach Jay how to run it. He'll be able to keep the grass mowed and it'll be good for him."

We? Did she hear Phil right? Did he say *we?* She felt butterflies but squelched them as quickly as she recognized what was happening to her.

They began to look at more upscale homes throughout the south end of the Salt Lake valley. Huge homes Jennifer imagined were for Phil's benefit. He commented on the rich cherry wood cabinets, or the privacy in a nicely landscaped backyard. He made little remarks about the convenience of a laundry room by the garage entrance once. He mentioned that he didn't care for the color scheme in one home, or the carpet in another. Jennifer was enjoying the looking process with Phil now and noticed how much his comments reflected her own taste. She knew none of these homes were *meant* for her although all of them were affordable for her.

"The last home on the list is smaller than the others, but located on a larger parcel of ground—one acre, in fact," the agent informed them.

She hadn't seen anything so far that appealed to her enough to make any offers.

"We'll drive by this last one. If it looks interesting, we'll take a look at it. I've got a shift to work this afternoon, and I need to get back," Phil told the agent.

The real estate agent stopped across the street from the residence, "What do you think—do you want to give it a shot?" It was set back about fifty feet from the road.

Jennifer sucked in her breath and held it when she saw the house. The large porch had a ramp. There were two rocking chairs, a porch swing, and large pots of bright red tulips in bloom making it more inviting than she could resist. "Can we look at this one?" she asked.

The inside of the house was even more enticing than the outside. Stepping into the spacious entry, her focus immediately settled on a baby-grand piano resting ahead of them from where they stood in the entryway. The real estate agent pointed the way into the office off to their right. They silently meandered from the office to the entry long enough to notice the small sitting room with a bay window directly across from the office. Anxious to see further, Jennifer ventured past the baby grand piano into the cavernous vaulted great room, her eyes glued to the stacked rock fireplace off to the side of the room. The massive hand-carved mantle that adorned it had a scene of trees and elk carved in it.

Phil let out a whistle when he saw the fireplace.

The entry floor of hickory hardwood flowed throughout the kitchen area and on through the dining room. The area in front of the fireplace was carpeted in a beige frieze so thick, Phil took his shoes and socks off and wiggled his toes in it. Jennifer laughed heartily at his enjoyment.

The kitchen cabinets were built of honey oak with cherry wood crown moldings and the granite counter tops were rich in earth tones ranging from light wheat to ebony. There was no shortage of updated appliances in the kitchen either.

"I sure like the wood-tones in this house," Phil said.

"Me too," Jennifer whispered, as her attention turned to the outside wall of the dining room, lined with built-in china cabinets and hutches matching the kitchen cabinets.

At the rear of the great room was a double-wide set of doors with etch-trimmed windows leading out onto a large covered patio.

The windows along the back wall by the doors displayed a panoramic view of the beautifully landscaped yard with concrete curbing weaving around the circumference. At the side of the patio was a large waterfall cascading down into a clear fish pond. Beyond that on the side of the yard past the curbing were several fruit trees and along the other side was an area which appeared to be a vegetable garden. At the far back of the yard, the rest of the acreage wasn't landscaped, but had lots of trees.

"What kind of trees are in the back?" Jennifer asked.

"I'm not sure," the agent answered. "Without the leaves on the trees, it's difficult to identify what they are."

Jennifer could visualize Jay playing in the back yard with his friends and hiding in his imaginary fort in the trees. There was plenty of room for any outdoor activity he might want to do.

The vaulted master suite was equally impressive with a jetted tub, a walk-through shower that curved around the back of the jetted tub and didn't require a shower door. There was an off-white stressed-wood dresser that had been converted into a bathroom vanity with a granite counter-top and double-sinks. The walk-in closet was huge. *I could fit my clothing for all four seasons in half the space.* At her apartment, she had filled the two small closets available, dividing her clothes by season.

"Plenty of room for all my suits and scrubs," Phil said, "even shelves for shoes."

There were two other bedrooms on the other side of the house, each large enough for a king-sized bed. The bathroom between the two bedrooms had a tile shower that was built in a circular pattern reminding Jennifer of a snail shell. It had no raised edge at the entrance and the shower was behind the wall of the entrance. The floor gently sloped to the shower drain and once again, there was no shower door to clean. Jennifer thought the simplicity of it would make it easy for Jay to manage.

There was a wide hall behind the kitchen and off the triple-car garage entrance that led to the laundry room. This hall was lined with pantry doors all the way down one side of it. There was more closet space in this hall than Jennifer had ever seen in a house. *I could easily store a year's supply of food in here.*

She was having a difficult time trying to refrain from making comments revealing her *longing* for this house. It was much more space than she needed. Then the agent showed them more unfinished space above the garage that could be expanded into a recreation room or even two more bedrooms.

The perks of having things so convenient for Jay seemed worth the extra space. *Besides, someday I might have a husband and other children to share the space with me.*

This was a place she could find joy and relaxation in until she was old. She was so impressed with this house she was ready to make an offer even if she had to spend twice what she had planned. She knew she could afford it—although her nest egg would be pared down a little more. She could always hope the market returns would improve. She wondered how soon the sellers could be out of the house. She needed to get Jay settled as soon as possible.

Once outside, the agent pointed out that the driveway led back to another separate RV garage with a high door for large vehicles. This turned out to be a workshop area.

"I could keep five sports cars in here," Phil said with a little laugh, "and there'd still be enough room for the workshop."

Jennifer's stomach did flip flops when Phil took her hand and swung it back and forth as they walked to the real estate agent's SUV where this time he helped her into the backseat and then slid in next to her. He took her hand in his and squeezed it. Her stomach did so many somersaults; she thought she might lose her breakfast.

After they pulled into Denny's parking lot, Phil told Jennifer, "I'll catch up with you later. I'd like to visit with the agent for a few minutes."

Jennifer asked for the agent's business card as she excused herself and got out of the SUV. "I'll be giving you a call," she promised him as she left to go to her car.

Chapter Eleven

Claustrophobia overtook her in the small apartment after envisioning herself in the glorious house. She pulled the business card from her pocket and dialed the agent's number.

"How long will it take you to prepare an earnest-money offer on one of the houses we saw today?"

"I could probably have it ready in an hour if you're in a hurry. Otherwise, you'll have to wait your turn."

"Well, actually, I *am* in a hurry, I need to bring a child home from the hospital. He's ready to come home tomorrow, but I can't take him until I'm moved in," she explained. "How soon could we close?"

"Yikes Lady! The first thing you'll need to do is arrange and get approved for financing. That usually takes a few weeks. Then…"

"The financing is all taken care of," she interrupted. "How long will it take to close with cash?"

"With cash, you can take possession as soon as the wire reaches the bank. You could sign the papers as soon as Monday and take possession on Tuesday. You must have one of the *vacant* condominiums in mind?"

"No. The last house we looked at." There was a long silence at the other end of the line. "Hello? Did I lose you?" Jennifer asked.

"No, I'm still here. I think there might already be an offer on that house," he hedged, "but if you're paying with cash, the sellers might take your offer first but you'll need to give them a *reasonable* amount of time to move out. *If* they agreed to it, you might convince them to move out in a few weeks, but it's *doubtful*."

"I'm curious to know—what is the relationship between you and Phil Henson?"

"I suppose you could say we're good friends. We became acquainted at the hospital. He's one of the physicians attending the child I need to bring home."

"It's going to take me a few hours to put an offer together on *that* house. How about if I get things drawn up and meet with you at six this evening?"

"All right. Do you want me to come to your office?"

"That should work. What would you like me to specify in the offer?"

"I'll agree to the full price. We sign papers next week and they move out as soon as they can hire the movers. They leave all the kitchen appliances, and I'll even throw in an extra three thousand dollars if they'll leave the baby-grand piano."

<<<

"The sellers accepted your offer," the agent reported to Jennifer the following Monday. "They weren't thrilled with the fast move, but they have a mountain cabin thawing out from the winter freeze. They can stay there until they finish building their new home. Not having to move or store the baby-grand piano sweetened the pot a bit and they are happy to leave it. We should be able to arrange the closing on Friday."

Jennifer felt goose bumps on her arms and chills go up her back. *We have a home!*

<<<

Phil stopped in Jay's hospital room to visit with Jay and Jennifer the following afternoon. "How is my favorite patient?" he asked Jay.

"I'm good. I get to go home soon."

"Does this mean you have come to a conclusion on where to live?" he asked Jennifer.

After what had happened with Braxton, she did not want him to know her financial status. In the back of her mind, she was hoping something might develop between them, and she didn't want her money to be part of the equation. She was not prepared for this question and wasn't sure how to answer it *and* keep her confidentialities. "I decided to buy a house instead of a condo," she answered trying to be vague. Then she quickly added, "But I really *don't* want to talk about it."

Phil opened his mouth to say something then clamped it shut. He thrust his hands into his pockets and slouched his shoulders. Jennifer watched as he paced from Jay's bed to the door and back twice, as if he was about to say something, and then he stalked out of the room.

Chapter Twelve

Jennifer's mind was consumed with thoughts of Jay and their new home. Her anticipation became so overwhelming; she gave her notice to the school and made arrangements for a substitute to take her place the six weeks left in the school year. She threw her own going away party so the children wouldn't feel quite so bad.

She donated most of her apartment furniture to the Deseret Industries and shopped for new furniture that would fill her new home.

She picked out a new front-load washer and dryer set and an upright deep-freezer she planned to keep in the garage thinking she would visit the grocery store less if she could freeze more of her food.

When she finally went to the finance office to pay for all of her purchases, the cashier asked her if she would like to open an R.C. Willey credit account.

"I'll just put it on my debit card," she answered.

"This week we're offering a twenty percent discount on everything you buy if you open a credit account with us," the woman offered again.

Jennifer realized that twenty percent of all she was purchasing would be a sizeable amount. "Well, in that case, I'll open an account. How long before I can pay the account off?" she asked.

"You should receive your card within thirty days, and you will probably receive your first bill in the mail thirty days after that."

"Will I be charged interest for those sixty days?"

"No, we offer the first ninety days interest free."

"Very well," Jennifer said, and she filled out the credit forms.

The cashier at the window entered her information into the computer and in less than five minutes, she told Jennifer that the credit card had been denied.

Frustrated that she had wasted so much time filling out all the paperwork, she just paid for it with her debit card. "Could you tell me *why* the card was denied?" she asked the cashier.

"We don't have access to that information," she answered. "They just approve it for a certain amount or they deny it. We never know why."

Jennifer decided to investigate the reason. She'd have to remember to send letters to the credit bureaus to check her credit.

Before she left the store, she took pictures of bedroom furniture for Jay's room and allowed him to choose his own. He picked out a bed shaped and painted like a race car in bright red and a black dresser with bright primary color drawers. He asked for a bean bag instead of a chair. Jennifer wasn't sure he'd be able to get in and out of it easily, but decided to let him try, thinking it might be good physical therapy.

When Jennifer made arrangements for the utilities, she requested an unlisted telephone number. She didn't want anyone to contact her without her personally giving them her phone number. She felt vulnerable as a single woman, and now with Jay needing her protection, she felt even more need for the security of anonymity.

<<<

Jay was more than excited to leave the hospital. Jay's caseworker, his guardian at litem, Dr. Henson, Dr. Killpack, Dr. Green, and the nurses on duty were having their own farewell party for Jay. The room quieted when Jennifer walked in to take him home. Jay scurried over to her and hugged her fervently. Her eyes were moist as she personally thanked everyone for all they had done for Jay. She and the guardian at litem signed the paperwork to release him into her custody.

Jennifer handed Jay some new clothes to wear home from the hospital. Dr. Henson helped him put them on. "You look great in your new clothes," Phil told Jay with a scratchy voice as he wiped a tear from his eye and hugged him.

"I don't have to wear hospital pajamas anymore," he said with a wide grin.

Jennifer and Jay walked out of the hospital taking only a small bag of Jay's balloons and class pictures, the pair of pajamas he'd been wearing that the hospital let him keep, and a sheaf of papers with medical instructions.

Phil walked them out to Jennifer's car. Jay waved wildly at Phil as they drove off down the street.

Chapter Thirteen

Jay ran from room to room when they arrived at the house. "Yahoo," he called as he discovered each new room. "This house is awesome!" It was only minutes until he discovered the patio with the Koi swimming in the pond. "Cool," he said, and he sat down to watch them for over an hour.

Jennifer filled the office with her school books and tutoring supplies and put a small sign in the window of the office which simply read "Tutoring" and her cell phone number. She didn't get a lot of calls, but she let the local elementary school know she offered her services and that she was a state licensed school teacher. She relaxed and concluded she had done her part, now the rest was up to the Lord.

On a quiet evening, she recalled Phil Henson wiggling his bare toes on the carpet in the great room. She thought about him frequently and wondered what he was doing, but more than anything, she was engrossed in her relationship with Jay. They spent hours reading together. She had him work math problems on a white board by telling *her* what to write, but letting him do the calculations in his own mind. He got so good at it, she couldn't write as fast as he could tell her the answers. By his ninth birthday in July, he was ready for third-grade work.

Jennifer had wanted to share the gospel with Jay, but at the same time, she didn't want to pressure him into something he didn't want for himself. She discussed her situation with the Relief Society president in her ward.

A couple of weeks later, Jennifer received a phone call from Alice Horne, a member of the ward.

"I received a phone call from the Primary president explaining about Jay and his unusual circumstances," Alice explained. "Apparently the Relief Society president called her, and she felt my son, Ben, who is Jay's age might make a good companion for

Jay. I was calling to see if it might be all right to bring Ben over to meet Jay?"

Jennifer didn't hesitate for a moment. "Oh, we'd love to have you *both* come over."

"Would tomorrow afternoon be a good time for you?" Alice asked.

"We'll look forward to it. And I'll be grateful to get to know someone in the ward myself. I'm afraid it's been a bit difficult for me to socialize with Jay, and being new in the ward hasn't helped."

<<<

Jennifer introduced Ben to Jay and Ben immediately asked, "What happened to you?"

"My mother set me on fire," Jay answered.

Ben's eyes widened. "What did you do to make her that mad?"

"I didn't do anything. I was asleep and she was drunk."

"What kind of games can you play without any fingers on your hands?"

"I can read books, listen to books on tape, watch movies, and I do lots of math with my mind. Come here and I'll show you."

The boys disappeared into Jay's bedroom leaving Jennifer and Alice to get acquainted.

"I love your baby grand piano," Alice said. "Do you play?"

"I do, actually. How about you—do you play?"

"Yes, and the flute, but I don't have a lot of time to practice. More than playing either, though, I love to sing."

"Me too!" Jennifer marveled.

"Are you a soprano or an alto?" Alice asked.

"I'm a soprano, what are you?"

"I sing alto. I guess that means we could sing a duet."

"Well, let's give it a shot," Jennifer said as she led Alice over to the piano. Grabbing the Hymn book from the piano bench, she fanned through the pages until she reached the section of hymns written for women. She stopped when she reached *How Gentle God's Commands*. She began playing the introduction and Alice joined her in singing at the beginning of the song.

"Oh, that sounds so good," Alice shivered after they finished.

"We're not half bad together," Jennifer admitted.

"Wouldn't it be fun to get several women together in a singing group?" Alice asked.

"I have always wanted to do that."

"Well, what's stopping us?"

"Who do you know that would like to sing with us?" Jennifer asked.

"I know a couple of women who like to sing. I could ask them if they'd be interested."

"That's wonderful. Do you know anyone that would like to play the piano for us?"

"Not really, but I'll bet we can get suggestions from one of the women we invite to sing with us," Alice said.

Chapter Fourteen

Jennifer arranged for surrogate foster care on Sundays while she attended her Sacrament meetings. She didn't quite know what the state's requirements were for taking children to church when they had no religious affiliation. After three weeks of going without him, she decided to call Lucy and ask her if it would be okay to introduce Jay to her own religious beliefs.

Lucy said she would like to come and make a home visit and discuss some things with Jennifer. They set an appointment for the following Wednesday in the afternoon.

When Lucy arrived, she was carrying a briefcase full of papers. Jennifer had been slightly concerned about this visit, but seeing the briefcase, she was now fearful she might get the book thrown at her for attempting to do something wrong. To her complete relief, the visit proved to be the opposite. After taking a full tour through the house and visiting briefly with Jay, she sat down with Jennifer in the office and paused only briefly to make sure the door was closed and Jay was busily distracted in another room.

"Jennifer, it's obvious that you and Jay have bonded and are doing well. Jay seems happy here. Dr. Green has reported back to our agency that Jay seems to feel secure with you. Our concern that you would lose your job has obviously not been an issue. As a matter of fact, you have a beautiful and well-furnished home. Are you financially able to keep up with all of this?"

"Finances are not an issue," Jennifer admitted. "Everything you see is paid for. I only have our monthly living expenses to cover."

"Jennifer, if you weren't receiving foster parent compensation, could you still meet your expenses?"

"Yes. I don't *need* the money."

"Then may I ask why you haven't petitioned the state to adopt Jay, or is that something you don't want the responsibility of—I mean, I realize you already have a tremendous burden taking care of him now—but if you adopted him, you wouldn't need to call me to see if it was okay to take him to church or on a vacation out of the state. I don't think anyone in our agency would stop you from doing either one, but if he were legally your child, you wouldn't even feel the need to ask."

"I'm still single. Does that matter?"

"No more than it mattered to be a foster parent."

"But if I adopt him, his medical expenses might run my funds dry in a hurry."

"His medical bills will be paid for by the state even after adoption. Because of the circumstances, Jay will have a medical card until he is eighteen years old.

"Really?" Jennifer asked in surprise. "If that's the case, then tell me what I need to do to get started."

Lucy pulled papers out of her briefcase and began having Jennifer read and sign them. "I'll contact the Guardian at Litem, and we'll get the process going. You and Jay will need to appear before the family court judge and answer a few questions, but in your case, I don't think there will be any doubt or question about the benefits of this adoption."

<<<

Jennifer asked Jay if he wanted to change his name to Heaps or if he preferred to keep Borky for a last name. She pointed out there was always the possibility she might marry some day and her last name would no longer be Heaps.

Jay thought about it and asked, "So, you will be my mom, right?"

"Yes," Jennifer answered.

"Does that mean I can call you Mom then?"

"Yes, Jay, *then* you can call me Mom."

"Shouldn't a kid have the same last name as their mother?"

"Well, usually. But there are lots of children who have step-fathers and their last names don't match their mother's. Do you remember Tyler Smith from school?"

"Yeah. He had orange hair," Jay clarified.

"Yes...well, his mother had remarried after she divorced Tyler's father and her last name was changed to Barksdale. So her name wasn't Smith like his. The same thing could happen if I ever get married. My last name would change to match my husbands, but that wouldn't change your last name." *Unless my husband decided to adopt you too*, she thought, but didn't dare mention this and set Jay up for future disappointment. She knew the likelihood of her ever marrying was slim, and she didn't know how someone else would feel about adopting Jay.

"My sister might want to find me some day," he said. "If my name was different, would she be able to find me?"

"I don't know. Jennifer hadn't even thought about Jay's sister. "Do you miss Emily a lot?" she asked Jay.

"Yeah, a little. Do you think she changed her name when *she* got adopted?"

"I have no idea, Jay. I'll check with Lucy and see what I can find out. If she didn't change her name, would that influence your decision?"

"No. I *want* to change my last name."

<<<

Jennifer called Lucy. "Jay would like to see his sister, Emily. Is that possible?"

"As you know, your adoption will be a closed adoption due to the circumstances. Emily also had a closed adoption to protect the children from ever being found by their mother. I cannot give you any information about her adoption. The best I can do is call and ask the adoptive family if they would be willing to allow Jay to visit. If they are willing, we can set it up through our office, but if the adoptive parents do not agree to it, I'm afraid I can't help you."

"If they refuse to give their name or number to us, would you mind terribly giving them my name and number in case they change their mind? I'm afraid Jay will never have closure on this until he sees Emily and knows she's happy."

"I'll make a note in your file that if Emily or her parents ever wish to make contact, that it's okay to give them your name and phone number. That's the best I can do. I'll check with them and see if they're open to it."

Chapter Fifteen

Every time the phone rang over the following week, Jay would wait expectantly by Jennifer's side hoping for good news that the call was from Emily. By the end of the week, his anticipation had worn off and he no longer ran to the phone when it rang.

The Sunday following Lucy's home visit, Jennifer offered to take Jay with her to church. He was delighted to go and expressed how he had felt left out on the Sundays she had left him with someone else. Jennifer sat by Alice and Jay sat next to Ben. There were many stares from ward members. Jennifer swallowed hard and realized she had to toughen herself up for the reality that Jay would experience this kind of shock from others all through his life.

She heard parents hush their small children who were asking questions about the ugly boy wearing the mask—then they would stare themselves.

<<<

Jennifer was pleased when Alice called and enthusiastically announced, "We have takers on the singing group."

"How many do you have?"

"Four so far. What do we do now?"

"I don't know. I've never done this before. What do you suggest?"

"Well, I guess we should decide when we could get together to practice."

"Did you get any suggestions for a pianist?"

"Yes, Kate Sorensen recommended IlaRae George. I don't know her, but Kate gave her raving reviews. She was concerned about her arthritis being a bit of a problem, however. She wasn't sure how her health would affect her ability to play for long periods or in the months to come."

"Hmmm. I guess we'll have to ask her and see. Let's set up our first practice about the fifteenth of September. Jay is scheduled for some reconstructive surgery and should be out of the hospital by then."

"Okay, do you want to call IlaRae?"

"Sure, give me her number and I'll see what she says."

Alice gave Jennifer the number and the two friends ended their call.

<<<

"Is this IlaRae George?" Jennifer asked.

"It is," the woman responded.

"This is Jennifer Heaps. I am calling because your name was recommended by Kate Sorensen as an excellent pianist. We're starting up a singing group and would be practicing once a week and will be accepting performance engagements during the holidays or for other special occasions. We're looking for an accompanist and wondered if you'd be interested?"

There was a long silence and then, "When do you practice?"

"That is still to be determined. When would be the best time for you?"

"Wednesdays or Thursdays in the mornings or evenings, or on Saturday mornings," IlaRae answered.

"Does this mean you're interested?"

"I might be. What kind of music are you planning to perform?"

"We, meaning myself and Alice, the other lady who is helping me get this started, would like to have a fun variety of popular and upbeat songs, some spiritual, and of course, lots of Christmas music. Does that sound like something you'd like to do?"

"I always wanted to travel the world and perform with a group like this. I just thought I'd get the chance when I was a lot younger. Now I'm just a gray-haired, frumpy old grandma. I'm like all the old ladies in nursing homes—the most exciting part of my day is having a bowel movement."

Trying to keep from bursting into laughter, Jennifer responded, "Whoa, nobody said anything about world-wide tours. I don't think we'll ever be famous… just a little group who loves music and enjoys each other's companionship. Are you with me?"

"Yeah," IlaRae said without enthusiasm. "But I still think we should go places and do things that might be exciting."

"Well, we'll see about that. How about September 15th for our first practice?"

Jennifer gave IlaRae her address and told her she was looking forward to meeting her before she hung up.

Chapter Sixteen

Jay's surgery was scheduled for September 7th. The hope was that after this surgery healed, he would actually have lips and be able to eat real food without having it fall out of his mouth.

Dr. Henson had finished his residency and moved on to his practice at the clinic. Jay missed him—so did Jennifer, but she didn't let anyone know. Dr. Killpack invited Phil to come back and assist him for Jay's surgery. Jay would never see Phil. He would be asleep the entire time.

When Jay was taken into surgery, Dr. Phil Henson stopped briefly to say hello to Jennifer on his way into the operating room. "How are you doing?" he asked.

Jennifer noticed the enthusiasm in his voice. "Good. I'm enjoying every minute of my time with Jay. I thought I'd miss my students more, but I have a fulltime student at home with Jay." Her heart was pounding but she tried to stay calm. "And how do you like your new job?"

"I like it a lot. I must say I've been looking forward to seeing Jay again—and you too. But Jay will probably be asleep most of the time I'm here."

"Well, maybe you'll have to come and visit him while he's in the hospital after he wakes up," she offered hopefully.

"I think I might do that," he countered. "Will you be here after he comes out of surgery?"

"Yes, I won't leave him here alone."

"Is there anyone else coming to see him?" Phil asked.

"Not that I know of. His caseworker might show up, but I doubt it. She's pretty well left all of his care up to me at this point."

"Is that all right with you? Or are you wishing you could have more support?"

"Oh no, I prefer it this way. Jay seems pretty much like my own child now."

Phil hurried off to surgery saying he'd see her after they were finished.

<<<

Jennifer read a novel while Jay was in surgery. The hours dragged on for what seemed like forever. When Doctors Killpack and Henson came through the surgical doors to the waiting room, they appeared to be tired, but in good spirits.

"It went really well, Jennifer. He won't look like Phil here, but I think he'll be able to chew real food when he heals," Doctor Killpack said.

Jennifer had to admit that even with Dr. Henson's hair disheveled from the cap he'd been wearing, his five o'clock shadow, and his towering height, he was a handsome man.

Dr. Killpack told Jennifer that Jay was in the recovery room and would be there for about another hour, then he excused himself and left. Phil asked Jennifer if she would like to join him in the cafeteria while she waited. "I don't know about you, but I'm hungry."

"Actually, now that you mention it, I am rather hungry," Jennifer said.

"So, how do you like yard work? Or did you decide to hire it out?" Phil asked Jennifer.

"I hired it out. Although after watching the lawn care folks do the trimming and mowing several times, I think I could actually do it myself if I had the equipment. Quite honestly, I didn't even know how to take care of a yard. My Dad always did that sort of thing when I was growing up. Mom and I were a little more domestic. How about you? Did you find yourself a house? Or are you still renting?"

"I'm still renting. Quite frankly, I lost all interest in buying a house when I lost the deal on that last house we looked at in the spring."

Jennifer choked on her water, and coughed until she almost turned blue. When she regained her composure, she blurted out, "*You* made an offer on that house?"

74

"Yeah, somebody else made an offer at the same time and they were paying with cash. The owners took the other offer. I can't blame them, but I haven't been able to imagine a house as nice as that one since."

Jennifer felt flushed and she wondered if her face was crimson red. She hadn't even considered her offer on the house might have trumped *Phil's* offer. She should have known Phil would make an offer. He loved the house as much as she did. *Would* she have made an offer if she had known *he* was making an offer too? What would he do if he knew *she* had made the cash offer? She was still holding on to the idea that maybe he'd realize he was madly in love with her and *then* she could tell him she was wealthy. If she told him she owned that house now, he'd either marry her just to get the house, or never speak to her again! She changed the subject at lightning speed.

"So how is the new job working out?"

"I like it. I enjoy the doctors I work with and we have a nice staff."

The word staff conjured up visions of several young women who might be attractive and provide lots of competition for the good Doctor's attentions. "How many people are on your staff?"

"We have six ladies that work in our office. Nadine is our office manager, Gladys does the insurance billing, and the other four are our office assistants."

"What does an office assistant do exactly?"

"Well, they're each assigned to assist one of the doctors. They set up the examining rooms, take blood pressures, get injections ready, take things to the lab and test them, and they stay in the room with us during an examination if our patient is a woman—which most of them are."

Jennifer could feel her blood pressure rising and she was ashamed of herself for feeling jealous unlike anything she had ever felt before. She had been irate with Braxton when he got jealous thinking she was flirting with a policeman. Now here she was visualizing Phil, a man who she had no real claim on, flirting with the women in his office, and she didn't even know anything about them! What was *wrong* with her?

"Tell me about the other Doctor's in your office," she groped for coherent things to talk about.

"They're really great. We have Dr. Sharp. He's exactly that—sharp in his dress, his work, and his personality. He's a likeable guy. Then there's Dr. Blomquist. We all call her Dr. Blonde for short. She has blonde hair and she's witty as can be. Fortunately she takes our teasing quite well. Then there's Dr. Halverson. He's kind of like the father of the group. He'll be retiring next year. That's why they offered me my position. I'm his replacement. I have a long way to go to get his experience, although he seems to think I have the advantage because I have just finished my residency and learned the newest and latest procedures in our field. I'm the youngest, the only unmarried doctor, and definitely the most inexperienced of the group."

"You have a *woman* doctor in your group?"

"Yes, and she's wonderful! She definitely has an advantage over the rest of us since the female patients seem more at ease with her than with a man."

Jennifer sensed she might be better off talking about politics—she couldn't believe how sensitive she was. This was completely out of character for her. "So, what have you been doing in your spare time since we last saw you?"

"Not much of anything. How about you? Anybody *new* and exciting in your life?"

"Just Jay. It's been fulfilling to have him living with me."

"How has he been adjusting to the changes in his life?"

"I think he's been grateful to be out of the hospital and have a little freedom. Dr. Green, the psychiatrist, has been working with him and said Jay's making great strides in overcoming all the fear and anger he had toward his parents for abandoning him and abusing him. He said Jay's using humor as a coping mechanism. He's done well in his studies. I believe he'll actually pass up his age group soon at the rate he's learning."

76

"So Jay and Dr. Green are the *only* men in your life?"

"Well, I guess you and Dr. Killpack would have to be in there somewhere," she smiled.

"I'm afraid I wouldn't qualify as a man in your life. I haven't even seen you since Jay left the hospital. I've wanted to call you several times, but I wasn't sure you wanted me to."

"Why wouldn't I want you to call me?" Jennifer was surprised.

"I got the idea that maybe you didn't want me interfering in your life."

"Well, here's your opportunity to interfere all you want to. I imagine we'll be living out of a suitcase in the hospital for the next week, so you can drop in and see us any time. Speaking of which, I think my hour is about up. Jay's probably in his room by now. I should get back."

<<<

Moving to a new condominium in an upscale high-rise, was Braxton's latest attempt at keeping up appearances. He found himself so absorbed in ways to get large quantities of money without working for it that he decided he didn't need a job any more.

Using searches for single women online, he began to wine and dine them with extravagance, always looking for new sources of income. He was hoping to find someone naive enough to fall for his charms and yet smart enough to have financial means.

He found it easy to get gift cards to the finest restaurants and theatres through the internet so there was never a question raised about the name on the credit card when it came time to pay.

Two credit cards were maxed out and so he began to use a third. When he got the credit card statements, he made minimum payments on the cards he hadn't maxed out already so they wouldn't freeze the accounts. But on the full accounts, he laughed and tossed them in the trash. "I'll milk them for all their worth before they shut me down! By the time they're all useless, I'll have a new trusting soul."

Chapter Seventeen

After a frustrating day of not being able to speak because of the bandages on his face, Jay had finally drifted off to sleep. Jennifer was reading a book when Dr. Phil Henson walked into the room dressed in tan slacks, a light yellow shirt with the top button undone, and a brown sports jacket.

"How is he?" he asked Jennifer in a quiet voice.

"He was pretty angry that his mouth was bandaged. He wants to communicate but doesn't know how. It would be easier if he could write what he wants to say, but for obvious reasons, that is not an option either. Fortunately, Dr. Killpack has ordered the nurses to keep him sedated so he's finally sleeping."

"The swelling will take several weeks to completely go down. The bandages will probably be there for about three days. Then he will get the opportunity to learn how to speak all over again. Meanwhile, I'm sure you could use a meal, and I could certainly use some company. Shall we?"

Looking down at her wrinkled shirt and old jeans, she asked, "What did you have in mind?"

"How about dinner at the Cottonwood Country Club restaurant?"

"I'm not dressed up for a nice restaurant. How about something a little more casual?"

"Burgers it is. But tomorrow night, it's La Caille for sure. *If* you'll have me, I would be delighted to have you accompany me at a dinner with the other doctors in my office and their spouses."

"La Caille?" she echoed. "Isn't that a bit extravagant for a peasant like me?"

"I beg your pardon? Anyone as lovely as Miss Jennifer Heaps and as kind as the *Teacher*, deserves the finest in life!"

"Will Jay be all right without me for that long?"

"He'll probably be sleeping like he is now."

"La Caille it will be then," she answered in a quiet voice.

At six-thirty in the evening, wearing a black pinstripe suit, white shirt, and his favorite black silk necktie with small red and white specks on it, Phil walked into Jay's room. Jennifer slipped on her black patent two-inch sling back heels and stood to meet him.

Phil caught his breath. Instead of her usual ponytail, her blonde hair cascaded down over her shoulders in soft curls. Her face seemed to glow with the addition of a little makeup. Her three-quarter length dress was a soft apricot color lightly frosted with iridescent beading around the neckline and on the lower edge of the elbow-length sleeves. With two-inch heels on, he still stood a foot taller than her. His heart melted. *She's what? Adorable? No, she's too classy for adorable. Is it regal? No. She carries no airs of importance. I'm not sure exactly how to describe her.* He lost all sense of propriety. Taking three broad strides, he pulled her into his arms, bent and kissed her.

Realizing what he had done, he let her go and cleared his throat. Jennifer's face flushed deep pink. She looked down at her trembling hands and swallowed hard several times as if trying to gain her composure.

"I'm sorry," he apologized, "forgive me. I don't know what got into me. You're just so….so…." again he was looking for the right word—"absolutely perfect!"

Jennifer smiled, "Then I guess I pass your inspection?"

"I'm sorry if I gave you the impression that I was scrutinizing you. I was actually prolonging my indulgence in looking at the exquisite sight before me."

Phil felt more relaxed than he had anticipated. Jennifer's dress was completely modest and there was no reason for him to be concerned about what his colleagues might focus on.

He observed Jennifer as she socialized with everyone. She spoke to everyone at the table using their names. Phil assumed she had developed this talent from teaching school and having to learn names of students quickly. She did nothing to call attention to herself, but instead, seemed to deflect the conversation back to the interests of others. He was amazed at how knowledgeable she was on such a wide range of subjects. It was evident by the end of the evening, that his colleagues and their spouses thought Jennifer was his superior. His admiration for her grew by leaps and bounds. She was so unassuming, and so *lovable*. He was definitely smitten!

<<<

Braxton's date excused herself to use the restroom, and since he was no longer confined to charming conversation and paying full attention to her, he glanced around the restaurant. When his eyes rested on the lovely woman dressed in the apricot gown, his mouth turned up at the corners. He waited until he caught her eye and then blew her a kiss. He couldn't believe how good his life was now because of her.

<<<

Jennifer faltered for only a moment. Seeing Braxton so unexpectedly in such a fine restaurant caught her off guard. *Why was he blowing me a kiss?* Then remembering who she was with and how lovely her evening was going, she tried to concentrate on the people at her table, but she found herself glancing over at Braxton every now and again. She couldn't help noticing the lady with the revealing black mini-dress that joined him at his table.

If she were to write her list of things she was thankful for now, there would be no question mark after "*I'm grateful I didn't marry Braxton.*"

<<<

As they were preparing to leave the restaurant, Dr. Halverson leaned toward Phil and winked as he whispered, "She's a *keeper*!"

When they were in the car, Phil asked Jennifer if she would like him to take her home or back to the hospital.

"The hospital," she answered a little too quickly then she softly added, "That's where my car is."

"Right," he responded. He reached for her hand over the console and held it all the way back to the hospital parking lot.

When he pulled the car to a stop, he raised her hand to his lips and kissed it before shifting into park and turning off the engine. "Jennifer, I can't tell you how much I've enjoyed your company tonight. You were the perfect dinner companion."

"Thank you. I enjoyed it, and you're right about the doctors in your office—they're all delightful. I can see why you enjoy working with them."

"Well, obviously they were impressed with you as well. Dr. Halverson especially seemed to find you charming."

"Whatever gave you that idea?"

"Because he told me you were a *keeper*."

Jennifer's face reddened. "No. That was my dad. He was a *beekeeper*. Did I ever tell you that?"

"No, I don't believe you ever mentioned it. You only said you have no living relatives."

"My parents were both killed in a plane crash three years ago. I was their only child, so now it's just me—and Jay."

Not wanting to dwell on a painful experience, he asked her, "Where were you raised?"

"Near Pocatello, Idaho—lived there all my life and graduated from Idaho State University. After I graduated, I decided it was time to grow up and get out on my own. It was as hard for my parents as it was for me since I was their only child, but I knew it was time. That's when I found a teaching position in West Valley and moved to Utah. I'd been teaching here two years when they were in the plane crash.

"What about you?" she asked. I'm guessing you are not originally from Utah?"

"No. I'm actually from San Jose, California. I have two older siblings—one brother and one sister. My parents still live in the same house in San Jose. Dad's retired now. Mom retired last year. My brother, Tim, is an attorney. He and his wife and two children live in Alameda. My sister, Ruth, has her Master's Degree in Comparative literature. She works for a radio station based out of Los Angeles and she can be a pain in the neck sometimes. Her

82

husband is an easy-going insurance agent in Orange County. I don't know anybody else who could put up with Ruthie. They have one son."

"Wow. I can't imagine what it would be like to have a brother and sister. I always wanted to have siblings, but my mother could never carry a baby full-term after she had me."

"That's too bad. It was kind of fun when we were growing up. Tim and I still get along well, but Ruth and I seem to clash a lot now. I go home to visit my folks once or twice a year for a few days—they're great."

"Are you happy here in Utah?" Jennifer asked.

"Yes, I like having the four seasons. I miss the beaches and the ocean, but not enough to let it pull me from where I am. I'd like to get settled a little more permanently in a home, get married and start a family. What about you? If you could pick any place in the world to live, where would it be?" he asked.

"I haven't been anywhere but Idaho and Utah. If I were to choose *any* place in the world, I'd have to see a lot more places to make an informed decision. I have nothing against Utah. It has become a comfortable place for me since my parent's death. My students became my family, and now Jay fills my life with purpose."

"I'm sure sorry about your parents' accident. It must be awfully lonely having no family."

"It has been. But I'm beginning to develop friendships."

"What are your hobbies?" he asked.

"I love music. As a matter of fact, my friend, Alice and I are starting a singing group. We haven't had our first practice yet, though. What about you?"

Phil's sense of delight was impossible to hide and he broke into a wide grin. "Oddly enough, I love to sing as well. I sing baritone in an all-male choir. Do you have any other hobbies?"

"Well, I love teaching children. I even enjoy cooking if I have a good excuse. I haven't done much because there is only myself to feed. But now Jay should be able to eat real food, I might get motivated. Strained baby food through a tube isn't exactly fixing him a meal."

"Well, it so happens I like to eat, and since I've been going to school, I've done most of my eating in restaurants. So a home cooked meal sounds perfectly wonderful. How about if I buy the ingredients and bring them over to your place and you can cook a dinner for me and Jay when he gets out of the hospital?"

"Uh…I have an even better idea. How about *I* provide the fixin's and we take Jay on a picnic?"

"You set the date and time and I'll see if I can manage to be away from work and the golf course."

"You golf?"

"Yeah—don't tell me, you golf too?" he asked in disbelief.

"No, but I've always wanted to learn how to golf and ski."

"Would you allow me to be your instructor?"

"I'd love it!"

"Excellent. When would you like to start?"

"Well, I don't imagine skiing would be real good until there's snow on the mountain," she said.

"Golf tomorrow?" he asked hopefully.

"What about Jay?" she asked with a chuckle.

"What *about* Jay? He'll be in the hospital for a few more days. Are you nervous about leaving him in the care of the nurses for a while?"

"I'm sure the nurses are capable. I haven't left him much since he's been in the hospital this time—tonight is the longest. I guess since I have applied for adoption, I feel so responsible for him— like he's already my child.

"You applied for *adoption*? You never mentioned it to me before now."

"Yeah. We have a court date set for the adoption hearing on October 21st. I'm hoping it'll be final after that."

"That's fantastic! I didn't know single people could adopt."

"Neither did I, until Lucy told me. About tomorrow, shouldn't Jay be awake more?"

84

"I believe Dr. Killpack is planning to take the bandages off."

"He'll be anxious to talk. What little he has been awake, I've played guessing games with him trying to ask yes or no questions. He raises his hand if the answer is yes."

Phil was enjoying Jennifer's company so much he didn't want it to end. "What about Monday?" he asked.

Jennifer seemed to give it some thought and agreed that Monday should work out fine as long as things were going well with Jay. "I suppose I should get back to him now. I really have been gone a lot longer than I had planned."

Phil knew this couldn't last forever, but he wished it could. He got out of the car and opened the door for Jennifer. When she stood up, he took her in his arms, lifted her chin with his hand, and looked into her eyes for a long moment. "I may have over-reacted to your stunning appearance earlier this evening, but would it be all right if I kissed you now?"

"I think it would be wonderful."

He leaned down and pulled her tightly into his arms. His lips sought hers, softly at first, and then more fervently, like he had never kissed anyone before. He felt her body relax—she seemed to melt in his arms and his head was exploding.

Jennifer pulled away from him, staggered back, and gasped.

"Are you all right?" he asked.

"I'm not sure," she said. "I think I need to breathe. But just to make sure it's what I think it is, could we try that again?"

He threw his head back in joyous laughter. "I knew it! You're feeling the same thing I am aren't you?"

"I don't know. What are *you* feeling?"

"Here, I'll show you," he said. Then he pulled her back into his arms and gave her a repeat performance. Again, she melted into his arms and he realized it was time to stop and take her inside before things got out of hand.

He released her from his embrace and she stood there with her eyes still closed and her head tilted upward as if waiting for more or maybe savoring the feeling a moment longer. To steady her from tipping over, he put one arm around her shoulder and said, "Here, let me walk you to Jay's room before I lose control of myself and decide to hold you hostage for my selfish desires."

Chapter Eighteen

Jennifer was reading to Jay out of The Book of Mormon each day now. He had asked her about the book after attending church with her three weeks in a row. He had not had any religious affiliation in his nuclear family, but he did understand the concept of God being a higher power. She purchased a paperback copy for him, had the binding trimmed off, and spiral bound, so it could rest open. He seemed to enjoy The Book of Mormon and was filled with questions. The book was often left open on Jay's bed stand so he could read out of it if he wanted. He was able to turn pages with his stubs, but he couldn't hold the book in his hands without dropping it.

Each day for the following week, Jay's hospital room became the rendezvous location for Phil to meet up with Jennifer. Phil had gotten into the habit of kissing her hello and goodbye, and he had fondly started to call her Jen, which she found endearing.

Jay's feeding tube was finally removed and he was able to eat almost anything. Jay felt more liberated than the first time he left the hospital. He struggled to learn to swallow and often choked on his food, but he soon got the hang of it. He was especially excited to taste ice cream again.

After three surgeries to repair his lips, this was the final one. The first surgery had taken place within the first few weeks after he was burned, but the graft didn't take. Another attempt was made, but the healing process had been long and slow. He was able to have the tracheotomy closed after the initial healing of his lungs and his lip graft. Jay didn't enjoy surgery, but it became so ordinary he became complacent and tolerant about the pain and inconvenience. Already there were plans being made to construct a nose and ears for him.

On Friday evening Phil looked at the open book on the bed stand and asked Jay about it.

"I'm reading The Book of Mormon," he proudly announced.

Phil looked questioningly at Jennifer. "Are *you* a Mormon?" he asked.

"Yes. Aren't you?"

"No. I'm a Christian, but I don't belong to any organized religion."

"Oh. I assumed you were L.D.S. for some reason—I'm not sure why. I guess because you didn't drink tea or coffee, smoke, or swear, I thought you were one of us. How much do you know about the L.D.S. Church?"

"I know they don't really practice polygamy like everybody says they do. And I know they don't grow horns like some people believe. Mostly they're nice people. All the other doctors in my office are Mormons. You know I like *all* of them."

"Would you be interested in knowing more about the church?" Jennifer held hopeful.

"Not really. I've been pretty content without any specific religion."

Jennifer's voice dropped showing her disappointment when she said, "Oh."

"Will this affect our relationship?" Phil asked.

"*Only* if you were planning to have our relationship become more than just a friendship."

He collapsed into a chair and looked into Jennifer's eyes like a scolded puppy. "Can we continue the golf and ski lessons?"

"I still want to learn how to do those things. If you don't mind spending the time teaching me, I'd appreciate the lessons," she said.

"Of course."

Jay, who had been quietly listening to the conversation now asked, "*Golf* and *ski* lessons?"

"Yes!" both Jennifer and Phil answered at the same moment.

"I told Jen I would teach her how to golf and ski when she told me she wanted to learn how. Is that okay with you? Or did you plan to keep her all to yourself?"

Jay grinned. "It's okay with me as long as I can come and watch sometimes. Maybe I could be your caddy—if I ever learn how to drive with these useless hands."

"Maybe we can invent a modified golf cart with handles so you could drive it," Phil suggested.

"That would be awesome!" Jay said with enthusiasm.

Phil acted funny and nervous before he said, "Goodnight," and slipped from the room.

"He didn't kiss you goodbye," Jay said.

"No. I guess that's because we can only be good friends and not date anymore," Jennifer tried to explain.

"How come you can't still date?" Jay asked.

"Well, Jay, I'm committed to my beliefs. I will never marry someone who isn't a member of the church and willing to take me to the temple to get married. So there's really no point in dating someone if you can't marry them. We can only be friends."

"You really like him, *don't* you?" It was more a statement than a question.

"Yeah. I'm afraid I like him a lot."

"He really likes you too. I can tell. My dad never said things to my mom like he says to you. They never kissed each other either. I thought you and Phil might get married and then he could be my dad. I would have liked that."

Jennifer held back the tears she felt surfacing. She hadn't realized before now how much her decision to marry would impact Jay. Could any other man *love* Jay like Phil did? Was it fair to Jay to marry someone that met her own criteria but might not be a good father to Jay? Wasn't Jay's welfare as important to Heavenly Father as hers? Phil was such a perfect match in every way except religion.

Could she ever *consider* compromising her religious beliefs? She couldn't. There were some decisions that were absolute and this was one of them—she was sure of that. Loneliness filled her at the realization she might never marry and she would only have Jay to keep her company until he grew up and left home.

"I would have liked that too, Little Buddy. But some things just aren't meant to be, I guess."

Chapter Nineteen

On Wednesday morning, Jay spiked a fever. Dr. Killpack examined him carefully, but could see no sign of infection around the graft area on the mouth or the area by his healing incision from the removal of the feeding tube. He ordered a strep culture. The quick test showed negative, but it would take twenty-four hours for the final test results to verify strep. His white cell count was too high—he had to have an infection somewhere. He checked Jay's abdomen for possible appendicitis. Jay winced and cried out in pain when the Doctor pressed and released his hand on Jay's right side.

"He's too young to have this happen," Dr. Killpack murmured. "This is the last thing this boy needs right now." He slipped out of the room and called a general surgeon, Dr. Call. "I need you to come and take a look at one of my patients at Primary Children's Hospital. I think he may need your laparoscopic expertise. There's one caveat—he's nine years old and has thick scar tissue from skin grafts. He's one of my severe burn patients."

"Geees, you sure know how to pick 'em!"

"This poor kid has been through the mill. How soon can you get here?"

"I have three patients in my office right now. I'll have my office staff call and reschedule my afternoon patients. Let me finish up with these three and then I'll be over. See if you can schedule the O.R. just in case. I should be at the hospital by one-thirty this afternoon."

"You got it. You want me to start an IV with antibiotics?"

"Wouldn't hurt."

<<<

Jennifer sat by Jay and wondered what more she could do. She put a cool rag to his forehead, but it wasn't helping.

Dr. Killpack entered the room. "Dr. Call will be here this afternoon. I've scheduled the O.R. at three o'clock for an emergency appendectomy. I'm relatively sure he's having an appendicitis attack. Dr. Call is one of the best laparoscopic surgeons I know. Jay should be feeling much better by tomorrow afternoon. For now, we're going to get him started on an IV with antibiotics and pain killers. He'll probably be drowsy in about five minutes until he comes out of surgery."

Jennifer took Jay's hand into hers and kissed it tenderly. "I'm so sorry, Honey," she said softly while the nurse inserted the IV into his other arm. *Poor kid must feel like a pin cushion.* Jay didn't complain when the IV went in. He didn't even flinch. Within seconds, he was dozing off to sleep.

Jennifer remembered when, as a teenager, she had seen her mother fall from the loft in the barn and hit the tractor with her head. Her lifeless body lay on the barn floor in contorted angles. Jennifer had been sure she was dead. She screamed for her father and witnessed her mother regain consciousness as soon as he gave her a blessing, and miraculously, she had no broken bones or any other negative effects. Because of that experience, she had great faith in the priesthood.

Jennifer called Alice, "Hey, do you think Dave could come to the hospital and bring someone with him to give Jay a blessing?"

"Sure. Is something wrong?"

"He's got appendicitis, and he's going in for emergency surgery at three this afternoon."

"Oh, dear. Dave won't be home from work until after six. Would it be okay if I call Brother Sheffield—he's retired?

"Sure. I didn't even think about it being a weekday. I kind of lose track of time here in the hospital. Come to think of it, tonight is our first choir practice."

"Do you need me to open the house and host the practice, or should we postpone it for a week?"

"No... don't cancel it. If I can't make it, you have my spare key. You can take care of it. Jay will probably be asleep anyway. If Dr. Killpack or Dr. Call say it's okay, I'll come home for choir practice."

"Honestly, Jennifer, I don't know how you do it all. You're something else! Isn't there something I can do for you?"

"Just get me a couple of priesthood brethren here to give Jay a blessing."

"Will do."

"Thanks, Alice. You're the best!"

Phil Henson appeared with Dr. Killpack at the door of Jay's room before one-thirty in the afternoon. "I hope you don't mind, but I called Dr. Henson and told him about Jay's condition. I know what a vested interest he has taken in Jay. I also thought you could use a little moral support," Dr. Killpack explained.

The look of concern in Phil's eyes didn't go unnoticed by Jennifer. He hurried over to her side and lifted her hand to his lips. "Are you going to be all right?" he asked with concern.

"I'll be fine. It's Jay I'm concerned about. Isn't there anything that can go *right* in his life?"

"Yes. He has *you* in his life," Phil answered.

Dr. Call entered the room, looked at Jay's chart, poked him in the side a few times and watched him wince through his drowsiness. "Yep. I'd say we're going to surgery. Have you got the room scheduled?"

"Yes, at three o'clock." Dr. Killpack said.

"Okay. Have the orderly bring him up at two-thirty to prep him," and then Dr. Call left the room with Dr. Killpack at his heels.

"What time is it now?" Jennifer asked Phil.

"It's about one forty-five, why?"

"I called and asked my friend, Alice, to send someone to give Jay a priesthood blessing before he goes into surgery. I hope they get here in time."

Phil took hold of her hands and pulled her up to her feet. She looked up into his eyes to discern what he was trying to do. He was gazing down at her and their eyes locked for a long moment. Finally, Phil pulled Jen into his arms and she willingly let him hold her close. He kissed her hair and said, "I wish there was some way I could make him better."

"I keep wishing I could too. The Lord must have something big in store for this little guy, for Satan to try so hard to destroy him."

"Makes you wonder docsn't it?" Phil whispered. He slowly lifted Jennifer's chin and then bent to kiss her softly. "Jen," he murmured into her hair "*What* am I going to *do*? I *love* you—*and* I love Jay. And yet, you have made it clear we *can't* be a family."

Tears began to trickle down her cheeks. Oh, how she had longed to hear him say those words—but under different circumstances. Now there was nothing she could do. "I love you too," she confessed, "but I know it would never work with different religious beliefs."

"Are they truly that different?" Phil challenged. "My mother is Baptist and my father is Episcopalian. *They've* made it through all these years."

"They aren't members of the Church of Jesus Christ of Latter-day Saints. There is a big difference—huge."

"Explain to me the difference," he begged.

"When I get married, I want it to be for time and all eternity, not just until death do us part. There's only one place and one way to have that and that's to be married in a temple by someone holding the authority of God to perform such an eternal seal."

"You mean—forever?"

"Yes. Forever. Not just for this life, but for the next life too."

"I've *always* believed that's what marriages *are*—never ending."

"Have you ever witnessed a marriage ceremony? They always pronounce the couple 'husband and wife until death do you part.'"

"Yeah, I have heard that, but I suppose I never analyzed the words that much" Phil admitted.

"Our church teaches that families are forever—father, mother, and children. I don't want to lose a husband because we didn't take the time to get married in the right place by the right person. You would have a *little* time together, but you couldn't enjoy the moments you had together for the fear of dying and losing each other. It would be settling for the crumbs of life when you could have had the full banquet."

"I think I know what you mean."

The door to the room opened and Brother Sheffield and Brother Cox peeked in the door. "Are we in the right place?" Brother Cox asked.

Phil let go of Jen and stepped back.

"Yes," Jennifer answered. "I'm so glad you could come. Jay is going into surgery in about half an hour. Could you please give him a blessing?"

"Be glad to," said Brother Sheffield. "I hope we weren't interrupting anything," he said as he looked at Jennifer and then at Phil with a little gleam in his eye.

"No. You're fine," Phil answered.

The two Priesthood bearers administered to Jay promising him a quick and healthy recovery from the surgery. Jennifer was relieved to hear it. She knew things would go well after that. The men wished Jennifer and Jay well.

"Is there anything else we can do for you?" Brother Cox asked Jennifer.

"Have either of you driven by the house and noticed if the lawn has been mowed? I have a fellow who is supposed to mow it each week, but since I wasn't there to pay him last week, he might not bother to come back."

"We'll drive by and take a look at it on our way home. If it looks like it needs work, maybe we can contact the Elders Quorum President. He probably needs something to do—it's been pretty quiet in the ward lately."

Jennifer cringed. She didn't like the idea of having others taking care of her. "Just give me a call here at the hospital, will you? If the mower didn't come, I'll call him—but please don't call the Elders."

"Well, if you insist," Brother Sheffield said.

"I do," Jennifer said.

"Well, best wishes to you and the boy again," said Brother Sheffield, and then turning to Phil, he said with a mischievous grin, "I wish *you* well, too, young man."

"Thank you, Sir," Phil blushed. Jen thought how cute he looked with pink cheeks.

The orderly came to get Jay and the two men quickly left. Jay was whisked off to surgery, leaving Phil and Jennifer alone. "How long do you think they will be in surgery?" she asked him.

"Probably not more than one hour if everything goes well."

"Did you have something planned for tonight?" Jennifer asked.

"I planned to be here with you and Jay if it's all right with you."

"Well, actually, I have a huge favor to ask of you, if you don't mind. I have a choir practice at my house at seven o'clock until nine. Would you mind staying with Jay while I go home and host our practice?"

"I don't mind," Phil said, "Although *Jay* probably won't be aware of my presence."

"Well, I'd feel much better knowing there was someone familiar here with him if he wakes up and needs something."

"Your wish is my command. Meanwhile, have you had anything to eat all day?" Phil asked.

"I had some cereal for breakfast. I haven't had much of an appetite since then."

"Well, how about I take you down to the cafeteria and we get a sandwich or something?"

"I think I'm about ready for that, thank you."

They walked to the cafeteria in silence. Once they purchased something to eat, they found a quiet table off in a corner.

"I feel so helpless at times, and yet I know Jay has a special mission here or he wouldn't still be alive. I hope I can help him realize his potential," she said.

"You're doing a great job, Jen. You need to take life one day at a time and be glad for the successes of each day. Today we'll be thankful Jay survived an appendectomy. Tomorrow we'll be thrilled to see him smile and able to walk again without severe abdominal pain. On Friday, we'll think about *Friday*."

"For someone who has always planned for the future and prepared well in advance, this is not an easy pill to swallow," she explained.

"I'm sure it's not. Right now, Jay needs your emotional support. My concern is for you. Who will give *you* emotional support?" Phil looked longingly into her eyes as if hoping she would choose him.

"I'm not sure," Jennifer admitted. "I'll have to rely on the Lord and Alice for now."

Phil let out a sigh. "I guess we'd better get back to Jay's room. He should be out of surgery soon."

Jennifer looked at her plate and realized she had only eaten about half of her food. She had no appetite. Then she noticed Phil's plate was about the same. "You must not be hungry," she commented.

"I brought you down to take care of *your* hunger, not mine," he said, then admitted, "I don't seem to have much of an appetite lately."

Jennifer wondered if his concern was about Jay. "Are you upset or worried about something?"

"Concerned about two very important people in my life," he answered dully without divulging names.

Jennifer didn't comment, but stood to return her food tray. Phil followed.

Jay returned from the recovery room before Jennifer had to leave the hospital to go home for choir practice. Jay was mostly sleeping and when he did wake up, he was groggy. Phil assured her he wouldn't leave Jay's side while she was gone.

Chapter Twenty

Jennifer stopped at the post office and sorted through her mail. There were credit reports from Equifax and TransUnion. She sucked in her breath when she looked at the long list of credit cards open in her name with high balances and late payments over ninety days. No wonder she had been denied credit at R.C. Willey's. But she had never opened any of these accounts! Obviously, her identity had been stolen, and she needed to do something quick, but what? A creepy feeling that someone was watching her made her skin crawl. She had never experienced such a feeling of violation. She noticed the opening dates on the accounts—all within a month of each other—starting in November—ten months ago. She couldn't believe someone had been using her name that long without her knowledge.

She wanted to kick herself for waiting so long to contact the credit bureaus. She should have contacted them in the Spring right after R.C. Willey's turned her down, but she had been busy getting the house set up to bring Jay home. She hadn't worried about it until August. It had just become routine over her years as a teacher to get things in order and follow-up on details before school started. She wouldn't put this off again. She'd contact an attorney in the morning.

She quickly took a shower and changed into some fresh clothes. She threw a batch of laundry into the washer, blew her hair dry and curled it for a change. She was so tired of sticking it into a ponytail for convenience. She felt much better after freshening herself up, and she realized she needed to take better care of herself. She turned the buzzer on the dryer up loud so she would be sure to hear it while they were singing when the clothes had finished drying.

At fifteen minutes before the hour, the doorbell rang. A woman in her seventies stood at the door. She was heavyset and clad in a worn purple housecoat with grape-colored canvas shoes covering her bare feet. Large swollen ankles poured over the edge of her sneakers. She had short, thinning gray hair that didn't seem to have any particular style except it was slightly curly.

"I'm IlaRae George. Now that you've seen me, do you still *want* me, or should I leave right now?" Her eyes were filled with mischief. Jennifer could see she would be a lot of spunk and fun to work with if she played as well as Kate had alluded to.

"Come in," Jennifer answered. "By all means we still want you."

IlaRae looked at her surroundings, and sat down on the piano bench. "Nice piano. Is it in tune?"

"I hope so," Jennifer answered. "Why don't you play a song or two until everyone arrives and tell me what you think?"

IlaRae began with a few scales and finger exercises. "I need to warm these old fingers up," she explained. And then she began to make magic with the keyboard. She played a medley of songs from Broadway musicals, including: "I'm Gonna Wash that Man Right Outa' My Hair", "Memories", "Climb Every Mountain", and she ended with "You'll Never Walk Alone". "I guess it's in tune enough," she concluded.

In the meantime, Alice and Nadine Archibald arrived and sat mesmerized with Jennifer listening to IlaRae play.

When IlaRae announced she was finished playing by dubbing the piano "in tune," the three ladies applauded at her performance.

The doorbell rang again, and three ladies were giggling at the front door when Jennifer answered it.

"I understand there's a gig goin' on here tonight," a striking woman with salt and pepper hair wearing a black pantsuit said. Her bright blue eyes sparkled. "Is this the right place?"

"Indeed it is. I'm Jennifer Heaps. Won't you please come in?"

The three women entered and for a brief moment, they stood in silence in the entry.

"Please come into the great room and meet the others," Jennifer said.

They trailed behind her to the great room like ants marching in a line toward a picnic laid out on a blanket.

When introductions were made, Jennifer learned that the distinguished looking woman who had spoken at the door was Kate Sorensen. Kate had apparently been cast in leading roles in musicals and had a beautiful soprano voice.

IlaRae had chosen songs that were a nice mixture of fun, spiritual, and girlish music. Jennifer decided she was a good barometer with her choice of songs and when to sing them.

After the second song, IlaRae asked Nadine to go around to the back of the piano and look toward her as they sang the next song. Nadine was dressed in blue jeans with red three-inch high heels, and a frilly white blouse with a scarlet velvet vest. She stood about five feet and nine inches tall—maybe less if you discounted the heels. Her long chestnut hair was clipped back over her ears and fell down her back in soft curls. With her soft brown eyes and tan complexion, she could have passed for a beauty queen. Undoubtedly, she held everyone's attention without saying a word. It was difficult for Jennifer to tell if they were awed by her beauty or just plain green with envy.

Three measures into the song, Nadine stopped. "Wait a minute!" she exclaimed. "You're not playing the music as it's written. Do you have different music than I do?" she asked rather puzzled.

"Just as I thought!" IlaRae exclaimed. "I transposed it up three keys. You have perfect pitch, don't you?"

"Yes I do," Nadine answered.

Jennifer darted a smug look of satisfaction toward Alice. *IlaRae* was more than an asset. If either of them had been playing, they never would have discovered Nadine's unusual talent.

"That's good," IlaRae said. "Whenever we perform, you can give everyone their pitch and I won't need to do it with the piano—it'll make us sound more professional—as long as the piano is in tune. Maybe we'll need to check that out ahead of time before the performance."

Choir practice went well. The song they ended with was "I Love to Laugh" from Mary Poppins. By the time they got to the end of the song, all the women were laughing uncontrollably.

Mitzi Bennett finally caught her breath long enough to sputter, "I think *that* should be our signature song. If it does this to us, think what it would do to our audience!"

Mitzi was all of five foot tall and might have weighed ninety-five pounds dripping wet. She had medium length, thick orange-red hair, green eyes, and facial features so petite they looked like they had been etched out of fine china. She had been a real surprise when her tiny frame boomed with a powerfully deep tenor voice. She had explained that she and her husband were both returned missionaries from the Venezuela South mission and both spoke Spanish fluently.

"We'll have to put that talent to good use and have you sing a solo in Spanish," IlaRae said, causing Mitzi to blush.

"We need to choose a name for our little group," Jennifer said. "Why don't we all think about it and maybe we can decide on a name."

With that said, the group dispersed into the cool evening air.

Chapter Twenty-One

Jay woke up and said he was thirsty. Phil held his hospital mug up to his lips and slipped the straw into his mouth. Jay took a couple of sips and then asked, "Would you mind reading to me? Jennifer always reads to me at bedtime."

"I'd be happy to. What would you like to hear?"

"The Book of Mormon would be good," Jay said.

Phil picked up the book from the nightstand and accommodatingly read to Jay. The marker was set on *Alma* Chapter Seventeen. Phil began to read, "*'And now it came to pass that as Alma was journeying from the land of Gideon southward, away to the land of Manti, behold, to his astonishment, he met with the sons of Mosiah journeying towards the land of Zarahemla.'*"

Manti—this must be where the Mormons got the name of the town in Utah. He read on… "'for they had undertaken to preach the word of God to a wild and a hardened and a ferocious people; a people who delighted in murdering the Nephites, and robbing and plundering them;" Nice folks! "… and their hearts were set upon riches, or upon gold and silver, and precious stones; yet they sought to obtain these things by murdering and plundering, that they might not labor for them with their own hands.

"'Thus they were a very indolent people, many of whom did worship idols, and the curse of God had fallen upon them because of the traditions of their fathers; notwithstanding the promises of the Lord were extended unto them on the conditions of repentance.'"

This describes how I envision the early American Indians.

"Keep going," Jay encouraged. "This is the cool story about Ammon. He's my favorite Book of Mormon guy."

In verse twenty-four, Lamoni offers his daughter to be Ammon's wife, and in verse twenty-five, Ammon refuses and offers to be Lamoni's servant. Phil could not understand the logic behind that, but he continued to read about Ammon guarding the sheep with Lamoni's servants.

"'Now they wept for the fear of being slain…..and they did gather the flocks together again to the place of water….And those men again stood to scatter their flocks; but Ammon said unto his brethren; Encircle the flocks round about that they flee not; and I go and contend with these men who do scatter our flocks…..behold, every man that lifted his club to smite Ammon, he smote off their arms with his sword; for he did withstand their blows by smiting their arms with the edge of his sword, insomuch that they began to be astonished, and began to flee before him.'"

Phil was so engrossed in the story he didn't notice Jay nod off to sleep and he continued to read the story with enthusiasm. When he reached chapter twenty-two verse fifteen, he read Lamoni's father's response to Aaron, "'…Behold, said he, I will give up all that I possess, yea, I will forsake my kingdom, that I may receive this great joy.'" Phil set the book down in his lap unable to see the words clearly through the tears welling up in his eyes. Something inside Phil warmed his soul. He realized that he too, wanted to have this great joy. *What was this book anyway? Who wrote it? And where did it originate from? Who was this Ammon and Lamoni? Was this real? Or was this a figment of some imagination to sound like scripture?* Phil wiped his eyes and looked down at the book again. He looked more closely at the layout of the page and realized in the bottom right-hand corner of the page, in parenthesis, it said, "(Between ninety and seventy-seven B.C.)" *Wait a minute! Didn't Ammon talk about the coming of Christ in there?*

He backed up a few pages to find what he remembered reading. Chapter eighteen, verse thirty-nine said, "But this is not all; for he expounded unto them the plan of redemption, which was prepared from the foundation of the world; and he also made know unto them concerning the coming of Christ, and all the works of the Lord did he make known unto them." Then again, he read where Aaron taught the same message to Lamoni's father in chapter twenty-one, verse nine: "Now Aaron began to open the scriptures unto them concerning the coming of Christ, and also concerning the resurrection of the dead…" How could they have known about Christ seventy-seven years before he was born? The more Phil thought about it, the more questions rose in his mind. He turned to the first of the book and began to read the account written by the hand of Mormon upon plates taken from the plates of Nephi. How could someone write on plates? Phil was visualizing earthenware. He proceeded to read the Introduction and then the testimonies of the witnesses and the testimony of the Prophet Joseph Smith. He gained more understanding when he read the brief explanation about The Book of Mormon after Joseph Smith's witness. This explained that the book was a record of people in ancient America…so it might really have been about the American Indians! This book is indeed a curious and unique writing. Phil wasn't sure he bought the whole story of God and angels appearing to Joseph Smith, but he had to admit, it made a fascinating premise for a story. After what he had read in Alma, a very compelling story at that.

Chapter Twenty-Two

Jennifer returned to Jay's room shortly after ten o'clock. Phil was watching the news on the TV. "How is he?" she asked, startling Phil.

"He's fine. Wow, you sure look nice. Have you got a *hot* date or something?"

"It's amazing what a shower and clean clothes can do for a girl," she said, ignoring his question.

"You know, I really like it when you wear your hair down like that. You look fantastic."

"Thank you," she blushed. "Did Jay get anything to eat?"

"No. He had a sip or two of water, but the IV will feed him the necessities for right now. He only stayed awake for about fifteen minutes. He's been asleep the rest of the time."

Jay aroused at the sound of Jennifer's voice. He smiled at her and said, "You're back. I missed you."

Jennifer looked at Phil with a bit of guilt in her eyes.

"No you didn't! You weren't even awake enough to know she wasn't here! You didn't even stay awake for the rest of the story!" Then turning to Jennifer and offering an explanation, Phil said, "He had me read to him since you weren't here."

"I did?" Jay asked. "I don't remember," he mumbled and then dozed off to sleep again.

"See what I mean? By tomorrow he'll never remember you were gone," Phil said.

"I really appreciate you staying with him. Obviously he felt secure with you here if he asked you to read to him."

"It was my pleasure I assure you. But I really had better get going, I have to be to the office early tomorrow morning." Phil rose, squeezed Jennifer's hand gazing into her eyes, and then quietly left the room.

Chapter Twenty-Three

Phil couldn't get the story of Ammon out of his mind. Here he was trying to help people improve their bodily appearances, and Ammon was amputating arms right and left. In his mind, Phil was thinking of all the nerves, bones and muscles that would have to be reattached to restore all the arms of the men at the well. "It would take at least twelve months to heal," he mumbled aloud.

"What?" Dr. Halverson asked.

"Oh, nothing," Phil said. "Just talking to myself out loud. I was thinking about how long it would take an arm to heal if it had been completely cut off and had to be sewn back on. Do you think it's possible to completely restore an amputated arm?"

"Why amputate it if you want to sew it back on? Or is this a rhetorical question?"

"I read a story about a man who cut off a bunch of arms with a sword. I can't stop thinking about it and was going through the procedure of restoring the arms in my mind."

"Have you been reading the story of Ammon?" Dr. Halverson asked.

"Yeah, how did you know?"

Dr. Halverson laughed out loud. "Well, if the story got to you *that* much, you should read *Third Nephi*. That's the best part of the whole book!"

"Really? Where can I find a Book of Mormon?"

"There's one in my office if I can find it under all the papers. Remind me before I leave for lunch to look for it."

<<<

Phil ordered lunch at the drive-through so he could go read The Book of Mormon in privacy. He took his burger and drink to a park where he sat in his car and devoured *Third Nephi*. He was so engrossed in the story his food got cold. He stopped and reread chapter seventeen, verse seven, *"Have ye any that are sick among you? Bring them hither. Have ye any that are lame, or blind, or* halt, or maimed, or leprous, or that are withered, or that are deaf, or that are afflicted in any manner? Bring them hither and I will heal them, for I have compassion upon you; my bowels are filled with mercy."

Just like that! No surgery or months to heal. He did it that instant! How would it be if I could do that? Then he read on… "Behold your little ones…and they cast their eyes towards heaven and they saw the heavens open, and they saw angels descending out of heaven as it were in the midst of fire; and they came down and encircled those little ones about….and the angels did minister unto them."

Phil's eyes were damp again as he thought about Jay and what a wonderful thing it would be for him to experience such a blessing and healing from Jesus. Phil felt so much love and joy fill his heart and soul he couldn't contain himself and he wept like a baby. His mind rushed from thought to thought. He remembered Lamoni's father being willing to give up the entire kingdom to have joy. Phil identified with that joy at this moment. Then he remembered he would have willingly given up his own professional practice to care for Jay if Jennifer hadn't been willing to take him. He knew the kind of love Jesus was describing when he said His bowels were filled with compassion. Phil was so overwhelmed it took him an hour to regain his composure.

He walked into the office thirty minutes late, and got a chastisement from Nadine, who had tactfully tried to deal with a waiting patient.

Phil took care of his patients for the remainder of the day with renewed concern.

Chapter Twenty-Four

Jay walked a little stiffly and said that compared to the pain he had experienced from the burns and grafts, these three little incisions didn't hurt that much. He was bright-eyed and full of questions. Dr. Killpack seemed pleased he was doing so well. "Jay should be able to go home this afternoon if you'd like to take him. I think the healing process will go fine from here on as long as he doesn't have *gallstones* or a *heart attack*," he said. "You'll need to watch his incisions for infection, but if you keep him covered with clean clothing and shower him regularly, he should be fine. You will need to make sure he gets completely dry after showering, so his incisions stay as dry as possible. I'll need to see him in my office in about one week."

Jennifer felt such a relief sweep over her. She was beginning to hate living in a hospital, but she would miss seeing Phil each night. Perhaps it was for the best they didn't see each other anymore. She debated about the golf lessons. She wondered if they were really such a good idea now. Though she had agreed to continue the lessons, the temptation to get close to him was too compelling. It had been a strain on both of them the past two times they had gone to the golf course. She felt like some kind of an addict. She wanted to be with him more than anything, yet she knew it would lead to trouble if she did. Willpower had never been so difficult for her. Before she lost her resolve, she called Phil's office and left a message for him.

"Please tell Dr. Henson that Jennifer won't be golfing anymore and that Jay is going home from the hospital."

"Jennifer?" Nadine recognized her voice. "Jennifer, this is Nadine Archibald."

"You've got to be kidding me! *This* is the doctor's office you work in? *You're* the Nadine that is the office manager?" Jennifer was connecting all the conversations from the past.

"Yes, this is the office I work in and…*you're* the Jennifer Dr. Henson has been golfing with!"

"Oh my heck! Nadine, you haven't told him you know me have you?"

"No. Until right now, I didn't realize I did."

"Nadine, you can't let him know we're friends! You especially can't tell him anything about where I live. Please promise me you'll keep this confidence."

"Well, okay, but you're definitely going to owe me an explanation on Wednesday night."

"Make it easier on both of us... call me tonight when you get home from work."

<<<

When his last patient left the office, Phil hurried to find Dr. Halverson, but he had already left the office for the day. Phil decided to take The Book of Mormon home with him and spend the night reading. If it was *this* good, he wanted to read it *all*.

"Oh, there was a message for you, Dr. Henson," Nadine called to Phil as he headed out the door. "*Jennifer* called and said she won't be golfing anymore and she said Jay was going home from the hospital."

Phil felt panic. He quickly came back into the office and placed a call to the hospital. When he talked to the nurse's desk outside Jay's room, they informed him that Jay had checked out of his room about three o'clock that afternoon. They were gone. All he had was Jennifer's cell phone number. He didn't know *where* to find her. He rushed to the hospital and asked the desk if he could take a look at Jay's charts for a minute.

"I'd like to review Dr. Killpack's notes if it's all right."

The nurse looked skeptical. She asked him to wait a moment while she checked with Dr. Killpack. When she hung up the phone, she handed the chart to Dr. Henson. He thumbed through it and then looked further back in the records to see if Jennifer's address might be listed in there. It wasn't, but her home phone

112

number was listed as an alternate contact number. He quickly jotted it down.

"Thank you," he said as he handed the chart back to the nurse. "I think I got what I needed—oh, maybe you would know where I could find Miss Heaps' address? I'd like to send her some flowers and a card to Jay."

"You know I can't give that information out."

"I'm a physician! Who are you trying to keep the information from?"

The nurse had to admit he was definitely within the guidelines of HIPAA for getting the information requested. "Well," she said, "I don't have her address, but I'll bet you could get it from the billing department."

Phil knew they were closed for the day, but on the off chance that someone might still be in the office, he went downstairs to see who might be around. Everything was locked up tight and there weren't any people staying late. "Darn," he mumbled as he headed back out to his car.

Once he got home, he sat down with the book he had brought home from the office. He began to read and totally forgot all else. Dinnertime came and went without even a thought of eating.

Chapter Twenty-Five

Jennifer felt rejuvenated to be home with Jay. She opened the windows for some fresh air and Jay sat out by the fish pond enjoying the cool fresh September air, while she called an attorney and made an appointment for the following day to discuss her case of identity theft.

Meals were simple for a while. Jennifer thought about the picnic she and Phil had planned to have after Jay got out of the hospital, but she quickly put it out of her mind, determined she would not think of Phil again... ever—not even for a minute... well, maybe a second, but definitely no longer than that!

At six o'clock, Jennifer's phone rang. Checking caller ID first, Jennifer answered, "Hello, Nadine."

"Okay, girl, out with the story! What is going on with you and Dr. Henson?"

"It's a long story, but the long and short of it is I'm madly in love with him, but he's not LDS. I had to break it off before I lost my ability to reason."

"Jennifer, *you* are all he has talked about at the office for the last six months! It's been Jen this or Jen that. I knew about his patient named Jay and how much he cared for him, but somehow I never put Jay's name together with yours. I don't know how I could have been so dense. Knowing Jay had been burned and was going through a lot of therapy and surgeries, I still didn't connect *him* with Dr. Henson. When you called today and I recognized your voice, it only took half a second to connect the dots."

"Well, now you know. I've had such mixed emotions over this whole thing. I love him dearly and miss seeing him every day, but I can't marry someone without the Gospel."

"Oh, Jennifer, I am so sorry. That's got to be tough. Dr. Henson is such a sweet guy; I didn't even realize he wasn't LDS. I thought everybody in our office was. But there's one thing I don't get—why can't I tell him I know you or where you live?"

"He made an offer on a house that he fell in love with several months ago and someone else's offer got accepted. He's been quite disappointed about that and I think he resents the person who got the house."

"So, explain to me what that has to do with you?"

"It's *my* house he wanted to buy. I'm not sure what his reaction would be if he found out it was *me* who took it away from him."

"Where does he think you live?"

"He doesn't know. We've always met up at the hospital. It seems we both practically live there."

"And I'm supposed to pretend I don't know you?"

"If he finds out you know me, he'll want you to tell him where I live. You'd be in a position to betray my confidence, or put your job in jeopardy. I don't think you want to do that."

There was silence on the phone. Finally, Nadine said, "No, I don't suppose I would want to be in that predicament. I won't say anything."

<<<

Once inside Mr. Finch's office, she explained the situation as much as she knew, and handed him the credit reports.

"This is quite a large sum of money," he said. "What is your financial situation that someone could get this many cards in your name and run them up this high?"

"I have a large inheritance," she explained.

"*How* large?"

"It's down to about two-and-a-half million now. But if I have to pay all those credit card bills, it'll definitely go down from there."

Mr. Finch asked for a sizeable retainer fee, and said he would launch an investigation. "For now, we will file a police report and contact all the credit card companies listed. They need to know the accounts had been fraudulently opened so they won't allow any more charges."

<<<

Jay and Jennifer spent time playing around with Dragon Dictate. Jay was excited to be able to talk and have his words printed out on the screen. He was frustrated when the computer typed different words than what he had said. "How come it thinks I said that?" Jay asked.

"Those are 'speakos'. Kind of like what we call a 'typo'," Jennifer explained. "Maybe Dragon Dictate needs a hearing aid!" They both laughed. *Imagine a machine hearing at all.*

Jay spent hours on end talking into his microphone and training the program to recognize his words on the computer.

Jennifer had to remind him to come to the dinner table and to take a shower once in a while.

Once Jay had the system trained to his voice and working quite well, Jennifer had tutor prompts installed on the hard drive, and Jay took off on his own. His learning curve went straight up. He was consuming information at such a rapid speed Jennifer couldn't keep up with the software needed to stay ahead of him.

They discovered there were some voice activated books that actually read aloud through the computer speakers so Jay didn't even need to look at the screen.

He kept himself busy trying to make his stumps fit around things to grasp them while listening to a book. He showed a great deal of determination to master the use of his hands again.

Jennifer filled her time with sewing projects, learning how to make new recipes, and playing the piano. Afternoons were taken with tutoring, although she didn't tutor on Wednesdays because that was choir night.

Chapter Twenty-Six

After what had seemed like a long time, October twenty-first arrived. Jay and Jennifer arrived at the courthouse and waited for Kimberly, the guardian at litem to arrive. The State also had an attorney to represent them. Dr. Killpack, and Dr. Green, Jay's psychiatrist, had submitted depositions.

They still had not heard from Emily. Jay became resigned to the fact that he might never see her again. Grateful to rid himself of the name Borky, he seemed excited to assume Jennifer's last name of Heaps.

After all the waiting for a court date, it only took fifteen minutes in the courtroom for the judge to hear the story and grant the adoption.

The judge set his gavel down and watched Jennifer and Jay with admiration.

"Now can I call you Mom?" Jay asked.

"Yes, Son. Now you can call me Mom."

The judge took a handkerchief out of his pocket to wipe his tears and blow his nose.

Jennifer wiped a few tears from her own cheek as she led Jay from the courtroom.

Jay beamed as he marched out as if he'd been crowned prince.

<<<

Halloween was coming up and Jennifer brought up the subject at dinner on the evening of the twenty-fifth. "Would you like to go trick-or-treating on Halloween?" she asked. "Or would you prefer to stay at home and help pass out candy to the trick-or-treaters who come to our house?"

"Could I go with Ben?" Jay asked.

"Why don't we ask Alice on Wednesday when she comes for choir practice?" Jennifer proposed. "What would you *like* to be?"

"I could go as a freak. I wouldn't even need a costume. I could take off my elastic mask and I'd pass for a real scary one."

Jennifer suspected his previous environment had been unsafe to show his own wants and needs. "Jay, we can easily afford any costume you might like. I could probably even make you a costume if we get started right away."

She saw Jay grin. He rarely allowed himself any pity. He made light jokes about his ugliness every now and again.

"Jay, do you really want to go as a scary person? This is one time you could wear a mask and be prince charming."

"Who'd be afraid of prince charming?"

"Halloween isn't just for scaring people, you know."

"Sure it is. That's what makes it fun. I have another question," Jay ventured. "When can I get baptized?"

"Are you sure you want to get baptized this soon?"

"I'm sure. I've been waiting for the adoption to be final so you could give permission for me to get baptized. It should be final Friday, shouldn't it?"

"I'll double check, but Kimberly said it would only take a week to be recorded. I would imagine there won't be any delays. The missionaries would be delighted, I'm sure."

She couldn't express her gratitude for his growing testimony. He had such a genuinely delightful personality that she often marveled he could be so good-natured after having gone through so much.

The following morning, Jennifer called the courthouse to see if the papers had been signed and filed by the judge. She was told they had actually been recorded the day following the hearing on the twenty-second. The adoption had been final for four days.

"Guess what?" Jennifer asked Jay, "We could have planned this *four* days ago!"

"Really? You mean I'm all yours now and you're *really* my legal mom?"

"Yes. Shall we call the missionaries and the bishop to make arrangements?"

"Yeah. Can *I* call the bishop?"

"I don't see why not." Jennifer let Jay push the numbers on the phone with his stubs and then he pushed the speaker button so he could talk without needing to hold the handset. Bishop Bowen's wife answered the phone and when she found out it was Jay and he wanted to get baptized, she gave Jay the phone number to call him at work.

Jay dialed the work number and pushed the speaker button again. "May I speak with Bishop Bowen?" he asked. There was a chuckle at the other end of the line. In the background Jay and Jennifer could hear, "Hey, Roger, you've got a call on the line— it's a church call." "Thanks," Bishop Bowen replied, and then into the phone he said, "This is Roger Bowen."

"Hi, Bishop. This is Jay Borky… umm, I mean Jay Heaps. My adoption is final now and I want to get baptized."

"How soon did you want to do this?"

"Can we do it right after church on Sunday?"

"I think that can be arranged—but we may need to wait until after six o'clock to provide enough time to fill the font. Why don't you and your Mother call the missionaries to let them know and make sure they can schedule it. I'm assuming you want one of the Elders to baptize you?"

"Yeah, I'd like Elder Manning to baptize me."

"Do you have their phone number?"

"Yep. I'll call them right now."

"Very well, Jay. I'm happy for you. I'll call you this evening to make sure about the scheduling."

Jay pushed the button to disconnect the call and then punched the numbers to call the missionaries who were equally delighted with the news. Elder Manning had known it was only a matter of time until the adoption was final and the baptism could take place. He had previously commented that if Jay's adoption didn't go through by the end of November, he'd be released from his mission and wouldn't be able to perform the ordinance.

Elder Manning wanted to interview Jay before Sunday, so they set up an interview for Thursday at ten o'clock in the morning.

When Jay was finished with his phone calls, he looked at his mother and asked, "Can we invite *anybody* we want to come to my baptism?"

"Yes. Who would you like to invite?"

"I want Ben's family to come. I'd like Brother Sheffield and Brother Cox to come." He hesitated for a minute, "and I'd really like Dr. Phil Henson to come."

Jennifer froze. She didn't know what to say. First of all, she hadn't wanted to see Phil again. Secondly, she didn't want him to know where she lived, and she had assumed they would invite guests over to the house for refreshments after the baptism. As she considered this reason, she realized it didn't *matter* if Phil knew she was living in his dream house *now*. There was no chance for romance anyway. She still didn't want to flaunt it in his face, however. Thirdly, Phil had made it clear he was not interested in knowing anything more about the church. She didn't want to appear pushy by inviting him to a baptism. She looked into Jay's expectant eyes. *How could she tell him no?*

"Pleee-ase, Mom," Jay begged. "I know he'd come for *me*."

Jennifer knew he *would* too. "Oh, Jay, you're asking a lot of me. Can I think about this for a bit?"

"I guess," Jay said dejectedly, making Jennifer feel even worse. He slipped off into his bedroom.

Jennifer went to her office where she began to format some simple invitations on her computer to mail out to the Primary president, her counselors, the bishop, his counselors, Alice's family, of course, and the women in her choir, Brother and Sister Sheffield, Brother and Sister Cox, and an extra.... in case, for Phil Henson. She left the time blank until after their visit with the bishop that evening. As she contemplated her dilemma, she considered deleting the information about gathering at the house following the baptism for refreshments on Phil's invitation. That way he would go to the baptism and never know for sure where she lived. She thought better of it when she considered Jay's feelings. She knew he would want Phil to come for refreshments more than any other person in attendance.

Chapter Twenty-Seven

It was nearly ten o'clock when Jay was finally asleep and Jennifer was tossing and turning in her own bed trying to feel at peace with the situation when her cell phone rang. She kept it plugged into the charger each night right by her bed. She reached for the phone, unplugged it, and looked on the caller ID screen to see who was calling. PHIL HENSON! Her stomach did a somersault. She was unbelievably excited and yet fearful at the same time. *I can't believe this! Why now? What could he possibly want? Should I answer it? Should I ignore it until I decide whether to invite him to Jay's baptism?* With unbearable trepidation she finally answered, "Hello?"

"Hello," the familiar voice resounded making Jennifer's heart skip a beat. "I have been meaning to call you for about a week now, but I either didn't have the courage, or I didn't know what to say."

"Any special reason?" Jennifer asked.

"Well, yeah. There are several things I wanted to talk to you about. First of all, I know you had a court hearing on the twenty-first. How did that go?"

"Very well—Jay's adoption is final. He's legally mine."

"That's good to hear. Secondly, how does Jay feel about it?"

"He seems quite content. I'm not used to having him call me *Mom* yet. I like it, but it still seems odd."

Phil chuckled, "I'll bet. But I think you make a wonderful caring mom, so you deserve it." After an awkward silence he continued, "Jen, I have something important I wanted to ask you."

Jennifer tensed. *I've already left the message that I won't golf or ski with him. I was emphatic about our relationship being nothing more than a friendship...and I pretty much ended even that. What could he possibly want to ask me? This can't be happening!* Her heart practically pounded out of her chest with nervous anticipation. *No! I won't get involved. I can't!*

"I'm getting baptized in the L.D.S. church this Sunday, and I wondered if you and Jay would come to my baptism?"

"Ehh…excuse me? S-s-say that again," she stammered.

"I said I'm getting baptized on Sunday and I wondered if you and Jay would come to my baptism—please? It would mean a great deal to me."

Jennifer took a few seconds to respond, then all she managed to say was "Why?"

"*Why* would it mean so much to me?"

"No…I mean *why* are you getting baptized?"

"Do you *object* to me getting baptized?"

"Of course not. But I really need to know *why* you're doing this."

"Because it's *true*."

"When did you decide this?"

"Remember when I stayed with Jay while you were gone to your choir practice?"

"Yeah."

"Well, Jay asked me to read to him from The Book of Mormon. He said that's what *you* do each night and I had no objections. I picked it up and read from where the book was laying open. It so happened to be the story of Ammon. Jay fell asleep within a few minutes, but the story was so compelling I couldn't put it down. One thing led to another: Dr. Halverson loaned me his Book of Mormon the next day and I couldn't put it down until I finished it. When I read Moroni's challenge in chapter ten, I decided to pray about it. I think I already knew it was true by that time, but I decided to pray anyway. I got my answer; I knew for sure it was true."

Jennifer was about ready to scream with excitement. With the most controlled, sober voice she could muster, she said, "I'm sorry, Phil, we can't come. Jay and I have an appointment on Sunday evening at six-thirty. We'll be tied up all evening."

"Oh," he said with great disappointment. "Would it work better if I did it on Saturday evening?"

"That's trick-or-treating for the kids. I promised Jay he could go this year."

"That's right, it is." Phil sounded like he was about to cry.

Jennifer couldn't stand it any longer. "I may have a solution to the problem," she offered.

"What is it?" Phil asked, sounding hopeful.

"Out of curiosity, about how many people have you invited to your baptism?"

"My family, but only my parents will be coming, the missionaries, and my colleagues at work, a few friends, and you and Jay. Why?"

"Well, I was thinking. Maybe you and Jay could use the same baptismal font and have a joint baptism. The appointment Jay and I have at six-thirty is *his* baptism."

"Seriously?" he asked sounding shocked.

"Seriously," she laughed.

"Can we arrange that? I'm not sure exactly how these things work, but having a joint baptism and being able to attend Jay's baptism would sweeten the excitement of my own baptism more than I can imagine."

"Give me the names and the phone number of your missionaries, and I'll find out in the morning." She purposely didn't mention refreshments afterward. Perhaps Jay could be baptized in Phil's church and then refreshments could be eliminated, served at the church, or served at Phil's apartment. She would have to see what the missionaries said first.

"Jen," Phil said in a husky voice, "I've missed you and Jay more than you'll ever know. I've missed feeling like I had something to look forward to every night after work. If it weren't for my discovery of The Book of Mormon and my excitement about the church, I think I would have died this past month."

"I've thought a lot about you too," she confessed. "I made a promise that I wouldn't allow myself to think about you for more than one second at a time. Every three minutes I had to remind myself to keep that promise."

Phil laughed, sounding delighted and relieved at the same time. "You know," he reminded her, "You promised me a picnic dinner after Jay got out of the hospital. Do you always break your promises?"

"I thought about that too. I couldn't put myself in a situation I knew would tempt me to compromise my values. I had hoped you would understand."

"I didn't at first. I was devastated. When you explained how you felt about eternal marriage I felt something tug at my heart. I knew your feelings ran deep and I have to admit that what you were saying seemed right to me. That was probably the first time I ever questioned my own beliefs. Then when Jay asked me to read The Book of Mormon to him, I got caught up with curiosity. Now I understand your decision completely and I respect you all the more for it. I'm hoping you'll reconsider and give me a second chance."

Jennifer laughed heartily. Realizing that Phil's baptism changed the entire dynamics of their relationship, she was concerned anew about him knowing where she lived. *What if he got angry knowing I was the person who out-bid him? The whole relationship could blow up in my face.* She considered how much she loved Phil, and how much she felt he loved her. For now, she'd keep her secret.

"Jennifer, are you still there?"

"It's probably a little too cold to have a real picnic now, but maybe we could have all the trimmings and eat indoors?"

"I'd like that very much. Would tomorrow be too soon?"

"I think that might be fine. Why don't you call me when you're ready to leave the office and Jay and I will meet you at *your apartment* with a picnic dinner? We might even be able to bring you good news about a double baptism."

"Wonderful! I'm scheduled to get off around five-thirty. Why don't you plan to arrive at six? If there are any problems, I'll call you, but otherwise, plan on six. Is that all right?"

"Sure enough," Jennifer answered. "Give me your address and we'll be there."

At the mention of an address, Phil realized he still didn't have Jennifer's address. "I'll give you mine if you'll give me yours."

Jennifer didn't know how to respond. *Think fast.* "Okay, what's your address?" He gave her his address and she took her time writing it down and making sure she understood how to find it. Then as if she had some emergency occur, she abruptly said, "Oh my gosh! I've got to go—we'll see you tomorrow!" and she hung up the phone.

Chapter Twenty-Eight

First thing in the morning, Jennifer discussed with Jay the possibility of a joint baptism with Dr. Henson. She had never seen him smile so broadly.

"Really? That would be awesome!" he said with excitement. "Will we still come to our house after, for the food?"

"I was thinking maybe we'd have them at the church. Then people won't leave and go home instead of joining us for the refreshments. How does that sound?"

"Okay, I guess," he sounded a little doubtful.

"Are you sure? We could forget about refreshments altogether, I suppose."

"No. I think it will be okay to have them at the church," he answered more confidently after being given the alternative.

"Oh," said Jennifer as an afterthought, "We're going to have a picnic dinner with Phil tonight at his apartment. *We're* taking dinner—what would you like to have to eat?"

"Can we have ice cream?"

Jennifer embraced him. "Honey, you can eat all the ice cream you want! But would you like something for dinner first?"

"How about fried chicken and potato salad, and Jell-O, and watermelon, and potato chips, and that cooked bean stuff?"

"Cooked bean stuff?" she questioned.

"Yeah, my mom used to make something out of pork and beans with bacon in it. It was really good."

"You must mean Boston Baked Beans."

"Yeah! *Baked* Beans—that's what she called it. I don't think she ever mentioned they were from Boston though."

"Well, Buddy, I'm in an exceptionally good mood today, baked beans it will be then—along with all the other trimmings you wanted."

Jay skipped off to his computer to do more reading.

Knowing Jay approved of the joint baptism idea, Jennifer called the missionaries who had been teaching Phil. She got the details of time and place for his baptism, and asked if it would be possible for Jay to get baptized at the same time. They were okay with the idea, but would need to get approval from the mission president and her bishop. They exchanged phone numbers of bishops, the other missionaries, the mission president, and agreed to each make the appropriate calls to get approval for such an arrangement.

Jennifer called Bishop Bowen first. It took a little explanation about Jay's relationship with Dr. Phil Henson and the desire each of them had to have the other in attendance at their baptism. The bishop was amiable and said there should be no real problem as long as the mission president was in agreement with the idea.

She waited only thirty minutes until the Elders called her with the good news that the mission president had approved the joint baptism. Then Jennifer called Elder Manning and his companion to let them in on the plan. They didn't seem to mind the change. The time was a little different. The baptism would begin at seven o'clock instead of six-thirty. They had not made any other appointments for that evening, so there were no changes in their schedule.

Then she called Phil's bishop to get approval for serving refreshments after the baptism. Bishop Lander laughed heartily. "What would a Mormon function be without refreshments? I think it would be fine. Do you need to get into the building a little early?"

"No, I think I'll be fine as long as I know where to find the kitchen and the multipurpose room. Do I need to call anyone in particular to reserve those rooms?"

"I can see to it that's taken care of. I'll even have the Elders Quorum set up some chairs and tables in the multipurpose room if you'd like."

"Thirty chairs and a banquet table to serve from would be all I need."

132

"Consider it done, Sister Heaps. I'm sure I'll be delighted to meet you Sunday evening."

Jennifer realized her week was filling up quickly with things to get done. She sat down at the computer in her office and began to make a list. She revised the invitations to fit the new circumstances listing the new address, time, and names of both baptismal candidates, and then printed one. After scrutinizing the finished product, she deemed it reasonable. She stuck the printout of the new version in her purse to present to Phil that evening and then began preparing for dinner beginning with the baked beans Jay had requested. After getting those going in the crock pot, she worked on the potato salad so it would have time to cool in the refrigerator before dinner. She quickly set a red gelatin salad with shredded apples and crushed pineapple in it. By noon she was ready to go to the store to pick up fresh chicken, a watermelon, ice cream and potato chips.

"That smells good," Jay said as he came into the kitchen to watch after the smell of the baked beans wafted into his room.

"Jay, what would you like to drink tonight?" she asked.

"How about lemonade?"

"Plain, pink or raspberry?" Jennifer asked.

"Raspberry!"

"Do you want to come with me to the store, or do you want to stay here?"

Jay agreed to go with Jennifer and they left in a hurry. Realizing it was lunchtime; Jennifer drove through the McDonalds drive-in and picked up a chicken sandwich for her, some chicken nuggets with fries for Jay because they were easy for her to feed him while she was driving.

When they passed the big display of pumpkins in front of the store, Jay asked, "Are we going to carve a jack-o-lantern for Halloween?"

"Maybe we could do that tonight after dinner with Phil? What do you think?"

"I think we should!"

133

"Let's get two pumpkins so Phil can do one of his own and keep it at his house. We'll, have to clean up after ourselves when we're finished though—he might not appreciate the mess."

Jay picked out two of the biggest pumpkins he could find. One was quite misshapen and the other was tall and round. Jennifer put two carving kits in the basket. She was almost ecstatic thinking about this evening.

As they passed the bakery, she stopped to see if she could order a special sheet cake for the baptism. She explained to the plump gray-haired lady in the bakery that she would like a sheet cake decorated with white frosting. "I'd like it to say 'Congratulations Phil and Jay' in blue writing," she explained.

"Would you like it scored with blue roses on that?" the lady asked.

"Can you decorate it similar to a wedding cake without any scoring? You know, put some fancy grill-work on it or some stripes or plaids with white frosting—*no* flowers for these guys," she said.

The bakery clerk raised her eyebrows. "And you want it to say 'Congratulations *Phil* and *Jay*' with no flowers and no scoring?"

"Yes, that would be perfect. Could I pick it up Saturday afternoon around four o'clock?"

"We'll have it ready for you," the lady grumbled.

"Thank you," Jennifer replied sensing the woman's disapproval. "Is there a problem?"

"I guess not," the woman said with a scowl on her face. "This is the first time I've had a request for a wedding cake for a gay marriage."

"Oh dear!" Jennifer gasped. "This isn't for a gay marriage! This is for a baptism of a man and my son. I'm so sorry if I gave you the wrong impression."

"Oh, I see," the woman said rather cheerily. "My mistake. We'll have it ready for you by four o'clock Saturday afternoon."

Jennifer shook her head in disbelief as she walked away to continue with the shopping. She let Jay pick out his choice of potato chips and they finished up in the meat department choosing cut up chicken she could dip in her famous batter to fry.

<<<

On the way home from the grocery store, they stopped at an office supply store and Jennifer ran in leaving Jay with the groceries long enough to pick up several boxes of invitation-sized envelopes.

"Have you decided for sure what you want to be for Halloween?" Jennifer asked Jay when she got back in the car. "Would you like to go shopping for costumes?"

"I don't think so. I really think it would be cool to go trick-or-treating as a freak and not wear my elastic mask. Nobody would have the same costume as me."

Jennifer was surprised Jay wanted to be different. Most children want to be like everyone else, and yet they want individual attention for being unique. *I'll have to ask Dr. Green about that. I'm hoping this means Jay is well-adjusted.* She wanted him to perceive himself as brilliant and capable—not ugly.

"What do you want to wear for clothing? It might be a rather cool night."

"How about if I wear my hospital pajamas over my other clothes to make me look bulkier?" Jay asked.

"*Bulkier?*" Jennifer echoed. "Where did you learn that word?"

"I don't know. I know it means fatter, bigger, or fuller. That's what I want to look like—*bulkier.*"

"Well, all-righty then. Bulkier it is!" Jennifer laughed with sheer delight at his adult-like vocabulary mixed with his child-like expectations.

Jennifer showed Jay how she dipped the chicken pieces in the flour and seasoning mix before she fried it. Then when it was brown, she cooked it in her pressure cooker for fifteen minutes at fifteen pounds of pressure and then turned off the heat for the pressure gauge to drop.

While the pressure was releasing, she decided to shower and change into some clean clothes.

135

Chapter Twenty-Nine

On their way over to Phil's apartment, Jennifer broached the subject of Jay giving out their address to anyone. "Jay, I need to discuss something important with you. For right now, I don't want you to give our address to anyone who doesn't already have it. If anyone asks you, I need you to tell them they will have to get it from me. Do you understand?"

"Sure, but why?"

"Well, there are certain people that I don't want to know how to find us—like your biological mother, for instance. I want to make sure you're safe—does that make sense?"

"Okay. I don't want her to find me either. Dr. Green says she's sick and she's not safe to be around."

"Yes, well, there are other people who aren't sick, but for other reasons, I think they would not be happy knowing we live in such a nice home. So even if it's a good friend, don't tell anyone your address except a policeman trying to help you get home if you get lost or kidnapped, okay?"

"Who wouldn't like us to live in a nice house?"

"Maybe someone who wanted to buy our house as much as we did, but we beat them to it."

Jay seemed to accept this at face value and said, "Okay. I won't tell anyone."

They pulled up in front of Phil's apartment at five-fifty-five. It wasn't difficult to tell they were both excited and anxious to see Phil.

Phil pulled into his assigned parking space at two minutes after six. He jumped out of his car and ran to theirs. He flung the backdoor open and grabbed Jay out in a gigantic hug. When he set Jay back down on the pavement, he turned to Jennifer who was out of the car and watching this joyful reunion.

"I've been looking forward to this all day!" he said. Then he stepped forward and embraced her tightly, kissing her hair first and then lifting her chin, he looked into her eyes momentarily before he kissed her hungrily like a man being offered food after days of fasting.

Jay watched quietly and grinned. "We have a special surprise for tonight after dinner. And I got to choose the whole menu!" he said, reminding them they were not alone.

"Is that right? Well, what did you choose for our picnic?"

"Fried chicken, potato salad, Jell-O, baked beans…"

Phil raised his eyebrows at Jennifer, "Baked beans?"

"Yeah," Jay continued, "and potato chips, watermelon, and ice cream."

"Baked beans are my favorite," Phil said. "Let's go eat! What can I help you carry?"

<<<

After several attempts to get gift cards online, using five different credit cards and being denied, Braxton paled realizing that the end had come and someone had discovered his game.

"They're on to me," he whispered to himself. He counted the gift cards he had in his possession and checked his bank balance. He would run dry in three months. "Hmmm, now what?"

<<<

"Are you sure you didn't buy this chicken at KFC?" Phil asked after eating Jennifer's fried chicken.

"No!" Jay answered for her. "I helped make it."

"You did? What part did you do?" Phil asked.

"I *watched* her," he answered proudly.

Phil and Jennifer both laughed.

"So, what's the big surprise?" Phil asked.

"We brought pumpkins to carve!" Jay said enthusiastically.

"I didn't see any pumpkins in the car," Phil said.

"They're hiding in the trunk until we get your permission to make the mess in your kitchen," Jay said almost beside himself with excitement. "We promise we'll clean up after we're done! Can we do it?"

"May we do it," Jennifer corrected.

138

"May we do it, pretty pleee-ase?" Jay begged.

"Absolutely! And I don't even mind doing the cleanup," Phil answered.

They hustled out to the car where they retrieved the pumpkins and the carving kits. With newspaper laid out on the table and the counter, they were discussing the options on who would carve which pumpkin and what they wanted the face to be.

Jay and Phil chose the misshapen pumpkin. As it turned out, they worked together on that one, and Jennifer worked on the more perfectly shaped pumpkin. Phil and Jay turned their pumpkin on its side so it rested on a flat spot and used the stem as the nose. Then they proceeded to cut an access hole in the back toward the upper part of the pumpkin as it rested. Phil insisted they save and rinse the seeds so he could roast them. Then he and Jay decided on a grotesque face that utilized all the blemishes on their pumpkin.

Jennifer basked in contented satisfaction as it became obvious they were both enjoying themselves immensely. She carved a more traditional jack-o-lantern, using the stem as a hat. She carefully cut out a toothy smiling face with triangular holes for eyes and a nose.

When they were all finished carving, Jennifer insisted on cleaning up the mess and wiping down the counter tops and the table. She even offered to mop the floor, but Phil refused to let her.

"I can do that later," he insisted. "Right now, I think we should admire our artwork." He pulled two candles out of a cupboard and lit them after setting one in each pumpkin, then turned off the lights.

They stood back and looked admiringly at the happy pumpkin and the frightening pumpkin. Jay asked Phil, "Which one are you going to keep and which one are we going to take home with us?"

"Hmmm. Which one would you like to take home?" he asked Jay.

"I like the scary one!" Jay answered.

"Perhaps your mother ought to choose."

Jennifer's heart swelled when Phil referred to her as Jay's mother. "That would be a good one to scare all the trick-or-treaters," she said thinking it would remind her of Phil and Jay having so much fun creating it. But then she thought of Phil housing a sweet smiling pumpkin, and she realized it might be a little too feminine for a guy. "Which one would you prefer to keep here, Phil?"

"I'll gladly keep the happy pumpkin," he said. "Then it will remind me of the happy time we had making them."

With that decision made, Phil carried the grotesque pumpkin out to the trunk of Jennifer's car, and returned to the apartment where they ended their evening with ice cream—Jay eating three bowls full.

"I understand there is a great haunted house in town. Would the two of you like to go with me tomorrow evening?" Phil asked.

"Tomorrow is choir practice," Jennifer reminded him. "IlaRae has arranged for us to have our first performance sometime in December, so I'm sure she'll have us start practicing Christmas music tomorrow night."

"What about Thursday evening?" he suggested.

"I'm not sure," she hedged. "The missionaries have set up an interview with Jay that morning, and I have so much to get done before the weekend. OHH! I almost forgot." She ran to her purse and produced the invitation to the baptism. "Take a look at this and tell me what you think."

"Do they normally serve refreshments at a baptism?" he questioned after reading it.

"Not always," she admitted. "I don't think they do it with convert baptisms much, but when eight-year-old children get baptized, parents usually bribe their families to come with the promise of refreshments. I had planned to have refreshments for Jay even though he has been nine since July and is technically considered a convert baptism."

As if his memory had been jogged, Phil suddenly asked, "Did you have some emergency happen last night while we were on the phone? You hung up in such a hurry when I was about to get your address from you."

All day, she had been considering her response to this question should it arise. "I heard something that sounded like someone coming in my front door and I wanted to make sure I had 911 dialed on my phone if I needed it. I'm so paranoid about being alone and responsible for Jay."

"So was there anyone?"

"No. I was overly sensitive to noises and was mistaken. Everything was fine."

"That's good. So let me get your address now," Phil stated.

Jennifer feigned a look of sheer terror on her face.

"Is something wrong?" he asked.

"Oh, Phil, this is really embarrassing, but I think my monthly cycle just started and I don't have any feminine supplies." Turning to Jay, she said, "Jay, get to the car—hurry!" Then she turned back to Phil and quickly said, "I'm so sorry to run out on you like this, but I really must get home." She ran to the car, opened the door for Jay and slammed it shut as soon as she buckled him safely in his seat. Then she jumped into the driver's seat and drove off.

"Mom, what's a monthly cycle?" Jay asked when they were on their way home.

Jennifer was wishing she had come up with a better escape story. Now she was stuck. "Well, it's something older girls and women have once every month," she answered. "It's nothing to worry about, but if they don't attend to it when they start, they get their clothes dirty."

"Oh," Jay said. "So Phil is one of those people you don't want to know our address."

Jennifer had been caught red-handed. She couldn't believe Jay perceived her motives so accurately. "Yes," she confessed. "I'm afraid he is."

"Did he want to buy our house?"

"I didn't know it at the time. I found out after we bought the house and were living in it that Phil had also tried to buy it."

141

"Wouldn't he be happy for us?"

"I've wondered that myself. Or would he be mad *we* got it instead of him. I don't dare say anything until I know how he'll feel about it."

Chapter Thirty

The next morning Phil thought about Jennifer's embarrassing moment and decided to surprise her by sending some flowers to cheer her up. *She was so darling*. The fact that her body was cycling reminded him of her femininity. His longing to have her by his side indefinitely was driving him crazy. He determined that soon after he was baptized, he would propose marriage to her.

He still hadn't gotten her address, so he decided to be devious and get it from another source. He stopped in at the hospital on his way to work and went to the billing department. "I need to check an address of one of our patients, he told the woman. I need the mailing address for Jay Borky in care of Jennifer Heaps."

The lady at the desk returned minutes later with a post office box number written on a piece of paper. "Is this the only address you have? Don't you have a physical address listed?"

"No. We only have a phone number and a post office mailing address for contact information. We don't need a physical address for our billing purposes."

"You've got to be kidding!" he mumbled and then walked out of the hospital. *I guess I'll have to figure out another way.*

On his way to the office, he remembered his real estate agent had sold her a house. Surely he could get the information from him. He made a mental note in his mind to call the agent between patients later in the morning.

When he had his first break between patients, he called the real estate agent. "Hi, this is Phil Henson."

"Oh, yes! Are you ready to buy a house now?"

"Well, I might be in the market sometime soon, but right now, I needed to get some information from you. Do you remember the young woman who looked at houses with us—Jennifer Heaps?"

"Yes, I remember her well."

"Well, I'm trying to locate her and I was wondering if you could give me her address?" Phil got a little concerned when the agent seemed to have a choking spell and was unable to speak amidst his coughing. "Are you all right?" Phil asked.

"Yes, yes—I'll be fine. A little something caught in my throat," he excused himself. "Actually, I don't seem to *remember* which house she bought."

"Don't you keep records of which houses you sell?"

"I can't say that I do. I keep track of the income I get from the sales, but not the information on the houses. Is there something else I can help you with?"

"No. I guess I've struck out again. I'll call you when I get ready to look for another house."

<<<

Dr. Halverson and Phil were consulting about one of their patients when Dr. Halverson stopped talking for a moment and said, "Phil, you seem to be distracted. Are you worried about your baptism this weekend?"

"Oh, no. I'm still excited about it. I should be getting some invitations out to you...." his voice dropped as he realized he didn't know if Jennifer was going to make some for him or not. "Well, actually, it's this Sunday at seven o'clock. I'd like you to speak, but I guess I'll have to get the rest of the information to you... " again, his voice drifted off wondering when.

"You don't seem to be yourself today. Are you sure you're okay?" Dr. Halverson asked.

"I seem to be having a difficult time putting things together in my mind. Do you remember Jennifer Heaps, the lady I took to dinner with us at La Caille?"

"Yes. Delightful woman. Are you still dating her?"

"Well—sort of. You see, she broke off the relationship because I wasn't a member of the church. In the meantime, I became converted to the church because of Jay, the young boy she was providing foster care for. I thought maybe if I was a member of the church, she would give me a second chance—and I still believe that, but when I called to invite her to my baptism, she said Jay,

144

whom she has now adopted, was going to get baptized the same night.

"Anyway, she has made all the arrangements to have both baptisms at the same place together so we can both attend each other's baptism. She made some invitations and gave me one last night, but I don't know if she was planning to give me some to give to everyone in the office, or if she was going to give them to her friends for her son.

"Furthermore, I have been trying to get her address to send her some flowers, but I haven't been able to get an address anywhere!"

"Have you considered *asking* her for her address?" Dr. Halverson asked as if it shouldn't be such a difficult thing to do.

"I have—twice!" Then he remembered the first time he had asked her which house she bought and how defensive she had become. "No, actually, I've asked her *three* times, and she still hasn't given it to me."

"It sounds like she doesn't want you to know where to find her. Perhaps you should be careful about getting too close to a woman who is so unavailable. Have you ever considered the idea she might be married to someone else?"

Phil almost laughed out loud. "No. I'm sure she's not. There was quite a bit of discussion at the hospital about her being able to do foster care if she wasn't married. I know she's not. But why wouldn't she want me to know where she lives?"

"I don't know. She didn't seem to be such a *proud* woman that she would be ashamed of her situation if she were living in a house below *your* means. But who knows—maybe that's exactly why." Thoughtful silence hung in the air for a moment before either of them spoke. Finally, Dr. Halverson said, "You've got her phone number—why don't you look it up in the reverse section of the phone book? You should be able to find the address there." He handed Phil the phone book off the desk.

Phil looked in the back section of the telephone book where phone numbers were listed in numerical order followed by the coinciding address, but cell phone numbers were not listed. Phil checked his notes from the hospital when he had jotted down her home phone number. He searched the listings for that number, but her number was nowhere to be found in the reverse listings. "Not there!" he said.

"She must have an unlisted telephone number," said Dr. Halverson. "I'd say you're in a real pickle. You might not want to get too serious about a girl who doesn't want you to find her!"

"How can someone be so invisible? There must be a way to find her address!"

Dr. Halverson sat back in his chair with his hands folded thoughtfully. "Maybe you should hire a private investigator."

"If I don't get her address soon, I might have to!" Phil responded and returned to his next patient.

Chapter Thirty-One

"Hello, is this Jennifer Heaps?"

"Yes it is," Jennifer answered.

"This is Valentino Finch from Crawford and Finch."

"Oh yes, Mr. Finch. What have you found out?"

"Not much, I'm afraid. It looks like a real pro stole your identity. All the transactions and charges have been done by mail or over the internet. The mailing address all the credit card companies had, turned out to be a vacant trailer house that hasn't been lived in for two years. It appears the mail hasn't been picked up for weeks."

"I see. Is there anything you need me to do?"

"Short of staking out the trailer house twenty-four-seven, I don't believe so. Have you seen any recent activity on the accounts?"

"How would I know if there was?"

"You will need to contact the companies and ask them for current balances to make sure they're complying with the request to shut them down."

"Okay. I'll do that. Let me know if you find out anything more."

<<<

Nadine arrived for choir practice a few minutes early to tell Jennifer she had overheard Dr. Henson tell Dr. Halverson he might possibly hire a private detective to locate her address.

"You have got to be kidding me! Would he really do that?"

"I don't know. *He* said if he didn't get your address soon, he would consider it."

IlaRae bustled into Jennifer's house with her arms full of music, ending any further discussion on the matter. "We have a date!" she said excitedly.

Alice and the other ladies arrived and were caught up in the excitement. They began perusing the music IlaRae had selected.

Most were familiar Christmas carols. Some were funny songs like "Santa, I've got the measles."

Jennifer handed out sheet music to the song "My Baby, Jesus." "At first glance, this looks a little complicated," she said, "but it was written by a friend of mine, and I think you'll love it."

When everyone gathered together, they offered an opening prayer and then IlaRae took charge.

"There's more music here than we can sing in a one-hour performance, but I'm betting we'll have other opportunities to sing during the holidays, and we might want a few varieties for different occasions." She played the accompaniment to "My Baby, Jesus" first so she and the ladies could get an idea of the melody.

"Kate, would you like to take the solo in this one?" IlaRae asked.

"I will if I can sing it without bawling my eyes out!"

"If you'll notice, there is a flute accompaniment through the middle two pages. Does anyone here play the flute?" IlaRae continued.

"I'm a little rusty, but I think I could pull it together for a trial run by next week," Alice said.

"Good. Now that that's all settled," IlaRae continued, "the rest of you can do the oohhing and aahhing that makes this music really sound Middle Eastern."

They ran through the number three times to get a feel for it, and then moved on to the song "Carol of the Bells." They sang several others and they ended with "What Child is This?"

"All right, Ladies, get your day planners out and let's go through our schedule," IlaRae said. They all scurried to get their cell phones, iPhones, or day planners.

"We have a performance planned for the eighth of December at six-thirty in the evening in my Ward. It will be two ward Relief Societies combined. They will be serving dinner in the cultural hall and we are the dinner-time entertainment. This gives us five weeks to get our music ready. How many of you could squeeze in an extra practice on the Saturday morning before our performance?" After some discussion back and forth, they all agreed it would work.

"Next week we'll add a few more Christmas hymns, but mostly we'll be working on 'My Baby, Jesus' to get it perfected. Kate, you work on your lyrics and melody this week. Alice, you work on the flute accompaniment. Maybe when we get together next week, we'll sound a little more organized."

When IlaRae finished with her comments, Jennifer took the lead. "Ladies, we still need a name for our little group. Does anyone have any suggestions?"

"What about 'Supercalifragilistics?'" Mitzi recommended.

"I was thinking about 'Sisters in Zion,'" Alice said.

"I like both of those suggestions. Why don't we take a vote on it?"

There were four votes for "Sisters in Zion" and three for Supercalifragilistics.

"That was very close," Jennifer said. "There's one other subject we haven't discussed before now—mostly because it wasn't needed—and that is costuming. What are your feelings about matching outfits, or should we all wear Santa hats? What do you think?"

"Well, it's for darn sure Mitzi and I can't wear the exact same thing and come even close to matching," IlaRae said.

Mitzi grinned and blushed slightly.

"Yeah, well I don't know if I can wear anything to match Nadine," said Alice. "She'd look sophisticated in a bathrobe, and I'd still look like a hick in an Oscar de la Renta!"

Kate piped up, "Since I sew—how about if we buy a bolt of red fabric, and then we can each choose a pattern for a top that fits our personality. We can wear black pants or skirts and I can make all our tops out of the fabric. That way we will all match and yet maintain our individuality."

"Can my top be black?" IlaRae asked. "I'm much too large to be dressed in red! Besides, I'm supposed to be invisible since I'm only the accompanist." Everyone laughed.

"What do you mean ONLY THE ACCOMPANIST?" Kate scolded. "You're the most important part of our group!" They all cheered in agreement.

Jennifer spoke up on IlaRae's behalf. "I think black would be appropriate for IlaRae. Especially if she'd feel more comfortable wearing it. We wouldn't want her to be out of sorts—she might play the music off key!" There was laughter again.

"Is there anyone else that feels terrible about wearing red? We might be able to get a combination of red, green, white, or even silver or gold. What do you all think?"

Nadine spoke up with authority now, "I think we would look much more united and uniform if we all wear the same color, and if red isn't an objectionable color, it would certainly look festive and be eye catching. It's also a flattering color on most complexions."

Jennifer wasn't sure if anyone dared question the fashion queen's opinion, but they unanimously voted for the idea.

"Now to find the fabric!" Kate said. "How much money can we afford for fabric?"

Each lady called out a different number—some thinking of the total cost of the tunic, and others thinking of fabric by the yard. Kate explained, "Fabric is sold by the yard. The total cost of your top will depend on your size and the pattern you choose. Nice fabric can run anywhere from five dollars a yard to twenty dollars a yard. IlaRae, I don't want to single you out, but you'll probably need two-and-a-half to three yards for a top. The rest of you would need less down to Mitzi who probably would drown in more than a yard. So think in those terms"

Jennifer had a brainstorm and without explaining it she suggested they each write a number they felt they could afford on a piece of paper with their name on it. Then she and Kate would work out the details and see what they could find for the price that would best suit the majority. They all agreed and when they had written down their numbers, Jennifer collected their papers and at the same time handed each of them an invitation to Jay's baptism.

"I know this is late notice, but I wanted each of you to know you were invited. If you can't come, I will understand."

Everyone seemed satisfied with the outcome of the evening and voices were buzzing.

Kate quietly asked Jennifer, "So, how much am I supposed to spend on the fabric?"

"I want you to go out and find a fabric that would look great, feel great, and be easy to sew on. Don't worry about the price. I wanted the ladies to feel they wouldn't be spending more than they could afford. When you fall in love with the perfect fabric, buy it! Don't worry about the cost. Make sure it is a solid color—not a print, and classy! I'll reimburse you and then collect from the ladies."

"What if it's more than they can afford?" Kate asked.

"It won't be—I promise," Jennifer said knowing she might pick up the tab for most of it.

"Yes Ma'am!" Kate said with a salute and then she sauntered out the door.

"Alice," Jennifer caught her as she was heading out the door, "Jay was wondering if he could go trick-or-treating with Ben on Saturday."

"Oh, that would be wonderful—I think. I'll have to check with Dave and make sure he can handle one more trick-or-treater in the group. He's going to take them out while I hand out candy to the kids coming to our door. I know Ben would love it, but Dave would really be the one to veto or approve it. I'll check with him and let ya know."

"Thanks, Alice. I don't know what I would do without you and Dave sometimes."

"No problem. What's Jay going to be for Halloween?" Alice asked.

Jennifer chuckled. "You'll never guess—he wants to be a *freak* and go without his compression mask. He figures his face is so grotesque to look at that he won't need a mask to look scary, and then he wants to wear his hospital pajamas over his clothing to look '*bulkier*' he said."

Alice laughed out loud. "Bulkier, huh? Was that the word he used?"

"Yeah. I got a kick out of it too. He really cracks me up."

"He's really a gem. Sometimes I forget he's disabled or disfigured. He has such a positive attitude about life. Some of the rest of us that haven't had near the trials he's had should take lessons from him."

"Amen to that," Jennifer agreed.

"I'll call you as soon as I get home and ask Dave. He'll probably agree to it because he loves to spend time with Jay."

"Sounds good," Jennifer answered and waved as Alice left out the door.

Chapter Thirty-Two

At ten o'clock on Wednesday night, Jennifer's cell phone rang. Jay was asleep and she hurriedly answered it without looking at caller ID hoping to keep from waking him up. "Hello?" Fully expecting Alice to be the caller, Jennifer was surprised to hear Phil's voice.

"Hi, Jen. I have two questions for you—well, make that three. First of all, I need to know if I can get some of those invitations for the baptism Sunday to give to the folks I'd like to invite?"

"Oh, sure. I was planning on making some for you, but I forgot to ask you how many you needed."

"I'd like twenty if you could manage it. And then that leads me into my next question—I don't think I got a real firm answer from you about you and Jay going with me to the haunted house tomorrow night. I could get the invitations from you then."

Jennifer considered her list of to do's. "Hmmm," she mused trying to organize in her mind. "If we don't leave for the haunted house until after seven, I should have enough time to get dinner after my last student leaves at six… okay, you talked me into it. I'll have to be organized in the morning. I'll start making my to-do list tonight. I'm not leaving myself any wiggle room to forget anything."

"Are you sure you can sandwich *me* in?"

"I told you I had a busy schedule this week." Then she remembered, "Oh my gosh! I forgot I have to pick up the sheet cake on Saturday afternoon at four o' clock. Trick-or-Treaters will start coming about six."

"Where are you supposed to pick that up?" Phil asked.

"I ordered it at Harmon's."

"Which Harmon's?"

"The one on Redwood Road south of Jordan Parkway."

"How about you let me pick up the cake? It sounds like you're doing all the work and here it is *my* baptism."

"Oh, but *you're* the guest of honor! I *couldn't* make you pick it up," Jen protested.

"Sure you could. I'll do it for Jay—he's a guest of honor too! It's the least I can do. And how about if I get paper plates, cups, and plastic forks while I'm at it. I feel guilty having you do all this while I'm doing nothing but trying to distract you tomorrow evening."

"Are you sure you don't mind?" Jennifer asked, realizing this could save her a ton of time and trouble.

"Absolutely! I insist," Phil answered.

"Well, all right then. I guess we took care of questions one and two—what was question number three?"

"Could I get your address? It seems every time I ask you for it…" Jennifer's cell phone beeped indicating there was another call on the line.

That must be Alice. "Phil, I'm sorry to cut you off, but Alice is calling me and I really need to take her call. Jay and I will come over to your apartment tomorrow night as soon as we get through with our dinner. Bye." She quickly answered the call on the other line, "Hi, Alice. What did Dave say?"

"Like I thought, he loved the idea! He wants to take the video camera and record people's responses when they see Jay."

"You're kidding, right?"

"No—I'm serious. He can't wait! He cracked up when I told him what Jay had said. I sure hope you're writing all the cute things down he says. Someday you will have forgotten them if you don't."

"Good idea! I'll add a journal to my shopping list. I don't know why I didn't think of it myself a long time ago."

"Jennifer, you're such a natural at being a mother. You're awesome with Jay. I know he has a genuinely sunny disposition, but putting the two of you together is almost like putting chocolate and peanut butter together. You make a perfect treat!"

"Thanks, Alice. Your family has been such a blessing to Jay and me. I really want Dave to know how much I appreciate him

154

taking Jay trick-or-treating with Ben. If he really does video tape people's reactions, I expect to get a copy of the video."

"No problem. I'm sure we could have a great family home evening night together sometime to watch it."

The two women laughed as they bid each other "Good night."

Jennifer was sporting a wide grin as she grabbed a pencil and a pad of paper to make her shopping list:

For the Pumpkin Rolls:
1 lrg can pumpkin
8 oz. creamed cheese

For the mock turtles:
Rolo Candies
Little square pretzels
Pecan halves

Candy for Trick-or-treaters
A Trick-or-treat bag for Jay that he doesn't need to hold with his hands
Baptism gift for Phil and Jay
Journal
Pattern for tunic

It was nearly eleven o'clock when she turned off the light and collapsed on her bed. Then remembering her prayers, she slid to her knees. Her heart was so full of joy she spent the majority of her prayer time thanking the Lord for his goodness to her and Jay.

She lay awake for quite some time wondering how long she would be able to put Phil off about knowing where she lived. Unsure of what a private investigator did to procure such information, she wondered how long she would have before her address would no longer be a secret. *How ironic. Here I am attempting to stay undiscovered, yet going crazy trying to locate the person using my name. Could this be karma?*

Chapter Thirty-Three

Phil heard the click on his phone when Jennifer hung up and he stared at the phone in his hand for a long time. "She did it again!" *It seems every time I ask her for her address, something coincidentally happens to prevent her from telling me.* Then he remembered someone once saying, "How many coincidences can you rack up before it's no longer a coincidence?"

He still had a difficult time believing Jennifer was deliberately avoiding giving him her address. She was so open in her relationship with him in every other way; it seemed out of character for her. He resigned himself to the fact that he'd have to be patient until tomorrow night. If she didn't willingly give it to him then, he would torture her at the haunted house until he got her to confess!

Phil had trouble starting his car in the morning. Realizing he would be late arriving at the office, he called Nadine. "I'm not sure how long it will take me to get there," he said. "I've got to get my car towed and get a rental car until mine is fixed. I'll call and let you know as soon as I get more details."

"All right," Nadine answered. "Do you want me to cancel your morning appointments?"

"At least until ten o'clock. If I need longer than that, I'll call you in a while."

"Consider it done," Nadine said. "Good luck with your car."

"Thanks," he replied dryly. Maybe I need to look for that hot new car I've been wanting. I could afford it.

He called for a tow truck to haul his car into the repair shop. He asked if they had a "loaner" vehicle they could let him use until his car was fixed. They didn't, so he called the nearest rental car agency. "I need to rent a car for the day," he said, then as an afterthought, "what is the sportiest model you have?"

"You're in luck, Sir," the gentleman explained. "It so happens we got a bright yellow Corvette ZHZ yesterday. We thought

157

corporate was crazy to send it to Utah. We didn't think anyone would want to rent a sporty car like this one. Did you need it for only one day?"

Phil's imagination went wild. "What if I took it for a week? Could you give me a really good rate?"

"Well, it will be $73 on a daily rate, and it's $430 per week if you return it next Thursday morning by seven-thirty.

"I think I'll take it for the day and return it this evening by six-thirty."

The agent took Phil's name and said he'd have the car ready for him in thirty minutes.

When Phil got off the phone, the tow truck was pulling up to get his car. He rode in the tow truck to the repair shop, gave them his contact information, and then asked for a courtesy ride to the Hertz rental location on State Street in Draper.

Things went smoothly and he was back in operation by nine-thirty. Driving a Corvette was not like driving his Oldsmobile. He felt the strongest urge to push the gas pedal to the floor to see what it would do, but he restrained himself. *I could get used to this.* He pulled into the parking lot of the office at nine-forty-five.

"Well, I made it by ten o'clock," he said to Nadine.

"It's a good thing. You have two patients that were not happy to be rescheduled, so they're waiting in the lobby."

He felt his excitement about the car deflate. "All right, send the first in."

When noon arrived, Phil asked Nadine how many more patients he had before his lunch break. "None," she answered. "Your next appointment isn't until two this afternoon."

"HOT DOG!" he shouted. Dr. Halverson and Dr. Sharp both came out into the hallway to see what the excitement was all about. Dr. Blomquist stuck her head out of an examining room, "Is everything all right?" she questioned.

"Things couldn't be better," Phil answered.

"You know, for having car trouble this morning, you sure are in a good mood," Nadine commented.

Phil ignored the remarks and was out the door and gone in moments. He spent his entire break driving around town stopping at a Wendy's only long enough to go to the drive-through window and pick up some lunch. He loved the feel of this car. Only once or twice did he feel a little ostentatious when people stared as he passed them. Eventually it occurred to him that with the tinted windows, they were ogling the car and probably couldn't even see him.

When his two hours were about over, he headed back to the office.

<<<

Braxton scanned the obituaries for names of survivors, looking for unattached women who might be the benefactors of an inheritance. There weren't many, but if the deceased had been preceded in death by a spouse, and there weren't many children listed, he cut out the obituary. Comparing the deceased's name with the telephone book, he checked to see if they lived in an upscale neighborhood.

After a week of searching, he found a name of interest… Julianne Jordan, the only surviving child.

<<<

As soon as Dr. Henson left the office after work, Nadine called Jennifer. "Dr. Henson knows your address," she reported.

"You mean he hired a private detective and has my address *already?*" Jennifer asked incredulously.

"I don't know how he found out."

"Was he angry?"

"No, he seemed quite satisfied, actually."

"Dang!" Jennifer mumbled. *He's probably thinking that now he's joining the church and has me in his grasp, he won the jackpot with the house too.* "Thanks for letting me know, Nadine."

"No problem. I thought I'd better give you a heads up. Is it a problem if I divulge our relationship now?"

Something didn't feel right about this. "No, I'd rather you didn't mention it for now. I'll let you know when the coast is clear."

"Okay. You've got my word," Nadine said.

Jennifer hadn't known Nadine long enough to know how trustworthy she was. It was possible that she had spilled the beans herself and was trying to cover up her guilt by being the informant. She also knew that if Phil Henson wanted her address badly enough to hire a private detective, he certainly could afford one. After considering her options, Jennifer decided her best bet was to pretend this conversation never happened. She would let Phil be the one to divulge his knowledge of her location and then she would find out how he gleaned his information.

Chapter Thirty-Four

Phil called Jennifer on her cell phone when he realized she must be waiting for him at his apartment. "I'm on my way. My car was in the shop and I had to pick it up. I'm only three blocks away."

"Okay, we'll wait in our car."

After Phil had showered and changed into jeans and a polo shirt, Jennifer handed him twenty invitations to the baptism and they left for the haunted house on Thirteenth South in Salt Lake City.

The line was still short when they got there and they only had to wait fifteen minutes until it was their turn to go in. While they were waiting, another child saw Jay and screamed in fear.

Jay laughed. "Help me take my mask off—then I can really scare him," he told Phil.

Phil willingly obliged and whenever other people would look at Jay he would roar at them.

"Why don't you walk down the line and scare people?" Phil suggested to Jay.

"It's not safe to let him go alone like that!" Jennifer voiced her objection.

"I'll watch him from up here and make sure he's safe," Phil said, reminding her that he could see over everyone else's head. Just then, the line started to move, and they entered the haunted house.

Jennifer was startled several times and to Phil's delight, she clung to him possessively.

Jay on the other hand, seemed to take great pleasure in frightening other people. Phil had more fun watching Jay than seeing all the other spooks that were constantly popping out of crevices during the evening.

At one point, Jay was in front of Phil and Jennifer when someone in a ghoul costume jumped out to frighten them. Seeing Jay, he let out a shriek of fear instead of a growl to scare them.

Phil and Jennifer came out of the haunted house laughing while those around them ran out screaming.

"That was fun," Jay said. "Let's go through it again."

"I think you've scared enough people for one evening," Jennifer told him.

Phil took them all for hot fudge sundaes afterward. They recounted the people Jay had frightened and laughed through the rest of the evening.

"I do hope you don't intend to make this a lifelong practice," Jennifer said to Jay.

"Only as long as Phil lets me stay looking like this," Jay answered.

"Well, I doubt you will ever look like Brad Pitt," Phil said.

"Who is Brad Pitt?" Jay asked.

"Obviously we need to get out more or see more movies at home," Jennifer said.

"He's a famous actor," Phil told Jay.

"Oh," was all Jay said.

When they arrived back at Phil's apartment, Phil walked Jay and Jennifer back to their car. He opened Jay's door first, buckled his seat belt for him, and then gave Jay a hug. "Thanks for the fun time tonight," he said to Jay.

"You paid for it," Jay reminded Phil.

"Yeah, but *you* provided the entertainment!" Phil closed Jay's door and turned to Jennifer. He took her longingly into his arms and whispered, "Just three more days!"

"And then what?" she whispered back.

Phil kissed her long and fervently. Then he kissed her again until she relaxed and kissed him back. "Does that answer your question?" he asked her.

"Not exactly—does it mean you'll still teach me to ski and play golf?"

"Only if you are planning to have our relationship become more than just a friendship," he answered using her own words and in a tone of voice that matched hers when she had said them.

162

"How *much* more did you have in mind?"

"I think we should discuss this more in depth when we could be alone," Phil answered nodding toward the back seat of the car at Jay's wide grin as he watched them.

Jennifer turned to see what Phil was nodding at and burst out laughing.

"He's adorable, isn't he?" Phil asked. "But I think maybe this is a conversation that ought to be just between the two of us—what do you think?"

"I suspect you're right," Jennifer admitted. "I guess I'd better take him home."

"I could follow you and then when he's asleep we could talk," Phil offered.

"It's late Phil. You have work tomorrow and I have a full day ahead of me. Why don't we set up a time next week?"

"I'll see you on Sunday then, and I'll expect a commitment on a time when we can be *alone* together."

"Fair enough," Jennifer answered.

"In the meantime, can I call you?" Phil asked trying to prolong their moments together.

"As long as you don't keep me up all hours of the night," she said laughingly.

"I promise," he said holding two fingers up like a good cub scout. He opened her door and she slipped into the car. He leaned down and kissed her goodbye before he closed it and waved her off.

<<<

Braxton entered the mortuary dressed in his solid navy suit, a light blue button shirt with the top button undone, no necktie, and his tennis shoes. If he appeared to be under-dressed compared to the attending crowd, his tie was in the car.

He waited in line with the other grieving guests.

"Charlie was a great guy," Braxton heard someone behind him say.

"Sure was," another man answered. "Everybody at Frenetic is wondering who'll take over the company now."

"I heard someone say he had everything set up so the company would continue seamlessly," the first man said.

"I sure hope so," the second man said. "We have a great company with a good team of employees. It'd be a shame if someone took the helm and destroyed everything we've got going for us."

"Excuse me," Braxton cut in, "what exactly does Frenetic do?"

Gentleman number two said, "It's a software company—we specialize in creating customized software for manufacturing companies."

"I see. My name is Braxton Thomas, by the way… and you are?" he asked as he offered his hand.

"Alfred Morrison," the man answered with a handshake.

"Tell me, Alfred, where is your company located?"

"Twenty-first South and State Street."

"And how many employees work for the company?"

"We have twenty of us; all geeks, and we love it! How did you know Charlie?"

"I know his daughter, Julianne," Braxton lied.

"Charlie was sure proud of her. After his wife died, Julianne was all he lived for."

Conversation stopped as they reached the guest book. Braxton signed his name and entered the solemn room where Julianne stood next to the casket greeting people. *Well what do ya know? I scored okay on this one—she's a real looker!*

He turned to Alfred and said, "Excuse me, I see someone I need to catch. Why don't you go ahead of me—and it was nice to meet you, Alfred." With that, Braxton went to the back of the line and stepped in behind a couple of young women who appeared to be around Julianne's age.

After hearing them talk between themselves for a few minutes, he interrupted. "Excuse me, I couldn't help overhear your mention of Charlie's daughter, Julianne. How well do you know her?"

164

"We're sorority sisters," one of them said.

"Oh? Which university?"

"University of Utah."

"So you know her pretty well, then?"

"Oh, yes. We were inseparable during our senior year."

"Charlie spoke very highly of Julianne, but I don't recall him ever saying anything about her being a sorority girl."

"Well, she is. We're members of Alpha Chi Omega."

"Tell me about Alpha Chi Omega."

"It's the musical sorority. Julianne plays the piano, the harp, and the violin. She also sings opera."

"Really? What other hidden talents or hobbies does she have?"

"She plays a mean game of handball and she loves hummus," she said with a scrunched up nose as if she could smell something foul.

Braxton laughed at her expression and excused himself to visit the restroom.

He returned to the end of the line again and waited patiently to get to the casket.

"Hello. You must be Charlie's wonderful daughter, Julianne," Braxton greeted her. "Charlie was a great guy."

"Thank you for coming," she said.

"I'm sure this must be very difficult for you now with both of your parents gone."

"Yes. It has been."

"Charlie talked about you constantly. When we had lunch together, he bragged about your love of music."

"Really?"

"Yes. As a matter of fact, I happen to have a couple of concert tickets to the Utah symphony. I wondered if you might be interested in using them?"

"When are they for?"

"Well, actually, they're season tickets, so I'd need to look on the schedule for the next date. I don't have the tickets with me here, but if I could get your phone number, I could call you later and let you know."

<<<

Phil called Jennifer on Friday evening and they talked about places they would like to go and things they both wanted to see in their lives. He was faithful in keeping his promise—he ended the conversation shortly after nine o'clock when he said goodnight.

Phil had decided earlier to do something for Jennifer. He waited until ten o'clock to drive over to her house. When he could see all the lights were out and it appeared she and Jay were sleeping soundly, he got out of his car. As quietly as possible with crunchy dry autumn leaves, he bagged up as many leaves from her lawn as he could. He had purchased several huge leaf bags that looked like pumpkins. When they were stuffed, he tied the tops closed and quietly drove away feeling smug that he hadn't been caught. *I wonder if she'll figure out it was me?*

Chapter *Thirty-Five*

The next two days rushed by for Jennifer as she anticipated the upcoming baptisms. She still wasn't sure Phil's love would pass the litmus test. He had stopped asking her for her address, which would indicate he did know where she lived, but he hadn't mentioned anything about her living in the house he had wanted to buy.

Saturday afternoon, Jay was listening to another book on his computer while Jennifer was finishing up with the pumpkin rolls and the mock turtles when the phone rang. She checked caller ID before answering it. She rarely had a phone call on her home phone. She didn't recognize the number and there was no name listed. She debated for a long while about answering it, but finally decided she could hang up if she didn't want to talk to someone.

"Hello?"

"Hello," a woman's voice answered. "This is Tonya Simpson calling. You don't know me, but I understand you adopted Jay Borky?" Jennifer's defenses went up. She remained silent waiting for further explanation.

"We adopted Jay's sister, Emily."

Jennifer dropped with relief into a chair. "Oh, how is Emily?"

"She misses Jay and she worries about him continually. Her counselor thought it might be wise if we let her see him. Kimberly, from Social Services gave me your name and phone number and said you told her it was okay to call you."

"Yes. I'm glad you did. Jay has also been concerned about Emily and has wondered how he would ever find her again. Did you say your last name was Simpson?"

"Yes, but please call me Tonya."

"Tonya, what did you have in mind? Would you like me to bring Jay over for a visit?"

"Well, actually, I was hoping to take Emily out trick-or-treating tonight and I wanted to bring her to your house so she could see for herself where Jay lives and know he is safe and hopefully happy."

"Were you planning on surprising her or does she know about this?"

"No. I haven't told her anything yet—I didn't want her to get her hopes up. I decided to call you and see if it was all right if we showed up at your door to trick-or-treat and let Emily and Jay discover each other."

"I love the idea. What time were you planning to bring her by? I'll need to make sure Jay gets home before you come. He's planning to go trick-or-treating with a friend tonight."

"Really? I didn't think he'd be able to go trick-or-treating. From what Emily said about him, he was pretty disabled."

"He is. But he compensates for a lot of things, and he's had another surgery since Emily left the hospital. He no longer has a feeding tube, and he has learned to do many things with his limitations."

"I see. Emily will be relieved to learn that. What if we come at the end of her trick-or-treating, say about eight-thirty?"

"I'll make sure Jay gets home by eight, then," Jennifer said. The two women ended the call with the plan laid out.

Jennifer could hardly contain her anticipation. She called Alice immediately. "You'll never guess who called me!" After she shared the excitement with Alice and explained she needed Jay home by eight o'clock she asked, "Do you think Dave would mind staying here to videotape this reunion, or would he mind if I *borrowed* the video camera? I can plainly see I'm going to need more than a journal to keep good records for Jay. I know he'll want to see this again later in his life!"

"Let me talk to Dave and I'll get back with you in a few minutes," Alice said.

Jennifer waited impatiently for Alice to call back all the while trying to think of a way she could purchase her own video camera. There wasn't enough time to buy one before this evening and she

168

really hated to borrow technical things she could break. When the phone rang, she attacked it, "Hello," she answered expectantly.

"Hi," Alice answered. "Dave said he would be happy to stay and record the reunion for you. He'll try to be as nonchalant about it as he can. Since he planned to have the camera with him to tape Jay's trick-or-treating experience, he doesn't think it will raise any suspicions if he brings the camera in the house to show you after they get back. He'll drop our kids off here before he brings Jay home."

"If you promise not to get mad at me, tell Dave I'll kiss him for this!"

<<<

Dave arrived shortly after six-thirty and stood at the door with his video camera all ready to shoot when Jennifer answered the door. "He's coming," she told Dave. When Jay appeared, he got it all on film. It was the first time Dave or Ben had seen Jay without his compression mask. To their credit, they both kept their calm.

"Are you ready?" Dave asked Jay.

"Yep. Let's see if we can scare up some candy," Jay said. Dave burst into laughter and led the way to the car.

<<<

When Jay had been whisked away, Jennifer realized this was the first time since Jay came home from the hospital that she had been alone in the house. She quickly picked up and cleaned anything she thought needed it knowing there were guests coming. She had the candy ready to hand out when the first trick-or-treaters rang her bell.

The hour and a half went quickly with many interruptions at the door. She was hoping they would slow down by eight-thirty when Emily and Tonya arrived. She wanted Jay to have some uninterrupted time with Emily, and she didn't want to be distracted either. She wanted to participate in the discovery of his sister.

Dave pulled into the driveway fifteen minutes past eight. "Sorry I'm late," he said. "It took a little longer to gather all the kids up and get them in the car. I figured you'd want to take time to see some of the video we took," he winked at her.

She played right along, "Yes, how did it go?" she asked Jay. "Did you scare enough people to make yourself happy?"

Jay grinned. "It worked like a charm every time," he said.

Dave plugged his camera in and rewound the video a few feet.

As Jennifer watched an elderly couple's response to Jay, she couldn't help but smile. They had been so astounded by his undetectable mask they had refused to let him leave until he told them where he had obtained such a perfect mask. When Jay finally explained that he wasn't wearing a mask and he held up his hand with only two stubs and said, "I was burned in a fire—this is what I really look like," the couple both looked horrified and quickly shut their door.

For only a moment, Jennifer's heart felt rejection for Jay. Luckily, Dave had caught Jay's response. She heard Jay say, "Did you see their faces? Best one yet!"

The doorbell rang, and Jennifer slowly made her way to the front door to give Dave adequate time to forward the footage to the end of what he had recorded. When she opened the door, a woman about thirty-something stood before her with a young girl who appeared to be around twelve years old. The girl had a mask covering her face, but Jennifer noticed the burn scars on her hands.

"Trick-or-treat," the young girl said.

"Step inside, while I get the treats," she winked at the woman and then nodded to Dave. Jennifer stepped back out of the way as the young girl and her mother entered the house.

"What is your name?" Jennifer asked the young girl.

"Emily," she answered politely.

"EMILY!" Jay screeched.

Emily turned to see who had yelled at her and collapsed to the floor in sobs. Jay ran to her and hugged her, refusing to let her go.

"Emily, don't cry—it's me—Jay."

Emily grabbed Jay and held him tightly as she cried even harder. "I know who you are, silly," she said. "I just can't believe it's *you*."

Jennifer's shoulders shook and she had tears streaming down her cheeks as she watched this happy reunion taking place. She was grateful Dave was behind the camera and not her. Tonya seemed rather stoic and Jennifer wondered if she felt threatened by Emily's loyalty to Jay.

"Guess what?" Jay said to Emily.

"What?" she asked Jay.

"I'm getting baptized tomorrow!"

"What does that mean?" Emily asked with concern.

"I'm going to be a Mormon! I'm joining the Church of Jesus Christ of Latter-day Saints," Jay boasted proudly.

"You mean you're going to be a *real* Mormon?"

"Yes, would you like to come?"

"NO! Momma and Daddy would not be happy about this Jay Borky!" she chastised.

"They didn't know it was true, Emily. Besides, I don't care what they thought. They didn't care about us anyway," Jay said defensively.

"Jay Borky! Don't you talk like that!" Emily started to cry again.

Jennifer wondered if she needed to intervene and ask Tonya to take Emily home, but she held out a little longer to see how Jay would respond.

"I'm sorry if I hurt your feelings, Emily. But I'm glad I don't live with Momma anymore. After Daddy died, she got mean. I have a new mom now and she's really awesome. She helps me learn all kinds of things. She taught me about the Mormon Church. If you'd read The Book of Mormon, you'd know it was the true church too."

"Emily, I think we'd better leave now," Tonya said.

Emily clung to Jay. "Can Jay come with us?"

Jennifer tried to ease the tension, "Emily, would you like to come over and spend some time with Jay next week?"

Emily looked at Tonya, "Would that be all right?"

"I'll have to think about it," Tonya answered in a terse voice.

Jennifer asked Tonya for her address, so if nothing else, Jay could write letters to Emily. Tonya looked at Jay's misshapen hands, rolled her eyes, and gave Jennifer her address before they left.

Dave had been recording the interaction between Jay and Emily the entire time. When Tonya and Emily left, he turned off the recorder and in a monotone voice said, "Well, that went well."

"Do you think Emily's mom will let her come over next week?" Jay asked.

"I don't know, Honey," Jennifer's voice trailed off.

"I wouldn't bet on it," Dave said. "But you did some serious missionary work there, little Brother! I'm proud of you!"

"I know she'd wanna get baptized too if she read The Book of Mormon."

"I wish everyone was that easy to convert," Dave said. "Well, I'd better get home. I'll transfer this to a DVD and get it to you at the baptism tomorrow."

"Thanks, Dave. You're a real gem… I told Alice I was going to kiss you. Did she tell you that?"

"No, I don't think she mentioned it," he said with a smile as he winked at her and walked out the door.

Jennifer turned to look at Jay and saw his eyes brimming with tears. "Hey, did Emily's visit upset you?"

His lip quivered, "I wish she wasn't mad at me."

"I think Emily was glad to see you. She just wasn't happy about you joining the church."

"If Emily's mom doesn't let her come back, can we take a Book of Mormon to her house so she can read it?"

Jennifer smiled. "*May* we," she corrected. "And I think I have an extra Book of Mormon on the bookshelf you could give her."

Chapter Thirty-Six

At ten o'clock, Jennifer's cell phone rang. Jay had only recently settled in his bed. A little shiver of excitement went through her when she saw Phil's name on caller ID. She answered with a little giggle.

"I almost didn't dare call you this late after your demanding schedule today," he apologized.

"You don't know the half of it!" she said. Then she filled him in on the phone call from Tonya she had received in the afternoon and the reunion that had taken place with Emily and Jay.

"How is Emily?" Phil asked with concern.

"I'm no psychologist," Jennifer said, "but I don't think her adoption was a real good fit, and I don't think Emily is happy."

"I'm not sure Emily would be happy with *any* adoption. She doesn't have Jay's positive attitude. I wonder if she's so serious because she's the oldest and feels the need to take care of Jay, or if it's her personality. It may also be the fact that she's a girl and I believe appearances are more important to girls than they are to boys. I mean—you saw how Jay acted at the haunted house the other night. He capitalized on his appearance. I don't think Emily would ever be able to do that."

"I really feel sorry for her, but I still believe she could have a better support system. Tonya seemed rather insecure and threatened by the relationship between Emily and Jay. I've seen students with insecure parents in blended families, and it often makes the student resentful and rebellious."

"Which only confirms my belief, that you are absolutely the most wonderful influence on Jay that he could possibly have! As a matter of fact, I think I might say—you seem to have that same positive influence on me too."

"You're much too generous in your appraisals. Jay is amazing in his own right, and you are too. I feel lucky to be able to associate with each of you, and consider it some kind of a miracle that I know you both."

"So, how did the trick-or-treating go at your house? Did you do any special decorating in the yard for the occasion?" he asked.

"I usually dress up like a witch to answer the door, but because I knew Emily was coming and my time was running out before Jay left, I didn't bother to dress up this year. I did, however, have this monstrous-looking pumpkin lit up with a candle on my front porch. I'm not sure the trick-or-treaters could have taken it if I had been dressed really scary too—the pumpkin was scary enough."

"Any *other* decorations?"

"No. I guess I need to get more involved in creating a spooky entrance to the house. Maybe some spider webs and goblins or something. I'll have to think about that for next year."

"I had this really cute happy pumpkin on my porch. All the kids weren't nearly as afraid of me as they usually are this year— and I dressed up like Frankenstein. I have a tape recorder running with ghoulish sounds on it, and the kids were still smiling when they rang the doorbell. All I can figure is that the smiling jack-o-lantern that was carved by the most beautiful lady in the world counteracted all my attempts to scare them."

"I'm sorry if I ruined your fun," she said. "Maybe you should have kept the scary pumpkin and I should have taken the smiling one. It might have helped Emily feel a little better."

"But Jay wouldn't have enjoyed it as much. He really got into the spirit of being spooky for Halloween, didn't he?"

"He did. Alice's husband, Dave, videotaped him trick-or-treating tonight. Jay pretended to be a 'freak' by taking his compression mask off. He wore his hospital pajamas over his clothing to make himself look 'bulkier' as he put it. I didn't have time to see more than a little tiny clip of the video, but I can't wait to see how it went. Dave seemed excited about the results."

"So, I've heard you talk about Alice before. She must be a close friend?"

174

Jennifer explained how she and Alice had developed such a close friendship, and how they started the Sisters in Zion group. "She's a great friend. Dave has become a close friend too. I think he and Alice are as taken with Jay's charisma as I am."

"I think there are few people who wouldn't be taken with Jay's charm. I know he won my heart over really fast at the hospital," Phil said.

"And yet," Jennifer countered, "everywhere we go, people avoid him. I've noticed that they stare at him and then hurry away."

"Yeah, but that's only because they see the *injured* Jay. They haven't had the opportunity to discover his personality. How does he respond to people when they stare and then turn away?"

"He pretends not to notice, but he couldn't help but see it. *I'm* the one who takes offense and feels hurt for him."

"How do the kids in church treat him?"

"Well, at first, they stared and then got scolded by their parents who in turn stared themselves. But since Jay has become a regular attendee, they don't seem to treat him any differently than all the other kids. Every now and again I notice someone staring at him, but I guess he'll always have to deal with that."

"I rest my case. Once they get to know him, they will love him. Was he as loveable before the fire?"

"He was less outgoing. Dr. Green said his personality change is his way of coping. He was one of those students that kept to himself but did his work to perfection. I could tell he had an above-average intellect—way above average—but after his father committed suicide, he grew *more* withdrawn. When he disappeared from school, I went searching for him and found out about the fire. I wasn't exactly sure he had survived until December."

"But you sent balloons every week."

"That was my strategy to find out if Jay had survived."

"I'm not sure Jay would have rallied if you hadn't sent those pictures from the classmates and the photograph of you and the other students. He was in a pretty bad slump."

"When I finally got to see him, it was the best thing in the world for me," she said. "I found myself looking forward to every visit."

"So did Jay," Phil said. "So did I, but I didn't admit it at the time."

"You didn't even know I existed!"

"Oh yes I did. We *all* knew who you were—every one of the doctors and nurses. You were the subject of many discussions among us. 'How did she know Jay? Why is she paying so much attention to him? What are her motives?' Then after your picture arrived we had the explanation and a new series of questions started, 'Isn't she nice looking? I wonder if she's married. Should we let her into the inner sanctum?'

"I voted yes on that one. It probably wasn't very professional of me, but like you, I had grown attached to Jay, and seeing his positive response to your photograph, was desperately hoping to bring him out of his slump. If a pretty lady that I might be able to fall in love with happened to do it, then all the better."

"You rogue, you," she accused jokingly.

"Guilty as charged."

"Were you seriously scheming the whole time?"

"Why did you think I fought to sit in during your visits instead of letting the security guard?"

"I assumed it was because the security guard was unavailable at the time."

"He was unavailable because I hog-tied him in a linen closet down the hall!"

"You *are* a rogue," she laughed at his exaggeration.

"Yeah, but look where it got me. I'm madly in love with the most incredible girl in the world and tomorrow I'm getting baptized."

"Are you sure you're not getting baptized because of me?" she asked suspiciously.

176

"You know, I've given that a great deal of thought," he said more seriously. "If I couldn't have you in my life without joining the church, I might have considered joining for that reason. But Jay convinced me to read The Book of Mormon. After that, I was totally committed to the truth of it. If you refuse to speak to me after tomorrow, I'll still belong to the only true church on the earth today."

"So you're saying it's all Jay's fault?"

"The real blame goes to the Holy Ghost, but Jay's a close second."

"You'll never believe this, but Jay told Emily about his baptism tomorrow and invited her to come."

"Will she be there?" Phil asked with hope in his voice.

"No. She was adamant with Jay that he would be disappointing their parents, and *she* was *not* pleased about it."

"Really? How did Jay react to that?"

Jennifer started to laugh. "He told her *they*—meaning their parents—didn't know it was true, and if *she'd* read The Book of Mormon herself, she'd know it was true and want to get baptized too."

"Good for him! I'm proud of that boy! Oh, but how did *Tonya* take that?"

"I think if I remember correctly, that's the moment she told Emily they needed to leave. She seemed anxious to get out of here. Emily wanted to take Jay home with her—maybe to rescue him from the *Mormons*, but Tonya didn't seem positive about allowing them to get together again."

"That's too bad. It might be good for both of them to see each other occasionally."

"Well, I did manage to get their address from Tonya so even if she won't allow them to visit any more, Jay can write letters to Emily. I think it might be good therapy for him if not for her."

"I'm surprised Tonya gave you their address if she's so opposed to them seeing each other."

"Well, I told her it was so Jay could *write* to Emily. She took one look at his hands and shrugged her shoulders and gave me the address. I honestly believe she thought it would be impossible for him to write a letter to anyone. I'm sure she has no idea what he can accomplish.

"It upset Jay when Emily got angry with him, but get this—after they left, Jay asked if we could give Emily a Book of Mormon to read so she'd know it was true."

"I sure love that kid," he said.

In that instant, Jennifer *knew* that she would be Phil's wife and Jay would be their son and carry Phil's last name. *Phil was going to adopt Jay*! The vision was so real she asked Phil, "When should we tell Jay?"

"Tell him that I love him?" he asked sounding confused.

Jennifer immediately realized she'd been given a personal witness for her alone, and Phil had no clue what she was talking about. "Oh, sorry," she apologized. "I think I'm getting tired and not making any sense."

"Well, I'd better let you get some sleep. I've got to get up early tomorrow myself. I pick my parents up at the airport at eight-thirty in the morning. I can't wait to have them meet you." *I wonder how they'll take to Jay?*

Chapter Thirty-Seven

Jennifer and Jay pulled into the church parking lot next to Phil's car. She opened the door for Jay and he slipped his arm through the strap of his bag with clean clothing and a towel. He was becoming independent. She gathered a plastic tote filled with goodies and decorations to take into the church.

Phil and his parents were standing inside the glass doors when she and Jay reached the building. Phil immediately opened the door for them and kissed Jennifer as she passed him, carrying her burden. After walking through the doors, she set the tote down on the floor and met Phil's parents, Bob and Mary. Following the introductions, Phil hefted the large container into the kitchen.

Jennifer could sense Phil's parents' apprehension in this unfamiliar environment, so she asked Mary if she would help her with setting the serving table.

She invited Bob and Jay to follow them into the multipurpose room, where they sat down and watched. Phil was taken into another room by the Elders.

"So how many times has my son beaten you up to make you look like that?" Bob asked Jay. Jennifer, overhearing the conversation, was drawn to Bob's humor.

"I'm not sure. Only two that I know about. Probably a lot before I woke up. I was in a coma for a long time," Jay answered.

Mary and Jennifer had the table set with the tablecloth and an autumn leaf floral arrangement. Off to the sides of the basket of leaves, Jennifer added two newly purchased brown leather sets of scriptures monogrammed with the names of the two baptismal candidates as her gift to them. She placed the cake in the center of the table, then set the plates, cups, napkins, and pitchers of water on the left, with the mock turtles and pumpkin rolls at the right.

"Very nice," Mary said about the way Jennifer set up the table. "It definitely has a woman's touch and yet it's masculine enough for Phil and Jay."

Elder Manning and his companion entered the room and asked Jay to follow them, leaving Bob alone on the chairs.

Jennifer led Bob and Mary to the chapel for the opening exercises.

"You tell us what to do," Mary instructed Jennifer. "We've never done this before, so we don't know where we're supposed to go."

"Do *we* have to do anything in this ceremony?" Bob asked.

Jennifer realized they were both apprehensive about the part they might have to play in this baptism. To put them at ease, she explained, "You're guests of Phil's tonight. He wants you here to witness his commitment to Jesus Christ. You can relax. You don't have to do anything but listen and watch. Enjoy yourselves. And thank you, Mary, for helping me get the table set up so quickly."

Jennifer introduced Bob and Mary to Bishop Bowen when they entered the chapel, and then to Dave and Alice and their family. Bob and Mary seemed gracious and shook hands readily with each introduction.

A short bald man in a suit approached them, "I'm Bishop Lander, and you must be Phil's parents, Bob and Mary Henson," he said, extending his right hand to Bob.

"Yes, we are," Bob said.

When Bishop Lander extended his hand to Mary, she took it with both of hers and held it for a moment while she spoke. "I'm not sure why we are here, but it is nice to meet some of our son's acquaintances."

Bishop Lander responded to Mary's comment, "It's a tribute to you both that your son *wanted* you to be here and share this experience with him. He's a great man and I'm sure it's a reflection of the wonderful job you did in teaching him to be honorable from his childhood."

Bob and Mary nodded and appeared to be pleased. "Thank you," Bob said.

"You must be Miss Jennifer Heaps," the bishop said, turning to Jennifer.

180

"I am that, indeed," she said as she shook Bishop Lander's hand.

"I met Jay a moment ago. He's quite a special boy. He told me you were his school teacher before you were his mother, is that right?"

"That's true. I'm afraid our bond began before he was traumatized and burned."

"Well, from what I have heard from *Dr. Phil*," he said with a chuckle, "and from Jay himself, you're quite a girl!"

"Thank you for allowing them to blindside you," she said sheepishly.

With that, Bishop Lander headed toward the stand.

Jennifer led Bob and Mary to seats near the front of the center section.

"They're certainly a friendly bunch," Mary commented. "I thought church people were kind of pious."

"I think they're all a bunch of used car salesmen," Bob said.

Jennifer tried to suppress a smile as she overheard them talking more to each other.

Just then, Elder Manning escorted Jay into the chapel with Elder Benedict and Phil following them; all of them dressed in white. They took their seats on the center front row. Everyone quieted down and only the prelude music, played by IlaRae, could be heard.

"I think they'll be starting soon," Jennifer whispered.

"Good thing," Bob whispered. "Let's get this thing over with!"

The opening song was "How Great Thou Art." Jennifer noticed that Bob and Mary were pretty quiet and didn't sing until it got to the chorus. She nearly fell off the bench when Bob belted out the chorus in a strong tenor voice. She looked over at him and smiled appreciatively. She instantly felt a kinship with Bob.

Bishop Bowen spoke briefly about Joseph Smith at the time of his visit from God the Father and His Son, Jesus Christ, when he was only five years older than Jay. He bore witness of the truthfulness of The Book of Mormon and then sat down.

Bob and Mary seemed to be listening attentively.

Then Dr. Halverson spoke about his relationship with Phil and how such a miracle had taken place when little Jay had introduced his doctor to The Book of Mormon. He quoted *Alma 32:23* "'And now, he imparteth his word by angels unto men, yea, not only men but women also. Now this is not all; little children do have words given unto them many times, which confound the wise and the learned.'

"Phil Henson is one of the finest men in our office," he continued. "I would consider him a learned man. Yet it took the testimony of an innocent child to change the heart of this wise man whose spirit resonated with the truth when he read it in The Book of Mormon. We are told in the Old Testament by Isaiah that during the time of the millennium, a little child shall lead them. In 3 Nephi, we read: '...And again I say unto you, ye must repent, and be baptized in my name, and become as a little child or ye can in nowise inherit the kingdom of God.'

"Everyone in our office has watched Dr. Henson as he has embraced The Book of Mormon and his testimony has strengthened ours. The restored Gospel of Jesus Christ is on the earth today, led and guided by a living prophet. I know it, Jay Heaps knew it, and now Phil Henson knows it. To this I testify, in the name of Jesus Christ, amen."

Mary pulled a tissue from her purse. Bob quickly wiped a tear from his cheek with the back of his hand.

Alice's husband, Dave, was the last speaker before Bishop Lander's closing remarks. He spoke about the Spirit of the Holy Ghost and how to recognize it.

"Dr. Halverson mentioned that Dr. Henson's spirit had resonated with the truth—that's how the Holy Ghost works. It is something we feel. Sometimes it makes us cry. Sometimes it makes us so full of joy that we feel we might pop our buttons. Other times the Spirit might tug at us in the form of a thought or feeling of warning we can't seem to identify, yet we aren't able to shake it off. Most folks, when they are first introduced to the

182

church, have never felt anything like it before, so the first thing they must do is learn to recognize that feeling. Then they learn to acknowledge the feeling. Then, of course, as we see here today with Jay and Dr. Henson, they act on it, embrace it, and it changes their lives forever," Dave explained.

He finished with his own testimony and Bishop Lander stood to give his closing remarks.

"This is a delightful occasion; an account of two spirits, a man and a boy, who have both embraced the Gospel through their mutual love and association. I suppose there are more unusual conversion stories, but for me it has been such a joy to share in this event."

Jennifer and half the congregation were sniffling.

The bishop continued, "We will have our closing song, *I am a Child of God,* hymn number 301. Because of the unusual relationship between our baptismal candidates tonight, we're going to try to fit everyone that wishes to witness both baptisms in the room together. We'll now proceed with the closing song, and then we will dismiss to the font room."

Bob and Mary didn't sing any of the closing song, but both of them were following the words in the hymnbook closely and Bob's eyes were teary. Jennifer noticed Phil and Jay were both wiping tears as well. The Spirit had definitely borne witness to anyone open enough to feel it. Jennifer was pleased.

Elder Manning baptized Jay first. Phil sat on the front row with Jennifer and his parents to watch. When Jay came up out of the water, Phil and Jennifer were holding hands and both crying.

Jay was beaming. Elder Manning picked him up out of the water and held him to his chest. Jay threw his arms around him and hugged him.

Jennifer saw Bob and Mary wipe tears away from their eyes.

Phil and Elder Benedict stood to take their turn. After they walked down into the baptismal font, Jay reappeared on the top step of the font in his wet clothes with a white towel wrapped around him.

Jennifer's heart swelled when Phil winked at him and Jay gave a wave of his stubby little hand in return.

Elder Benedict lifted Phil out of the water and they gave each other a brotherly hug. Phil turned to Jennifer and smiled. She was beaming.

When he turned around to exit the font, Jay dropped his towel and practically leaped into Phil's arms in the water. Phil caught him and they clung to each other.

Many of the observers laughed, but not one of them were dry-eyed—even Bob and Mary. Jennifer didn't think there could ever be a happier moment in her life.

<<<

Everyone moved to the multipurpose room to visit and have refreshments. Jennifer asked that they not cut the sheet cake until the guests of honor returned from the dressing room.

Dave and Alice's children immediately took mock turtles and pumpkin bread not waiting for Phil and Jay to join them. Dave slipped a DVD into Jennifer's hand and said, "This will be priceless to Jay someday. I'm sure you'll find it entertaining."

"Thank you, Dave. I'm sure I will." Jennifer slipped it into her purse in the kitchen.

People mingled and commented on the wonderful Spirit they had felt. Bob and Mary seemed to be enjoying introductions to all the guests and were much more at ease than they had been prior to the meeting.

Jennifer overheard IlaRae ask Mary how long they were going to be in town. "We'll leave a week from today," she said. "Phil wanted us to stay long enough to see him get confirmed next Sunday."

"I see," IlaRae said. "In that case, what are your plans for Wednesday evening?"

Jennifer realized that IlaRae was about to invite Phil's parents to her house to be an audience for their choir practice. She felt uneasy about the confrontation that might ensue.

184

"We'll have to check with Phil, but unless he has other plans," Jennifer heard Mary say, "We'd love to come, wouldn't we Bob?"

Bob had snitched one of the mock turtles from the table and stuffed it into his mouth. He nodded his head in agreement.

Phil and Jay, along with Elder Manning and Elder Benedict, entered the room dry and well groomed. Jay had his compression mask back on. He ran to Jennifer with Phil right on his heels.

"Group hug," Phil said as the three of them embraced.

Refreshments were served and the crowd slowly thinned as people left the building to return to their homes. In the end, Jennifer and Jay along with Phil and his parents were the only people left. As they began to clean up the room and take down the table decorations, Phil asked Jennifer what her plans were for tomorrow.

"I actually don't have any," she said with a sigh of relief. "I have been trying to get through this past week."

"I was hoping I could take you and Jay to dinner with me and my parents tomorrow evening," Phil said.

"We'd love to. I guess I'd better ask where you plan to go—do I need to dress formally?" she asked teasingly, remembering La Caille.

"Dress nice, but comfortable—not formal," Phil said with a bit of mystery in his voice.

"Where are we going?" Jennifer asked. "That way I can determine what *nice* means."

"It's called *Log Haven Restaurant*. It's up Mill Creek Canyon. Ever been there?"

"Never even heard of the place," she admitted. "What time should we be at your apartment?"

"Could you come about five-thirty? You could visit with my parents until I get home from work, then we'll leave around six o'clock. Does that sound okay?"

"Sure enough," Jennifer answered.

She gave Phil's parents a hug as they parted and they left the church in their respective cars to go home.

Braxton called Abravanel Hall and ordered season tickets to the Utah Symphony, then dialed the phone number in his little black book.

"Hello, is this Julianne Jordan?" Braxton asked.

"Yes it is," she answered.

"This is Braxton Thomas. I met you at your father's funeral. I told you I'd call about the Utah Symphony tickets?"

"Oh, yes! Really, Mr. Thomas, you don't need to give your tickets to me. I'm sure they were rather expensive."

"Well, it just so happens that I'm currently unattached and don't have anyone to go with me. I hate going alone. So, I thought since you enjoy music so much, you might like to go and take one of your friends—maybe one of your sorority sisters?"

"Really? That's very thoughtful of you. How did you know about my sorority sisters?"

"As I mentioned at the funeral, your father talked a great deal about you when we shared an occasional lunch together. He was a great man and I'll miss doing business with him."

"What did you say your business with my father was?" she asked.

"I don't believe I mentioned it. I actually knew him from the software he designed for a company I used to work for. I was the technical liaison for the programming department of a composite manufacturer."

"Oh. So Frenetic Technologies designed the software," she said, indicating that she understood the connection.

"Yes, something like that. Would it be alright if I drop the tickets off at your house in about an hour?"

"I really feel guilty taking them. Are you sure you can't find someone to go with you?"

"I'm sure. And there's no need to feel guilty. I'll feel better knowing someone with an appreciation for fine music is using them."

"Well, all right then. I'll see you in about an hour."

186

He hung up, printed the tickets from his online order, showered and shaved, dressed in a pair of gray slacks and a navy polo shirt, and drove to Julianne's.

She was wearing jeans and a tee shirt, her hair piled on top of her head with tendrils of auburn curls hanging down around her face.

After an hour-long visit on the front porch, Braxton had set up a date to play handball at the gym he'd said he had a membership with.

He hummed happily back toward the Mercedes. Well, well, well. I guess I'd better get a membership at the gym before Saturday.

Chapter Thirty-Eight

Jennifer wore brown slacks with a cream colored blouse, ruffled at the V-neckline, and a multi-autumn-colored suede jacket. It accentuated her slim figure and she felt quite comfortable. She wore her brown loafers. "Nothing like what Nadine would wear," she said, thinking how she always wore three-inch high heels. *I don't know how she can walk in those things without killing herself. But then, if I dressed like that, I'd look like a clown—she looks classy. I guess that's the difference between a city girl and a country bumpkin like me.* Jennifer wore her hair down in curls around her shoulders.

Jay wore a pair of khaki pants and a blue plaid shirt. Jennifer buttoned the front placket for him. "I don't know why it matters what I wear," he said. "I still look like a sick puppy."

"At least you don't have to dress up to be noticed," Jennifer answered. "There are women who would kill to have enough personality they didn't need to worry about their attractiveness!"

Jay grinned. "You're just saying that to make me feel good."

"I'm saying it because it's the truth! Think about it, Jay, a lot of people love you. Dave and Alice, Ben, Elder Manning, Phil, IlaRae, Bishop Bowen. We all think you're remarkable."

Jay's face sobered. "You're right," he said to Jennifer, "I'm really lucky."

<<<

Jay and Jennifer arrived around five-thirty. They visited with Bob and Mary while Phil showered and shaved. When he walked out of the bathroom, Jennifer's heart skipped a beat. He looked so nice in his dark gray slacks, burgundy shirt, and navy jacket. His shirt was unbuttoned at the top, giving him a more casual appearance than normal had he been wearing a tie.

Phil paced back and forth from the living room window to his small kitchen. Jennifer wondered if he was a little concerned about combining his parents with her and Jay at dinner. *He hadn't seemed preoccupied with fears about them being together at the baptism.* She decided she was being overly sensitive. At six o'clock the doorbell rang, and Phil stopped pacing. "Here is our ride," he announced and quickly answered the door.

Everyone looked stunned. "Our ride?" Mary looked at the man standing at the door with curiosity.

Phil invited the man in and he tipped his derby. "My name is Regi," he announced. "I'll be your chauffer this evening."

"Cool!" Jay said with excitement.

They all followed Regi out to the stretch limousine double parked in the parking lot of the apartment complex. With a flourish, Regi opened the double back doors to expose six individual leather bucket seats—three on one side facing three on the other with enough leg space between them to fit a dinner table.

Jay climbed in first, followed by the rest. When everyone was seated, Regi pushed a button and a bar raised up out of the floor. "Perhaps you would like to begin your evening with a glass of Chardonnay?"

"We won't need the bar," Phil said.

"Very well, Sir," Regi said. "Would you prefer to have the bar down and perhaps view a movie while we travel?"

Jennifer noticed the small TV screens above their heads on both sides enabling them all to watch a movie.

"No movie tonight," Phil answered, "We'd like to visit if that's all right."

"Yes, Sir. Then I assume you are not interested in reading material. Would you like soft music in the background—we have several CD's to choose from—classical, pop, country, elevator music—the choice is yours?"

"If I tell you we'd like it quiet are you going to offer me something else?" Phil asked.

"Your wish is my command," Regi answered. "What is it you would like?"

"Just a driver to get us to our destination," Phil said with a chuckle.

190

"And so you shall have it." With that Regi politely closed the doors.

"I was beginning to think we'd never get out of the parking lot," Phil said. Everyone laughed but Jay.

"How come nobody asked me if I wanted to see a movie?"

"Would you like to see a movie?" Phil asked.

"No. I'll watch a movie some other time."

Jennifer thought she could read Jay's mind. It's that delightful curiosity of his that wants to absorb everything going on around him and internalize and learn from it.

"How was your day at work, Dear?" Mary asked Phil.

"It went fine. I had a patient from Guatemala with a cleft lip and palate come in today. He was sponsored by a charity that wanted to give him a new chance at life. I hope he will be able to see himself in a different light after the surgeries. Apparently the people of his country believe he is wicked or has done something terrible to be born with this curse."

Jay asked, "Will he look normal after he's operated on?"

"Almost completely. There may be a little scarring on his upper lip."

"How terrible for people to feel that way about a birth defect," Jennifer said.

"What would he say if he saw me?" Jay asked. "Do you think he'd feel better about himself?"

Four adults turned to stare at Jay. "One look at you and *anybody* would feel better about themselves," Bob chided. "Why don't you fix *him*?" Bob asked Phil.

Even Jay laughed at Bob's humor.

"He's a hopeless case, but I'm working on it—one operation at a time—I want to stretch the torture out as long as I possibly can." Then turning back to Jay, Phil said, "I wonder what someone in his circumstances *would* do if someone like you *did* talk to him?"

"I guess the only way to find out is to try it," Jay answered.

"He only speaks Spanish, Jay. He wouldn't understand you."

"How do *you* talk to him?"

"We have an interpreter come to explain what we say."

"Well, if he can interpret for *you* can't he interpret for *me*?"

"He's quite right, you know," Bob said. "Those interpreters usually can do their thing for more than one person."

"All right, Jay. You win. I'll see if I can set it up so you can meet him," Phil said with resignation. "Since when did I start taking counsel from a nine-year-old?" he asked Jennifer.

"That's what you get for fixing his mouth so he could talk!"

"I must say," Mary said, changing the subject, "I certainly enjoyed myself last night at your baptism—or would that be baptisms for plural?"

"It did go nicely," Jennifer agreed. "I certainly enjoyed getting reacquainted with Dr. Halverson."

"He gave a nice talk, don't you think, Bob?" Mary asked.

"I guess my favorite talk was by that friend of yours who spoke about recognizing the Holy Ghost."

"That was Dave Horne," Phil supplied his name.

"Have you ever felt the Holy Ghost, Bob?" Jay jumped right into the thick of the conversation.

"I can't say I've recognized it if I have," Bob answered.

"Then why were you crying during that song about being a Child of God?" Mary asked.

"Well, it touched my heart to hear the simple words of that sweet song," Bob answered.

"When you heard the words to the song, you *knew* you were a Child of God, didn't you?" Jay said it more as a statement than a question.

"Yes, well, perhaps that was it, Jay. It was nothing profound. It was acknowledging that God in his heaven is over us all and we are his children."

"So you cried, huh?" Jay prodded further.

"I guess I teared up a bit," Bob admitted.

"Remember what Dave said about the Holy Ghost? He said it was something we *feel*. He said sometimes it makes us cry?"

"Yeah, I remember something like that," Bob admitted.

"Well, there you have it!" Jay said with finality.

"I have what?" Bob asked.

"You cried. That was the Spirit of the Holy Ghost telling you it was true. You need to learn to recognize this stuff," Jay said authoritatively.

Jennifer was about ready to set Jay in his place and remind him that he needed to be more respectful to adults when Bob spoke humbly, "Maybe you're right, Jay."

Jennifer clamped her mouth shut.

Mary spoke up, "Perhaps we should look into this Mormon religion a little further, Bob."

"Perhaps we should," Bob said thoughtfully.

The Log Haven Restaurant was a delightfully quaint place with beautiful scenic grounds surrounding it. It was too dark outside to really appreciate the autumn colors on the trees, but from the window by their table they could see the waterfall and some of the surrounding trees with the help of several well-placed spot lights. "I'll bet this place is heavenly in the daylight," Mary gushed.

"We'll definitely have to come back during the summer when the evening light lasts longer," Jennifer said as if she expected Bob and Mary to still be here then.

After their server brought them their dinner, Phil turned to his father and asked, "So, Dad, what do you think about Jennifer, does she meet with your approval?"

Jennifer was embarrassed to have Phil so blatantly ignore her while he and his father had this conversation as if she didn't exist. She looked at Bob and realized he was in a more uncomfortable position than she was. How could he possibly tell Phil if he didn't care for her if she was right there listening?

"Would the two of you like me to leave?" Jennifer offered.

"Oh no, that's not necessary," Phil said with a smile.

"I don't know, Phil," Bob answered, "Maybe she should go powder her shiny nose if it would make her feel better. While she's at it, do you think we should let her know her entire face is bright red? Oh, and another thing, Phil, I don't think she's as funny looking as you said she was."

Jay and Jennifer both burst into the giggles. "I know when I've been had," Jennifer confessed. "Mary, do you have to put up with this all the time?"

"Yeah, and Phil's the worst. Bob is like this all the time, but when he and Phil get together, they feed on each other."

"Well, I guess that about wraps it up, Phil," Bob said. "If she can laugh at our tormenting her, you'd better marry her."

"Great idea, Dad. Jennifer, will you marry me?"

Jennifer laughed at the jest and then realized it wasn't a joke. Everyone at the table was looking at her expectantly.

"Honey, if your answer would be yes, now would be the time to say so," Mary said quite seriously.

Jennifer was so thoroughly caught off guard; she didn't know whether to laugh or to cry. Unbidden tears began to fall down her cheeks, and Bob said, "Well, I guess that means the Holy Ghost is telling her yes!"

They all laughed including Jennifer. "Of course I'll marry you, you crazy guy," she said quietly to Phil. He put his arm around her and pulled her close, giving her a long kiss.

"Hear, hear!" Bob said as he tapped his glass with his knife. Mary joined him. Jay was observing his mother with a smile.

Phil straightened himself up and cleared his throat. "There's one other little matter of business I need to take care of before we make the engagement formal. Jay, will you be my son? And if you'll allow me, I'd like to adopt you and change your last name to match your mother's and mine. How would you feel about becoming Jay Henson?"

"I'd like that," Jay said beaming.

Bob and Mary were both teary eyed. "There's the Holy Ghost again," Jay said. And they all burst out laughing.

Jennifer's heart swelled with so much joy that she felt she would burst her buttons. She contemplated Dave's words from his talk on the Holy Ghost. She had felt this feeling before when she had her personal witness that she would be Phil's wife, but now as the reality of it was settling in on everyone else seated at the table; Jennifer recognized the Holy Ghost's presence.

While they were comfortably riding in the limousine to go home, Bob with his arm around Mary's shoulder, and Phil holding Jennifer's hands with both of his, Mary invited Phil to bring Jennifer and Jay to California for Thanksgiving.

"I'll have to check my schedule," Phil said, "But I'm pretty sure I can arrange it. What about you Jennifer?"

"My only concern would be choir practice the night before Thanksgiving. Let me find out Wednesday what the Sisters in Zion would like to do for practice that week. Oh, that reminds me, are you all coming Wednesday night to our choir practice? I heard IlaRae invite you at the baptism last night. She's looking for an audience to perform for, I'm sure."

"I'd actually forgotten to mention it to Phil," Mary said. "Phil, did you have any special plans for us on Wednesday evening?"

"You mean we're actually invited to come to your house?" Phil asked Jennifer.

"Yes, I guess if we're going to be getting married, it's high time I finally give you my address," Jennifer offered hoping to discover how much Phil really did know.

"Dr. Halverson *told* me he thought you were intentionally holding out on me! How many times have I asked you for your address and you always seemed to have some emergency come up? *Were* you deliberately avoiding telling me?"

"Yes," Jennifer confessed. "I was grateful when you finally stopped asking me for it, but I'll gladly give it to you now."

"No need." Phil said smugly. "I quit asking because I found out where you live."

"How did you find my address?" she asked half expecting him to say Nadine had told him.

"I just happened to be parked behind you at a stop light when you were on your way home from shopping Thursday. I was in a rented car while mine was being worked on, so you didn't know it was me. I followed you home."

"You rascal, you!" Jennifer accused.

"That's my boy," Bob said proudly.

"So, does this mean you'll come on Wednesday evening?" Jennifer asked. "I'll even throw dinner in if you come early enough we can clean it up before choir practice."

"Will you make baked beans?" Phil asked.

"Yeah," Jay said. "We like baked beans, don't we Phil?"

"So, do you make baked beans, Jennifer?" Bob asked.

"Well, yes, but they're really nothing to brag about."

"Do tell! Mary and I love baked beans."

"Well, I'm sure I can think of something to make for dinner that will go with baked beans," Jennifer said. "Is five o'clock too early?"

"We'll be there," Phil answered.

Jennifer felt guilty for suspecting that Nadine may have betrayed her and relieved that she hadn't. *What if Phil proposed marriage because he knew we lived in 'the' house?*

Chapter *Thirty-Nine*

Jennifer had decided to make Sante Fe Chicken and baked potatoes. She made the baked beans early in the morning and got them cooking in the crock pot so they'd be done by five. Then she chopped cabbage and green onions to make her favorite crunchy coleslaw. *I hope they like cabbage.* She set the chopped cabbage and green onions in a nice serving bowl, covered it with plastic wrap and refrigerated it until dinnertime. She cut carrot sticks to add color to the meal and then made rolls and put butter out to thaw.

She clipped chrysanthemums from the backyard and arranged them in a vase for the center of the table and then set the dining room table with her mother's china, silverware, and stemware—something she hadn't used since her parents' untimely death. She placed a straw in Jay's glass and his special spoon by his plate that had Velcro straps to go around his wrist. The chicken and potatoes were ready to bake in the oven by three o'clock and then she made sure the house was straightened.

"It sure does smell good," Jay said.

"I forgot to make dessert," she realized. "Oh well, I guess we'll have to settle for ice cream."

"Yummm!" Jay said. "Hey, Mom, is there enough time to take that Book of Mormon over to Emily's house this afternoon?"

"I'm not sure her mother will be too happy if we show up with a Book of Mormon, Jay. She didn't seem very pleased about you mentioning your baptism to Emily Saturday night."

"But Emily has to read it; she just has to! Or she'll never forgive me for joining the church. Besides, I wanna tell her that I'm going to be Jay Henson. She still thinks my last name is Borky."

Realizing what this meant to Jay, Jennifer decided if Tonya and Emily got upset over a quick visit, an announcement of a name

197

change, and a free gift of love, then it was their problem—she didn't want it to be a problem for Jay.

"Let's go get the book off the shelf in the sitting room," Jennifer said. "Would you like it gift wrapped for Emily?"

"Yeah! Then her mom won't know what book it is until Emily has a chance to open it and maybe read it."

Jennifer quickly wrapped the book in some blue tissue paper she had in storage and then went with Jay to his computer to make Emily a little note. In the letter, he told Emily how much he loved her and missed her and how much he wanted her to read this special book. "Read it before you decide to throw it away. If you hate it after you have read it, then I won't be mad if you get rid of it. I love you, Jay." He had spoken the words into his microphone and then the words appeared on the screen of his computer. He said, "Click file," and then "Click print." At his voice commands, the printer produced his letter to Emily.

Jennifer found Tonya's address and they quickly drove over to their house.

Jennifer sat in the car while Jay walked up to the front door.

<<<

Emily answered the door. She let out a squeal of delight and hugged Jay. Jay asked her to reach in his shoulder bag and take out the gift and letter he had for her. Then he told her that his new mom was going to get married, and he would be changing his last name from Heaps to Henson. "Did you change your last name to Simpson?" he asked Emily.

"Yeah," she told him. "It was done when I was adopted."

"My mom gave me the choice," Jay explained. "But I was glad to change my name from 'DORKY' to Heaps," he said.

Emily laughed. "It was a terrible name, wasn't it?" she agreed.

"We have to go now. My new dad and his parents are coming to dinner soon. Read the letter before you open the gift," he said as he turned to leave down the steps.

"Jay, wait!" Emily called out. She ran after him and gave him a big hug. "I love you," she said. "I always will!" Then she ran back into the house and closed the door.

"I know she'll feel the Spirit when she reads the book," he said as they drove home.

Chapter Forty

Phil, Bob, and Mary pulled into the driveway of Jennifer's house right at five o'clock. The place had been cleaned up a bit since the night Phil raked the leaves. They all piled out of the car and walked up to the front door.

"Phil! Bob and Mary!" Alice exclaimed when she opened the door. "Won't you come in?"

"Hi, Alice. Did Jennifer invite you to dinner tonight too?" Phil asked.

"I don't think so. If she did, I didn't know about it. So what brings you here?"

"Jennifer invited us for dinner before choir practice," Mary said.

"Oh, that's nice." Alice said with a confused look on her face.

Dave walked into the living room. "Well, hello," he boomed when he saw who the visitors were. "Are you staying for dinner?"

"Yes," Bob answered. "Didn't Jennifer tell you?"

"No. I don't think she mentioned it. Hey, did you get a chance to see the DVD with Jay trick-or-treating?" he asked Phil.

"No, not yet," Phil answered.

"Well, come in and sit down. We can take a look at it while the girls finish making dinner. You'll love the reaction people had to Jay."

<<<

Jennifer and Jay were quite surprised when five-fifteen rolled around, dinner was getting over-cooked, and Phil and his parents had not yet arrived. She was getting ready to call Phil's cell phone when *her* cell phone rang. It was Alice.

"Hi, Alice, what's up?"

"Jennifer, did you invite Phil and his parents to dinner at *my* house tonight?"

"YOUR house? No, I invited them to dinner at MY house and they're fifteen minutes late!"

"They must have misunderstood the invitation. They're all sitting in my living room watching the DVD Dave took of Jay on Halloween and waiting for the dinner bell to ring."

It only took Jennifer a few minutes to figure out what had happened. "Oh my gosh!" She laughed hysterically. "And to think I thought he might have asked me to marry him because of the house I lived in!" she sputtered between guffaws.

"He asked you to marry him?" Alice asked. "Jennifer—you've been holding out on me! "When did he ask you to marry him?"

Jennifer could hardly speak between her uncontrollable giggles. "Monday night when he took Jay and me out to dinner with his parents."

"Congratulations!" Alice said. "Now what do you want me to do with them? Should I feed them or send them to your house?"

"If it weren't Wednesday, I'd play along and turn this into a great prank, but choir practice is in an hour and a half. You'd better give them my address with the explanation that Phil followed me to *your* house—not *mine*. I can't wait to see his face when he pulls into my driveway!"

"Am I missing something here?" Alice asked.

"No more than Phil is. It's a long story—I'll have to tell you about it later. You'd better send them over here quick or we'll all be late for choir practice."

Jay looked at Jennifer questioningly. "It must be good," he said. "I haven't seen you laugh that hard *ever* before."

"Oh, it *is* good," she answered. "Meanwhile, I think you and I might want to be sitting out on the front porch waiting to see Phil Henson's face when it dawns on him that you and I are living in HIS house!"

"Will he be mad?" Jay asked.

"I rather doubt it, but I guess we'll find out in a few minutes."

<<<

"I hate to interrupt your movie," Alice said loudly enough to be heard over the television. "But there seems to be a little misunderstanding about your dinner arrangements for tonight."

202

"No, I'm sure Jennifer said it was tonight," Mary said.

"Yes, it is tonight," Alice agreed. "Only it's not *here*. You see, Phil, you must have followed Jennifer here to *my* house—not *hers*."

"WHAT? You mean I raked up all *your* leaves?" Phil asked in disbelief.

"*You* did it?" Alice and Dave said simultaneously.

"We wondered who did such a nice thing for us. We thought maybe the ward was doing a service project and we were the beneficiaries." Dave laughed. "Nice of you to be so kind," he said, as he slapped Phil on the back.

"Oh, my—I'll bet Jennifer is a nervous wreck wondering why we're so late. And I imagine you were quite put out that we were dropping in for dinner unexpectedly," Mary said to Alice.

Alice laughed good-naturedly. "Actually, it turned out to be kind of fun. And I understand congratulations are in order for you and Jennifer," she said to Phil. "Or maybe it was supposed to be a secret that happened to slip out while Jennifer and I were trying to figure out what the misunderstanding was about your dinner tonight."

"It's quite all right for you to know. We were planning on making the announcement at choir practice tonight anyway. You deserve a heads up for being such a good sport about our imposing on you for dinner," Phil said with a sheepish grin. "The next time I try to play detective, I'd better make sure I get my facts straight."

Alice gave Phil the correct address and explained that Jennifer lived a few blocks away.

<<<

Phil's car crept up the street slowly. All of a sudden the car stopped in the middle of the road.

Bob rolled his window down and hollered to Jennifer and Jay sitting on the front porch, "If we can get Phil here to park this car, are we still invited to dinner?"

"What do you think?" Jay asked Jennifer. "Do you think he's mad?"

"I don't know. Let's walk out to the car and see what he says."

"This *can't* be Jennifer's house," Phil bellowed. "This is MY house!"

Jay and Jennifer both heard Phil's loud declaration.

"Yep, I think he's mad," Jay whispered quietly so only Jennifer could hear him.

Jennifer stuck her head in Bob's open window and said, "Well, that's true. It *will* be your house soon—that is if you aren't withdrawing your proposal."

"That's right, it *will* be my house, won't it?" he said and he smiled and laughed like a child.

Bob and Mary looked at each other doubtfully and Mary shrugged her shoulders as if to tell Bob she couldn't explain it.

"Dinner is over-cooked and now it's getting cold," Jennifer said. "Why don't you all come inside and let's eat."

Once inside the house, Phil slipped his shoes and socks off inside the door. He scurried to the great room and turned around in a complete circle looking appraisingly at the room.

Jennifer couldn't suppress a smile.

"It's more beautiful than I remember it. How did you manage to pay for all of this?" he asked.

"There are a few things we need to talk about," Jennifer answered. "But right now, we need to eat dinner and get things ready for the Sisters in Zion practice."

<<<

Braxton began to fill Julianne's calendar with dates and concerts. He called her daily. He had to admit, she was better than him at handball, but he was glad. He wouldn't have wanted to beat her anyway. She was a nice girl… with lots of money. He learned that she had a monthly dividend from the profits in her father's company in addition to the sizeable payment she had received from his life insurance. He told her he was currently unemployed and looking to replace the job he'd left with the composite company.

204

Chapter Forty-One

When Nadine walked in for choir practice, Phil bounded out of his chair. "What are YOU doing here?"

"I sing with the Sister's in Zion," she answered squarely.

"You mean to tell me that this *whole* time I have been trying to find Jennifer's address, *you knew* where she lived and had the information right under my nose at work!"

"Jennifer asked me to keep her information confidential."

Phil dropped back into his chair and shook his head, "I don't believe this—you work for *me*, not her."

"It seems to me," Bob directed his comment to Nadine, "you ought to *demand* a raise."

"I'm considering it," Nadine smiled.

The Sisters in Zion filed through the door a few at a time until they were all huddled around the piano listening intently to the conversation taking place.

"I ought to fire you," Phil said only half seriously.

A sinister smile crossed Jennifer's lips as she reached out and touched Nadine's arm, "If he fires you, I won't speak to him again."

Alice let out a loud gasp from behind the piano.

"That's blackmail!" Phil said.

"Yep. You lose your office manager, and me, and Jay…and the house. Just like that," she said as she snapped her fingers.

Everyone's eyes were on Phil. "You drive a hard bargain, Jen."

"Nadine has proven her loyalty and deserves to be treated better than this, Phil," Jen said.

"I guess you're right," Phil said in good humor.

"Does this mean I get that raise?" Nadine asked.

"I'll think about it," Phil said with a grin.

"Well, now that we're all friends again," IlaRae announced, "Can we get on with our practice?"

They gathered around the piano, Alice offered the opening prayer, and IlaRae instructed them to warm up with "It's Beginning to Look a lot like Christmas."

The soloists had their parts learned well for the "My Baby, Jesus" song. When the flute began to play the mysterious descant, making the song sound Middle Eastern, Mary sucked in her breath.

There was hushed silence after the song was finished. "I made it without crying," Kate whispered.

"That was beautiful!" Mary said. "I don't believe I've ever heard that song before."

"It was written by a friend of mine," Jennifer explained.

"Well let's not disappoint our audience," IlaRae said, "Let's turn to *Sleighride*."

When the choir began to practice some of the more familiar Christmas songs, Bob and Phil joined in with their deep voices and it turned into a fun evening.

<<<

When choir practice was winding down, Jennifer asked the women what their plans were for the Wednesday practice right before Thanksgiving. Most of them hadn't even considered the schedule that far ahead. Several of them were planning to be out of town, and IlaRae was going to have a house full of company as all her children were coming home for Thanksgiving. They all agreed they couldn't skip a practice because of the short time left before their performance.

After several suggestions and votes, it was decided that they would have two practices the week prior to Thanksgiving and then none the week of the holiday. The extra practice would be on Saturday morning.

With this arrangement made, Jennifer turned to Phil. He stood beside her to announce their engagement.

"When is the big day?" IlaRae asked.

"We haven't decided that yet, but I'm hoping it will be soon. Perhaps we'll know after tonight," Phil answered with a mischievous grin.

206

"Well, are we going to sing at your wedding reception?" IlaRae asked.

Jennifer looked up at Phil for an answer.

"Could you?" Phil asked.

"Just don't get married before our Christmas performance!" IlaRae ordered. "We don't want the bride to be on her honeymoon during our grand debut."

Kate made an announcement. "I have found the perfect fabric," she said. "I made my top out of it and I brought it with me so you could see it." She lifted her tunic out of a clothing bag and all the ladies "Ooohed" and "Aaahhed." It was a bright red shimmering polyester fabric. "IlaRae, I have enough of the same fabric in black to make yours. Now I expect all of you to have your patterns to me by next week, or your blouse might not be finished in time."

Jennifer produced the pattern she had shown Alice the day Phil had followed her to the wrong house, and Kate put her stamp of approval on it. "This will sew up nicely," Kate said. "It will drape well, and will look chic."

Jennifer was relieved to know she had chosen wisely.

"If you get your pattern before the weekend," Kate said, "please bring it over to my house and let me get started. Our time is short."

Everyone agreed and a closing prayer was offered. As they were filing out the door, Alice prodded Phil, "So, when you found out where Jennifer really lived, I'll bet you were surprised."

"He was surprised, all right," Mary answered for Phil. "At first we thought he was mad enough to kill someone. Then when Jennifer reminded him that this would be *his* house, he calmed down and seemed rather happy about it. We still haven't figured out why he was so angry at first."

"*Angry*? Phil, what gives with being angry?" Alice asked. "Were you hoping for a two-story with only a single-car garage like ours?"

Jennifer filled them all in on the story of Phil trying to buy the house at the same time she was making an offer on it. "We both wanted the house. I'm sure Phil didn't think I could possibly afford it, so he would never have guessed *I* was the person making the cash offer. I purposely didn't tell him where I lived for a couple of reasons, but once he had asked me to marry him I knew it was time to let him in on the secret. I offered to give him my address the other night, but he said he already knew where I lived, so I assumed he really did know. Obviously he had misjudged when he followed me to Alice's house last week."

"That brings up a good question that has been on the back of my mind all night," Phil said. "How *did* you manage to afford this house?"

"With the money from my parents' estate."

"You mean you own it free and clear?" Phil said with raised eyebrows.

"Yes. It was paid for the day I signed the papers. My only expenses are the utilities, taxes, and insurance."

"Well, Son, it looks like it was a much better deal for you to marry into it than to buy it!" Bob said with a smile.

"Don't feel too badly, Phil. If you really can't stand this place, you can still come to our house for dinner sometime," Alice said teasingly. She congratulated them again about their upcoming marriage and then excused herself to leave.

<<<

"Since you won't be having choir practice the night before Thanksgiving, does this mean you'll be joining us in San Jose for the holiday?" Mary asked.

Jennifer looked at Phil hopefully.

"We'll be there," he said.

"Good! I'm sure Phil's brother and sister will be anxious to meet you, Jennifer."

"Jen, I was wondering if you and I could go shopping together on Saturday. Maybe Mom and Dad could spend some time with Jay?" Phil asked turning to his mother.

"We'd love to, wouldn't we, Bob?" Mary answered.

"Sure. It would give you two some time together, and it would give me a little more time to harass Jay. He seems like a good sport that's up to my nonsense."

Phil looked to Jen for her answer.

"Well, it appears it's already decided," she said.

Chapter Forty-Two

Phil and Jennifer left Bob and Mary in charge of entertaining Jay knowing that it would probably be the reverse.

"Where are we going shopping?" Jennifer asked Phil.

"Well, there are a couple of places I have in mind," Phil answered. "First of all, I can't have my fiancé running around without a ring on her finger. I want folks to know I've already staked my claim on you!"

Jennifer had hoped that was part of Phil's plan—not that she wanted anything flashy, but she did want something.

When they were in the jewelers, Phil told Jennifer to look at everything before she made her choice. She looked and looked and looked. She saw nothing that enticed her. Finally she turned to the jeweler and asked, "Do you have anything that is a good companion with a plain wedding band? I will probably only wear the wedding band after we're married, but when we have special occasions, I would like to be able to add the diamond and have it look impressive together."

The jeweler scratched his head a moment and then looked up and sighed, "Ahhh, I think I have an idea that might work." He showed Jennifer a simple shiny medium-wide platinum band. Then he chose a two-carat solitaire diamond mounted on a thinner shiny band of platinum. The two bands together created a wide looking ring, but the two-carat diamond was large enough to make it look classy when put together.

Jennifer tried the combination on her hand and liked it but wondered if something smaller wouldn't suffice. She turned to Phil for his approval and asked, "Do you think the diamond is a little overkill?"

"I'm thinking it's perfect," he said.

Jennifer turned to the jeweler and asked, "Do you have a solitaire similar to this only not quite so large?"

"I have one that is about half that size. Let me get it for you."

Jennifer tried it on but before she could even comment, Phil said, "Nope. I like the larger diamond better."

"The two carat princess cut does balance the size of the wedding band," the jeweler offered. "This particular diamond is a nice piece."

"What is the price on something like this?" Jennifer asked.

The jeweler looked at Phil to see if he wanted Jennifer to hear the answer to that question. Phil immediately responded, "Whatever the price is, we'll take it. No price is too high for Jennifer!"

"Why do I feel like a ten-cow wife?" Jennifer asked.

Phil looked at her quizzically while the jeweler laughed heartily.

"I'll explain it to you later," Jennifer said. "Or maybe I'll let you watch the movie. Meanwhile, since we're here, why don't you look around yourself to see what you would like in the way of a wedding ring?"

Phil looked for a much shorter period of time. He chose a medium-wide band with five radiant-cut diamonds inlaid in the band. "Another fine choice," the Jeweler said.

The jeweler invited Phil into the back room where Jennifer overheard little of their conversation, but knew they were discussing the purchase of her rings.

When Phil and the jeweler returned to the show room, the jeweler asked Jennifer to step into the back room. "Would you like to get the wedding band for him that he likes, or did you have something else in mind?"

"Yes, I'm sure you could size it to fit him?" she asked.

"Yes, I can have it ready for you to pick up in a week."

The jeweler discreetly passed the bill of sale for the total price to Jennifer. She handed him her debit card.

Moments later, he told her the card had been denied.

"That's impossible," she said. "I know there's money in that account."

"You may want to check with your bank," he said. "Meanwhile, I can hold the ring for two days, if you'd like."

"I don't think that will be necessary," she said. "I can write you a check." Fortunately, she had one check from a money market account in her wallet. She rarely used that account.

With her mind preoccupied over the denial of her debit card, Jennifer blindly walked back out into the showroom to join Phil, and she clumsily bumped into another customer standing in front of the glass cases.

"Oh, excuse me!" she said, as she looked up to see whom she had practically knocked over. "Braxton! What are you doing here?"

"We're just looking," he said. "This is my friend, Julianne."

"Hello, Julianne, nice to meet you."

"Someone you know, Jen?" Phil asked.

"Yes, this is Braxton and his friend, Julianne," she answered without offering any other explanation.

"Hello," Phil said, keeping his hands tucked in his pockets.

He looked up at Phil, "I don't believe I caught *your* name."

"I'm *Dr.* Phillip Henson, Jennifer's fiancé." Jen stifled a snicker. She'd never heard Phil use his title as a trump card before.

"So how do you two know each other?" Julianne asked.

"She's my ex," Braxton said.

"Ouch!" Julianne said, sounding like she'd been slapped.

Jennifer felt the blood rush to her cheeks. She immediately looked to see Phil's reaction to Braxton's statement, but saw a perfect poker face.

"Nice to meet you, Braxton and Julianne," Phil said abruptly. Then he took hold of Jen's hand and led her out of the store.

<<<

Bob was curious to see all of Jennifer's beautiful home, so he asked Jay to take him on a grand tour while Mary sat reading on the couch in the great room.

Jay started the tour by showing him the house beginning with his own bedroom and ending in the office.

He explained that his mom was a teacher and she tutored students after school most week nights. "There's her sign," he said, indicating with the wave of his hand toward the window.

Bob noticed the orderliness of the room. He plopped himself down in the leather chair and rolled the casters up to the desk where he could look "official."

Jay followed his lead and sat in the other leather chair across the table and turned it toward Bob. "This is where the students sit," he explained.

As Bob scrutinized the neatly stacked papers on the desk, he noticed the credit report on top of the stack from Equifax. He lifted the paper off the top of the pile and saw the paper from TransUnion. Bile rose in his throat when he saw the staggering numbers and the late reports. *So this is how she afforded the house and nice furnishings. What was Phil getting into? Even with his sizeable income, he wouldn't be able to sustain this kind of debt! How can I tell Phil without appearing to be a snoop? Would Phil ever believe me? He'd be brokenhearted. We all love Jennifer so much.*

Bob asked Jay if his mom had a copy machine in this office.

Jay showed Bob the printer that also doubled as a copy machine and a fax machine.

Bob pretended to play with it while he experimented with trying to make a copy. At first he copied a picture of Jay, and then for "fun," he told Jay, he copied the two credit reports. "Yep, it'll copy several pages at a time," Bob said as he folded up the copies and placed them on top of the originals and set them neatly back on top of the stack. "Now what would you like to do?"

Jay got up and started to walk out of the office and Bob quickly slipped the two folded pieces of paper into his pants pocket."

<<<

After they left the jewelry store, Phil mentioned nothing about Braxton and drove to a car lot. "I've really been itching to get a new sporty car recently. How do you feel about having something fun parked in your garage?"

"You know," she said, "I somehow pictured you in a bright red sports car. But after paying for that ring, are you sure we can afford a car too?"

"Maybe not, but it doesn't cost any money to look."

They test drove two sporty-looking models, and then decided to go out for lunch.

While eating their food, Phil took Jennifer's hand with his left hand, and put his right arm around her shoulder. "Hey, Sweetheart, when would you like to become my wife?"

"How much time do you need?" she asked.

"*Me*? I thought *you* were the one that needed time. I could get married Monday as soon as the courthouse opens and we can get a marriage license. I could probably even talk my parents into staying an extra day to be here for the occasion."

Jennifer laughed. "Well, maybe I need a little longer than that. We'll have to wait a year to go to the temple to be sealed—and we can have Jay sealed to us too."

Phil groaned, "Do we have to wait that long? I don't think I can stand the wait."

"I guess we *could* get married civilly and then go through the temple in a year."

"Which temple do you want to go to?"

"Well, I've always wanted to be married in the Salt Lake Temple, but we'll have to see how we feel about it in a year."

"In that case, where would you like to get married in the meantime?"

"How about in our home?" Jennifer asked. "I think it would be fitting to have an intimate group of family and close friends and either my bishop or yours perform the marriage."

"Wouldn't you like to have a dinner or something?"

"I don't know, Phil. I always thought I wanted to have a big formal affair, but since I have a home, a child, and you in my life, I don't really care about all the trimmings and fanfare. I just want us to be a family. Would you feel cheated if we didn't have a big gala celebration?"

"How many people can we fit in the great room?" Phil asked.

"If we clear all the furniture out and put in rows of folding chairs, I think we could probably fit fifty people comfortably in the room. How many people do we need to accommodate? I obviously won't have more than twenty."

"If we invite both of my siblings, my colleagues, and the office staff with their spouses, some of my closest friends, my bishop and a few ward members, I'd say I probably have about fifty myself."

"I was thinking I would invite the Sisters in Zion and Dave and Alice's family. I don't think I'd invite anyone else from the ward except Bishop Bowen and his wife. There are others that I *could* invite, but I don't think they need to be there for the ceremony. How would you feel if we only had family and maybe the doctors from your office and their wives for the ceremony? Then we could take the chairs down and open the house up for an informal Open House for a couple of hours. All the other people you would like to invite could come by during that time and wish you well."

"You know, I like that idea," Phil agreed. "That would make the celebration private and cozy all at the same time. What day do you have in mind?"

"Well, we'll be at your parents' for Thanksgiving. When have you scheduled to get off work for that?"

"I thought we'd fly down on Wednesday, the day before Thanksgiving and come back on the Sunday after."

"The Sisters in Zion have a performance on the eighth of December…IlaRae would kill me if I didn't wait until after that. We're really cutting into other people's Christmas schedule if we go much later into December. What if we schedule a Friday or Saturday in January?"

"You know what? If people can't come because they're too busy in December, then that means we have less people to worry about fitting in the great room. Besides, how many people do we need there for it to be legal?" Phil asked.

216

"I guess six of us."

"Six?"

"Yeah. You, me, Jay, two witnesses, and someone to perform the marriage."

"So really, if we can get one of our bishops to agree, and my parents to come, we're all set!"

"You're right! So when would *you* like to get married?" Jennifer asked Phil.

"How about the tenth of December?" Phil asked, looking at his calendar on his smart-phone.

"How many weeks is that to prepare?" Jennifer asked. She and Phil counted the weeks from now to December tenth. Almost five weeks.

"Can we do it?" Phil asked.

"I don't see why not!" Jennifer giggled happily. Phil pulled her tightly into his shoulder and she looked up into his eyes to see him gazing into hers.

He gave her a lingering kiss. "Do you think there's anyone in the whole world as happy as we are right now?" he whispered.

Jennifer thought for a moment, and then smiled.

"Jay," they both said at the same time.

Chapter Forty-Three

When Phil and Jennifer arrived at Jennifer's house, they found Jay teaching Bob how to use Dragon Dictate on the computer. Bob seemed engrossed in Jay's demonstration on producing written work without the use of his deformed hands. Mary was sitting in the great room gazing out the windows. Jennifer noticed the Ensign magazine open on her lap while she seemed hypnotized by the leaves falling from the trees in the back yard. Someone had flipped the switch on the fireplace and a gas log gave warmth to the room.

"I didn't get much reading done," Mary confessed. "I've been soaking in the ambience of this beautiful autumn day in the peaceful setting."

"We have an announcement to make," Phil said. "Let me get Dad and Jay in here so we only have to say it once." When Bob and Jay joined them in the great room, Phil took hold of Jennifer's hand and with a wide grin turned to his dad and said, "We eloped this morning—I thought you'd like to know."

Mary let out a gasp and Bob said soberly, "Congratulations, Son."

"Phil!" Jennifer threatened, "You'd better tell them the truth."

"Okay," he said sheepishly. "We postponed it until December tenth."

"Oh, you!" Mary said with disgust. "Jennifer, when these two get together, you can't take anything either one of them say seriously!"

"I'll try to remember that in the future," Jennifer grinned.

"So, Jennifer," Mary said, "Since you're the only person to be believed here, have you *really* set the date for the tenth of December, or is he horse-playing about that too?"

"Me? Horseplay? Mother, you don't even believe your own son!" Phil said feigning innocence.

"I might if you weren't always trying to trip me up," she said.

"Yes," Jennifer finally answered Mary firmly. "We have set the date for the tenth of December." Then to Jay she said, "Are you ready to become a Henson in time for Christmas?"

"You bet!" he answered exuberantly and he rushed over to hug Jennifer. He then turned to Phil and wrapped his arms around his legs. Phil picked Jay up and the three of them embraced.

Phil and Jennifer shared their plans for an intimate wedding ceremony in the exact room in which they were standing. Mary wanted to know if they would be included and Jennifer assured her that all of the family was invited.

"We don't want to have a big elaborate wedding," Jennifer explained. "Family and a few close friends can be here for the ceremony, and then after, we plan to have an informal Open House for friends to call. I hope that meets with your approval. I guess we should ask your opinion before we make any final plans."

"That's a little soon, isn't it?" Bob asked.

"Dad, what's the matter? I thought you were the one encouraging me to not let her get away."

"Well, a fellow can never be too careful."

"Oh, Bob!" Mary scolded. "Of course we're delighted! I think your plans are perfect. I'm actually quite comfortable here in your home, Jennifer. I don't know much about the customs or protocol of a formal Mormon wedding, but an intimate group of family and friends here in this lovely setting sounds like a wonderful idea. Is there anything you need me to do?"

"Yes," Phil interrupted, "You need to keep Dad locked up somewhere so he doesn't eat all the food before the guests arrive."

"I really think we'll be fine, Mary," Jennifer said ignoring Phil's teasing. "I'm mostly concerned that you and the rest of the family feel welcome and comfortable."

"Does that mean I can wear jeans and a tee-shirt?" Bob asked.

"Of course you can't," Mary said, showing her irritation.

"You mean I have to wear a penguin suit?"

Jennifer laughed and said, "I hardly think you'll need a tuxedo, Bob. A suit would be nice, but if you really object, you could wear a sports jacket with slacks—you might even stretch it a bit and wear a tie."

"Maybe," he relented. "I think Jay and I will get back to our Dragon Dictate project while you women discuss this."

Phil plopped down in the leather sectional in the great room and found the remote control to the TV. After flipping through a dozen stations and apparently finding nothing of interest, he turned it off and joined Mary and Jennifer at the table.

"Afraid you'll miss out on something?" Mary teased when he came over.

"Afraid I'll be assigned to wear one of those penguin suits is more like it. I have come to defend my territory," he said as he pantomimed brandishing a sword through the air.

"What would you *like* to wear for our wedding?" Jennifer asked.

"I think I'd like to match the bride," he answered with softness to his voice and a look of pure admiration in his eye. "So I guess it all depends on how formally you dress."

"I'm not sure. I really can't see wasting hundreds or thousands of dollars on an elaborate wedding dress that I would only wear for a few hours. Yet, I really would like to have a wedding dress for pictures. I guess I'll have to think about it."

"Bob's comments aside—what would you like us to wear?" Mary asked.

"Would it be asking too much to ask you to dress up in something festive since you will be the parents of the… the only parents actually," Jennifer added quietly.

"Phil told us your parents were killed in a plane crash. I'm sorry. I'm sure they would have wanted to share in this occasion with you." Jennifer had tears brimming in her eyes but she said nothing. Mary continued, "I hope you'll feel comfortable allowing Bob and me to treat you like one of our own. I've felt such a warm connection with you since we met last week, and I know Bob feels the same way—if he didn't, he wouldn't give you such a bad time.

He seems to have bonded with Jay remarkably well too. I didn't expect that."

"It doesn't surprise me," Jennifer said. "Jay's an engaging child."

"Phil told me about him months ago when he was torn between taking care of Jay and finishing his internship. I couldn't understand how a young child could have such an overwhelming tug at Phil's heart at the time, but I'm beginning to see it now," Mary said. "I think it's wonderful that the two of you are getting married. I think you make a fine couple, but I also think it's a wonderful thing for Jay to have two parents that love him so much. I guess I can add grandparents to that as well," she smiled.

"Back to our original discussion," Phil interrupted, "Do I need to wear a suit or a tux?"

"Well, let's talk about this. Since we will be decorating the house for Christmas, we will have a lot of reds and greens. I think I'd like to fill the room with red poinsettias and have some gold trim. I think we'll have bright red be the theme color with gold and green as accents."

"And this has *what* to do with my apparel?"

"I'm trying to visualize the entire scenario," Jennifer said.

"Be quiet, Phil, let her think for a minute," Mary scolded.

"I think I'll go join Dad and Jay," he said. "Let me know when you have it all figured out. I can't stand the suspense." He leaned over to kiss Jennifer as he left to go to Jay's room.

"Typical male," Mary said. "Now we can really do some planning."

Jennifer reasoned that the bride and groom would stand out in the crowd if they were wearing white. So she decided on a bridal gown for herself, and a white tux for Phil.

When they entered Jay's bedroom, Bob and Phil were sound asleep on Jay's bed and both snoring. "Hey, Mom! Look how Dragon Dictate spells their snoring!" Jay said with delight. He was holding the microphone hanging by a wire looped over one of his

222

stubs as near to the bed as the cord could reach. Jennifer and Mary burst out laughing and the men woke up at the sudden noise.

"What's so funny?" Bob asked.

"You are," Mary answered. "Look at the screen of Jay's computer and see what you've been saying for the past few minutes."

Phil and Bob both looked at the screen and were confused. "It just has a bunch of words that don't mean anything. I don't see what's so funny." Bob said.

"That's because it spelled out your snoring," Jay explained.

"I don't snore!" Bob defended.

"Yes you do," Phil said. "You were snoring when I came into the room."

"Obviously you do too," Mary said to Phil.

"Yeah," Jay said. "I didn't start to record until you were both snoring. Look on the screen—these words are when Grandpa snored, and those words are when you snored. It could tell the difference." Jay said referring to the software program.

"*Grandpa,* huh?" Phil said with raised eyebrows.

"I may have jumped the gun a bit. I told him he could call me grandpa," Bob explained.

"Phil," Mary said, "Jennifer wants to know if you would object to wearing a white tux at the wedding?"

"White?" Phil asked.

"Yes, you know, the bride and groom would be dressed in white to stand out from the guests. Don't you think that would look nice, Dear?" Mary asked.

Phil took a minute before answering and Jennifer was a bit concerned that maybe it was not such a good idea after all. Suddenly Phil's face broke into a grin and he said, "Yeah, I like that idea. And we could get a white tux for Jay so he could match us."

Jennifer hadn't even considered what Jay should wear. She wasn't sure if he would want to stand out, or try to stay under the radar of attention. "What do you think about that, Jay?" she asked.

"Will it itch?" Jay asked. "I don't like to wear itchy clothes."

Jennifer thought of his tender scar tissue on his neck, arms and legs. "That's a good question. Maybe we'll need to check with the tuxedo rental store and try one on you. That's the only way to know for sure."

"If it doesn't itch, I'd like to wear what Phil wears."

Chapter Forty-Four

After returning to Phil's apartment, Bob pulled the folded papers from his pocket. "Phil, I think we need to have a chat."

"What's up, Dad?"

"Jay took me on a tour of Jennifer's house. While we were in the office, I happened to see something that concerned me. I made copies so you could see it for yourself." Bob handed him the credit reports.

Phil studied them for a long moment. His face blanched.

"Phil, if you marry this girl, that's a heavy debt to take on. She could break you awfully fast if she goes through that much money in a year. I'm even more concerned that she's not responsible enough to pay the bills."

"Jennifer has always seemed so responsible. This seems so out of character for her."

"I'm sorry to give you such grim news, but I felt obligated to tell you. I'd hate to see you get blindsided."

Tears welled up in Phil's eyes. "What am I going to do, Dad? I love her… and I love Jay. If I back out of this now, what will happen to that boy?"

"Perhaps you should talk to Jennifer about this. Maybe she's taken care of the balances by now and this is all cleared up," Mary suggested.

"Even if she's paid them all off, which I doubt, from the magnitude of the balances, it still won't make everything all better. The history of poor money management will still be an issue," Bob said.

"I can't talk to her about this—it would be too humiliating for her—especially in front of Jay. He looks up to her and respects her so much, I don't want to make her look bad in his eyes," Phil spoke through his tears.

Mary put her arms around him and gave him a squeeze. "I'm sorry, Phil. What *are* you going to do?"

"I don't know, Mom. I feel sick inside—like I've just lost everything. I don't want to give up what we had, but I can't go into a marriage with that kind of debt and deceit."

"Jennifer has invited us to dinner tomorrow after your confirmation. Will we still go?"

"We could say your flight has changed and we won't be able to make it."

"What about Jay's confirmation in the morning?" Bob asked.

"I can't disappoint Jay. I'll have to go. If it will make you feel better, I can go alone."

"I'd really like to see the little guy before we leave," Bob said. "I have a little something to give him."

"Perhaps we should keep our original plans and act as if this never happened. Then you and Jennifer can work this out after we're gone," Mary said.

That thought pleased him. For at least one more day, Jennifer and Jay could be his.

Chapter Forty-Five

Sunday was a full day. Jay's confirmation took place in the early morning and Phil's was in the early afternoon in his ward sacrament meeting. Following Phil's sacrament meeting, they had a roast beef dinner that Jennifer had cooked in the oven.

That evening, Jennifer and Jay rode along as Phil took his parents to the airport to catch their flight back to San Jose.

"We'll see you in two weeks," Jennifer said as she hugged Mary and Bob goodbye.

Mary glanced at Bob and then Phil and said, "Yes."

Bob pulled something out of his pocket and held it out to Jay. "I got you a little something that might be useful until my son here gets you a better one."

Everyone looked in Bob's hand and saw a plastic nose. It was obviously part of a Halloween disguise. They all burst out laughing—even Jay. Because he was unable to pick it up out of Bob's hand, Jennifer took it and asked him, "What would you like me to do with it?"

"Tuck it right above the breathing holes in my mask. Maybe it will look like I have a nose," Jay giggled.

Phil took the plastic nose out of Jennifer's hand and lifted his compression mask enough to slip the plastic nose up into place and then pulled his mask back down. The plastic nose was too large for his face, but it did look like he had a big nose. "Does it hurt your face?" Phil asked.

"No, I can't even feel it," Jay answered. "What does it look like?" Mary had come prepared with a small mirror and she held it up for him to see his reflection. "Hey! All I need now are some ears!"

<<<

After they were back at Jennifer's house, Phil removed the plastic nose from Jay's compression mask and checked his skin to make sure there was no irritation on his face. There was only a tiny red impression showing the outline of the nose from the pressure of the mask pushing against it.

Jennifer asked Jay, "Do you plan to make a habit of wearing this?"

"Only when I want to dress up—can I wear it at the wedding?"

"I'll work on it some and see if we can't modify it to fit better," Phil said.

Once out of Jay's room, Phil took Jennifer into his arms and held her tightly, tears welling in his eyes, knowing this had to end.

He breathed in deeply, memorizing her fragrance. "Your hair smells so good, and you feel even better in my arms than you smell. I hate to admit it, but my happiest days were when Jay was stuck in that darn hospital bed and you were staying there with him. I always knew where I could find you." *And I believed I could trust you.*

"You always know where you can find me now too, only the atmosphere isn't as sterile. Follow me," Jennifer commanded. "I want to show you something."

Phil followed her as she pulled him by the hand through the master bedroom. "You remember the fabulous bathroom and walk-in closet?"

"I definitely remember."

"Well, let me show you how I have set it up. If you prefer to have the other sink, I can switch sides." She took his hand and led him to the spacious closet.

The day we originally looked at this house together I visualized my shoes on those shelves at the end of the closet. Oh, how I love this house. "I remember thinking my suits and scrubs would all look wonderful hung in nice even rows along the back… " he stopped short when he saw the racks on the back wall were empty. He turned around and gazed at Jennifer.

"You see," she said, "there is plenty of room for your things in here." She took hold of his hand and pulled him into the bedroom area. "The bed is a king-size. Do you have a preference about which side you sleep on?"

Phil pulled her into his arms as tears filled his eyes. He wanted to scream out from the pain that seared through his chest. "No," he said. *I would have been happy to have any side just to be with you.*

"We're not through with the tour yet." She took him to the front of the house where she showed him the office. He peeked inside the cupboards on the far side of the desk and looked at Jennifer in amazement. "What are you planning to do with all this empty space?" he asked.

"If you must know the truth, I was hoping someday I'd be able to share it with you."

He agonized over his pending loss. On her neatly stacked papers, he spotted the Equifax report. He picked it up and looked at it for a moment, as if he'd never seen it before. "Jen, is this for real?"

"Someone has stolen my identity. There is an investigation going on to find the culprit, but apparently, they're quite professional. My attorney said they are having a tough time nailing them down. I'm just hoping I won't have to pay for anything more than the exorbitant attorney fees."

Phil let out a long breath. *It all made sense now. Jennifer really was responsible and wise with her money.* In his mind, he could hear his father say, "How do you know she isn't making this all up?"

"Jen, where is your attorney bill?"

"I haven't gotten one yet. So far, he's working off the two thousand dollar retainer fee I had to pay."

"Who is your attorney?'

"Valentino Finch from Crawford and Finch."

"I've heard of them before. Do you know how they base their charges?"

"He said it would be twenty percent of the amount recovered."

"So you'll be stuck with twenty percent of all these credit card charges just to pay the attorney?"

"I'm not sure how it works. I doubt whoever racked up these bills will ever pay it back, so I'm not sure how much will actually be recovered. On top of that, I'm not sure if the credit card companies will make me pay the bills. I didn't open any of the accounts, and my attorney called each one as soon as I found out about them to set up a fraud alert."

"Jen, I want to take care of you and Jay. I want to provide for you and give you joy and happiness. But if you end up getting stuck for all these credit cards, I'm not sure I'll have enough money in ten years to pay this all off."

"We really need to talk," she said as she took his hand again and directed him to the great room. "Phil, you know how frustrated you were trying to find out where I lived?"

"How could I forget? Every time I asked you for your address, you had some crazy emergency come up and you managed to escape without giving me any information! I thought at first it was a coincidence, but then after it happened repeatedly, Dr. Halverson suspected you lived in abject poverty and were ashamed to let me know it. He couldn't have been further from the truth."

"Did you ever worry that someone might seek you out or make a play for you because of your professional status or your income?" Jennifer asked.

"Not really," Phil answered honestly.

"How would you feel if you thought I only wanted to marry you for your money?" she asked.

Phil thought about it for a long moment. That thought *had* crossed his mind a time or two since yesterday. "I couldn't believe you'd be that kind of woman."

"Thank you for your belief in my integrity," she said, "But truthfully, if I had been in your shoes I would have been suspicious of any woman making advances toward me."

"You wouldn't have if they were as sweet and unassuming as you are."

"Now you're trying to butter me up!" she said as she punched him lightly in the arm.

"No I'm not. Do you remember when I invited you to the Country Club for dinner and you didn't feel dressed for it?"

230

"I was in worn-out jeans!"

"I know, but if you were a gold digger, you would have changed to go someplace exclusive. Then when I suggested La Caille, you said it was a little extravagant for a peasant like you."

"True," she admitted.

"Jen, one of the things I love about you is there has never been any pretense—you're authentic—you never try to be something you're not. You're a fabulous teacher. From everything I've tasted, you're an excellent cook. You have a beautiful voice, and you seem comfortable in all types of company. I couldn't believe how well you related to my parents—especially Dad. He can be difficult at times if you don't have a sense of humor. I've had dates dissolve into tears taking his attempts at sarcastic humor seriously."

"Well, there's one thing I *am* that I *have* hidden from everyone," Jennifer confessed.

"Besides being deeply in debt?" Phil asked.

"Even if I have to pay all of it, it won't kill me. I already told you about my inheritance, but I didn't tell you how *much* I inherited. You see, I'm a millionaire… twice." Her words hung in the air. "That's why I kept it a secret about where I lived. I didn't want anyone to know I had a lot of money. It was my way of protecting myself from being taken advantage of by someone. Only someone took advantage of me anyway."

"Did you think *I* was after your money?"

"No. I mean—I didn't know. I didn't want you to find out until after I knew you loved me for who I was. How was I to know you wouldn't have asked me to marry you to get the house you loved?"

Phil gave an insulted laugh. "You're serious!"

"Well, early on in our relationship I didn't know that much about you. I decided long before I met you that I would keep my wealth a secret and only spend money on bringing someone special into my life. I decided to spend a chunk of change to have the house of my dreams so Jay and I could share it.

"I promise, I had no idea you'd made an offer on this house at the same time as me. The real estate agent told me there was *another* offer on the house, but he never told me *you* were the one making the other offer. I didn't find out that little piece of information until months later when you told me yourself. When I realized how disappointed you were about not getting this house, I wondered what you'd do if you knew *I* was the one who'd bought it.

"Our relationship was much too young and fragile at the time to take any chances. Then I suffered with inner torture knowing you weren't LDS. I loved you. Jay loved you. I knew you loved both of us. The only thing our situation lacked was a common religious foundation. You know how I feel about that. When you asked me what you were supposed to do with your love if I wouldn't allow us to be a family, it nearly ripped my heart out. That was when I decided to call your office and leave the message about not golfing with you anymore.

"If you had known I owned this house, I could only believe you would have felt it a double slap in the face when things didn't work out between us."

"It's true it would have been a bitter pill to swallow if I had known I couldn't have you and Jay in my life, and then found out it was *because* of you I didn't get the house. But I still have a hard time thinking you thought of me as a gold-digger."

"I didn't. I thought of you as human, and because I'm a paranoid single woman who has had to learn how to avoid being vulnerable, I put up a lot of walls to protect myself. You must believe me when I tell you my reasons were not because of my suspicions about you, but because I was trying to protect Jay and me."

"That part makes sense to me. I wouldn't have been too happy if someone else had taken unfair advantage of you, so I guess I shouldn't be too upset that you protected yourself—even from me. There is one question I still have—where did you get all your money?"

232

"Plain and simple, it all came from my parents' deaths. There was a lot of payoff money from the airlines, life insurances, compensation from my Dad's employer, which was mostly guilt money since Dad was on a business trip when the plane went down—Mom had gone along to keep him company since it was to be an extended trip, Then there was the sale of their home and farm."

"I never would have guessed you had money from the way you acted. I had illusions of being your knight in shining armor and rescuing you and Jay from the poor house. I was going to give you the good life, and you already have it," Phil said.

"There's one thing money can never buy, Phil," Jennifer reminded him. "*Love* cannot be bought. Jay and I need you in our lives so we no longer have to worry about putting up protective walls. Being vulnerable is one thing for a single woman, but a single woman with an abused child in her custody and dependant on her protection, only multiplied the fears I've had. Don't ever think we won't be dependent on you for your protection and emotional support."

Phil wrapped his arms around Jennifer and kissed her tenderly. "I won't ever let anyone or anything hurt you intentionally,"

"I believe you," she whispered back. "So, are you ready to forgive me for buying *your* house and keeping it a secret?"

"Only if you promise to have our relationship become more than just a friendship," he said.

<<<

Phil called his parents as soon as he got home. "Dad, it's going to be alright." He explained the situation to Bob.

"Are you sure she's not making this whole story up?"

"I wonder how I knew you were going to ask that?"

<<<

As soon as the bank opened on Monday morning, Jennifer called to see why her debit card wasn't working.

"The IRS has put a freeze on your account," the man said.

"Why would they do that?"

"They don't give us that information. We just got notification and it went into effect last Thursday."

Jennifer numbly hung up the phone and dialed her attorney's office.

"What do I do now?" she asked.

"I will need to call the IRS and ask them why they locked your account. Have you paid your Federal taxes?"

"Yes."

"Do you owe any back-taxes for previous years?"

"No. Would your fees be less if I called them myself?"

"Yes, but don't wait. You only have twenty-one days after they lock the account to take care of it. After that, you won't be able to recover any of the money."

She spent three hours and twenty minutes going through a hundred different automated messages trying to get to a real person, and then nine different people before someone knew anything about how to help her.

"I'll get to the bottom of this and get back to you," the IRS agent said, taking her name and address.

"You should have received warning notices prior to the seizure of your funds explaining everything. Have you moved since filing your tax returns?"

"Yes. I moved the end of April."

"I see. Well, your notice would have been mailed to the address on… wait a minute… your social security number brings up two returns for the year."

Chapter Forty-Six

Wednesday evening the Sisters in Zion were thrilled to learn the wedding date had been set for the tenth of December—even more when they heard they were invited to sing five songs—one each half hour beginning at the start of the Open House. IlaRae offered to play soft background music on the piano the rest of the time. All the women had their patterns for their blouses, and Kate had Jennifer's top completed. It looked festive. The women marveled over each other's patterns. No two were alike. Each person would definitely have her own personality defined.

IlaRae waited until everyone was finished talking about their clothing choices to make her own announcement. She pulled her pattern out from under her sheet music and produced a tuxedo pattern. "I want a black tux top with tails and diamond buttons on the back like Liberace," she said. "Here are the buttons!" She produced two faux diamond buttons the size of silver dollars. Then she walked around the piano and brought out a huge shopping bag from under the piano. They all looked at each other in amazement. Nobody had even noticed the huge bag until now. IlaRae reached inside the bag, pulled out a large silver candelabrum, and she set it on top of the piano. She returned to the piano bench where she pretended to flip her imaginary tux tails back and sat down on the bench.

"Which songs should we perform for the wedding?" IlaRae asked.

They decided on Let it Snow, Sleighride, Have Yourself a Merry Little Christmas, The Christmas Waltz, and My Favorite Things—but not necessarily in that order.

<<<

Phil and Jay had been in Jay's bedroom working at a game of chess. When the Sisters in Zion began to sing *Sleighride*, Phil had a great idea pop into his mind. He quickly jotted a note down and slipped it into his shirt pocket to remind himself to arrange things tomorrow.

Chapter Forty-Seven

Phil did overkill on the Christmas lights in the back yard. He put lighted deer under the pine tree on the hill above the waterfall. He was like a little kid enjoying his first taste of candy. More seemed better. When he started to put lights on the patio furniture, Jennifer put her foot down.

"We're trying to decorate for Christmas and a wedding, not a fiesta," she chided him.

"You're right," he smiled smugly. "I think we should put this furniture in the garage to store for winter, don't you?"

"I hadn't thought about it—but that's actually a good suggestion. Are you planning to do something on the patio?" Jennifer asked.

"What would you like on the patio?" Phil asked in answer to her question.

"I don't know. Maybe we should put some lighted trees out there or something."

"I'll give it some thought," Phil said, knowing his secret plan would be a pleasant surprise.

"We need to get our pictures taken for the wedding invitations at the photographers this week. I arranged an appointment for Friday, is that all right?" Jennifer asked.

"Why can't we use a good photograph from our camera?"

"Because this will be a black and white winter scene with us dressed in red. Unfortunately, there isn't much snow yet, so we'd have a difficult time finding the right setting. The photographer I have lined up has the perfect backdrop for the picture."

"I see," Phil responded. "Are you always this detail oriented?"

"I seem to be. Organizational skills seem to be one of my strong suits."

"So, I imagine then, that you have been in contact with my mother and have made the reservations at a hotel for my parents and my siblings?"

"Well, yes, I did talk to your mother. It appears your siblings will be coming with their children for the wedding."

"Did you pay for their airfare as a bribe, or did they *voluntarily* agree to come?"

"No, I didn't pay for their airfare. I think they plan to drive up for the wedding. Meanwhile, I was able to get two rooms at the Shilo Inn in Salt Lake City."

"What about my parents?"

"I figured they could stay with you in your apartment until the tenth of December, and then after the wedding, they can stay here at the house with Jay until we return from our honeymoon."

Phil's eyebrows wiggled up and down and he gave her a wicked grin at the thought of being alone with her. "Does that mean you were able to arrange getting December off from your tutoring?"

"Yes, I did," she admitted. Phil chuckled as he watched her eyes drop to her now empty plate and her face turn crimson.

"Oh boy! Does that mean I get to have Grandpa and Grandma for baby-sitters?" Jay asked.

"My parents agreed to that?" Phil asked.

"They *volunteered* for the job, and yes, Jay, they will be your baby-sitters. Only I suggest you don't record everything they say with Dragon Dictate."

"Ohhh-kay," Jay said. "Does my name change to Henson on the tenth of December? Or do I have to wait longer?"

"Didn't I tell you? I guess I forgot to mention it. I sign the papers on the ninth of December, so you'll officially be a Henson one day before your mother." He looked at Jennifer for approval. She only smiled but said nothing. "If I didn't sign them on the ninth, I would have to wait until we got home from our honeymoon," he explained. "I knew Jay wouldn't want to wait. I'll need you to go with me to sign the papers at the attorney's office since you *are* his legal parent. After we're married, we'll both be Jay's legal parents."

"YIPPEE!" Jay yelled.

"Will this affect your relationship with Emily?" Jennifer asked.

238

"No. She already changed her name when she got adopted. We're both glad to have a different last name than Dorky."

Jennifer let out a gasp.

Phil tried to stifle a laugh. "Did you really get called 'Dorky' by the other kids?"

"All the time. We all did, and we hated it—even our mom."

"I find it interesting that it bothered you to be called *Dorky*, yet you aren't the least bit annoyed when people look at you and think you're ugly," Phil observed. "How do you account for that, Jay?"

Jay was silent for a long moment before he answered. "Everybody knew the Borky family was bad news. My daddy drank a lot and he beat up momma when he was drunk. We were ashamed to admit he was our daddy. When he killed himself, I was glad he was gone. Then momma started to drink and acted like him—only she did *more* than beat us up.

"When Daddy beat up momma, she'd have bruises, but after a few days, they'd disappear and people never believed her when she said she'd been hurt. I guess in a way, being ugly is my proof that she did this to me."

"Jay, do you think you will ever be able to forgive your mother for what happened?" Jennifer asked.

"Why should I? I'll look terrible all the rest of my life."

Jennifer got up from the table and returned with the Triple Combination. She turned to Doctrine and Covenants section 64 and asked Jay to read verses 8-10.

He read aloud:

"My disciples, in days of old, sought occasion against one another and forgave not one another in their hearts; and for this evil they were afflicted and sorely chastened. Wherefore, I say unto you, that ye ought to forgive one another; for he that forgiveth not his brother his trespasses standeth condemned before the Lord; for there remaineth in him the greater sin. I, the Lord, will forgive whom I will forgive, but of you it is required to forgive all men."

"Does that mean I *have* to forgive her?" Jay asked.

"No, you don't *have* to do anything. You have your free agency. I'm sure that all you have been through and will yet go through because of what she did isn't easy. I'm not sure I could forgive just like that," she said as she snapped her fingers.

"The sad thing is, if you don't forgive her, Heavenly Father won't forgive you for your mistakes either. Then there's always the problem of the dark hateful cloud that looms inside you when you don't forgive someone. It won't punish your mother at all if you stay angry with her for what she did. She won't ever know or possibly even care. But you'll know, and your hate will eat away at your own happiness."

"I always believed I wasn't really a Borky—I knew I was sent home with the *wrong* family when I was born. My *real* family had a last name like Smith that people didn't laugh at. Sometimes I pretended that I lived with Mr. and Mrs. Johnson who lived next door. When things got bad, I went to their house. They fixed me dinner and Mr. Johnson played checkers with me."

"Is that how you managed to stay focused on your school work and be happy most of the time?" Jennifer asked.

"Yeah. I was always waiting for my *real* family to find me. When I woke up in the hospital, I didn't know what had happened to Emily and me. I just knew we were burned and it hurt a lot. Our mom never came to see us, which was fine with me, but Emily asked about her, and Phil explained what had happened to both of us.

"When Emily left the hospital to be adopted, I was mad because *she* got to be adopted into another family, and I was still stuck with being a Borky."

"That's when you gave up and quit trying to get better," Phil interjected and he grasped Jennifer's hand under the table.

"I was afraid if I got better, I'd have to go back home and live with my momma and keep being a '*Dorky*'. It made me sick to think about it."

Chapter Forty-Eight

Jay convinced Jennifer that he was capable of taking care of himself while she took Alice with her to try on wedding gowns. She made sure he had access to food, and taught him how to call for help in an emergency.

She couldn't believe it when she could not find one dress that she would have felt comfortable wearing.

"What happened to the old-fashioned wedding gowns with sleeves and high necklines?" she asked Alice.

"Is there something I can show you?" the store clerk asked after she noticed Jennifer and Alice talking rather than looking at gowns.

"I'm afraid you don't have anything I would consider wearing," Jennifer answered. "Where do the girls who are getting married in the temple shop for their wedding dresses?"

The clerks face wilted. "There is a store in the Gateway Mall called *LatterDayBride and Prom*. They have gowns that might suit you, but you need to make an appointment ahead of time for a fitting session with them."

"Thank you," Jennifer said. She borrowed a phone book from the store clerk and found the phone number for *LatterDayBride and Prom*.

Once they were out in the car, Jennifer dialed the number on her cell phone. Someone answered after three rings and Jennifer asked when the next available appointment was for a fitting session.

"I don't have anything until a week from Tuesday," the lady on the other end of the line said. "Would ten in the morning work for you?"

Jennifer's heart dropped. That was the day before they were flying to California for Thanksgiving. "Is that the only option you have?" Jennifer asked desperately.

"We could schedule you later in the month if you would prefer."

"No!" Jennifer said emphatically. "I need it as soon as possible. You see, I'm getting married in four weeks."

"Oh, my—that doesn't give you much time for alterations then, does it?"

"No, I'm afraid it doesn't. What are the chances I can find a dress that will fit me and not need alterations?"

"Each gown is made by a different manufacturer so they all fit differently. If you happen to like one of the gowns made by a manufacturer that designs specifically for your build, it is possible. However, most of our customers fall in love with a certain gown that fits a different body shape and usually needs some modification. It's all a matter of what you end up liking."

"That doesn't help me much," Jen said.

"One thing I could do," she added as an after-thought, "if I have a cancellation before then, I could call you; but you wouldn't have much notice ahead of time. How far away from the Gateway Mall do you live?"

"I'm probably about twenty minutes away," Jennifer answered.

"Well, give me your phone number and if someone calls and cancels ahead of time, I might have enough time to notify you. Unfortunately, I don't usually have any advance notice that someone isn't coming until they are thirty minutes late and I call to see if they are going to keep their appointment. By then it would be too late for you to come. Otherwise, would you like the ten o'clock a week from Tuesday?"

Jennifer agreed to take the appointment, quickly disclosed her cell phone number, and said a prayer that somehow, some poor bride would call to cancel her appointment. She and Alice gave up on any more shopping and returned home by way of the jewelry store where Jennifer picked up Phil's wedding ring.

<<<

When Jennifer entered the house from the garage, she called out to Jay expecting him to answer from his bedroom. The house was ominously quiet. She checked Jay's bedroom to see if he might be napping, but he wasn't in his bedroom. She checked in the bathroom and found no one. She panicked and began to look through every room of the house calling Jay's name. As a last resort, she went to check outside, but when the double-glass doors to the patio were locked, she knew he hadn't gone out those doors to the back yard. Trying to remain calm, she pulled her cell phone out and dialed 911.

Tearfully she explained that her nine-year-old son was missing, and she gave the details, including her address, to the woman on the phone. The woman asked her dozens of questions, like how long had he been missing, and where would he go if he were hiding? Who would he go to if he wanted to play with a friend? Jennifer felt extremely agitated since she couldn't really answer any of these questions. The lady explained that most missing children were not really in danger, but were found within hours to be somewhere explainable. "Did he leave you a note?" the lady asked.

"He can't write!" Jennifer answered in exasperation—then she thought about Jay's computer. *If he were to leave me a note, it would be on the screen of his computer*! "Hold on a minute!" Jennifer ran back to Jay's bedroom and looked on his computer screen to see if he had left her a message. In large letters, she read, "Mom, I have gone to the office with Phil to help with one of his patients. I'll come home from work with him about five o'clock. Love, Jay."

Oh thank goodness! "Never mind, she said to the lady on the emergency line. I found him. He's fine."

"Where was he?" the lady asked.

"Gone to the doctor's office," Jennifer answered not wanting to answer any more questions. "He left a note—I just didn't see it."

"I thought you said he couldn't write."

"Well that doesn't stop him from talking," Jennifer said with a laugh and she flipped her phone shut.

Jennifer remembered that Phil had told them about one of his patients from Guatemala that had a cleft lip and palate. Jay had offered to visit with him and see if he could help the man feel better about himself. Jennifer assumed this was what Jay was referring to when he said he had gone to help Phil with one of his patients.

She thought it odd that Phil hadn't called her to let her know before he took Jay. *What was he thinking? Didn't he realize I would nearly have a heart-attack when I returned and Jay was gone?* She thought about it for a minute then realized that this was not like Phil or Jay to worry her—but they *had* left her a note of explanation. Obviously, they both thought she would look at the computer screen for an explanation. She noticed the bar on the right side of the computer screen and noticed a little square at the top of the bar indicating that this was only the first part of the message. She scrolled down the screen to reveal more of the message.

"Hi, Love! I hope you don't mind if I kidnapped Jay for a couple of hours. My Guatemalan patient is coming in this afternoon—his surgery is scheduled for tomorrow and he's an emotional basket case. I decided to take Jay up on his offer to help. I didn't want to interrupt your afternoon with Alice while you were shopping. I also thought if I could get away from the office early enough, Jay and I might get to the Tux Shop to get fitted in our wedding attire. Don't worry about fixing dinner tonight, we'll bring something home. I love you! Phil. P.S. While I was picking Jay up, the photographer called. He was reminding you about our appointment tomorrow at seven o'clock for wedding pictures. Call me if I need to wear my tux and I'll see if I can take it with me tonight. XXOOXXOO"

Jennifer relaxed with the explanation. She looked at the clock and realized she only had thirty minutes until her students began to arrive for tutoring. Grateful she didn't have to worry about fixing dinner, she took some time to go through her closet and decide exactly what to wear for their wedding pictures tomorrow evening. She visualized in her mind a black and white winter scene in the background with Phil and herself wearing bright red as the focal point in the photo. She wasn't sure Phil owned anything bright red. She wondered if they should wear formal clothes or look casual. She decided to call Phil for his opinion.

"Hello, Beautiful!" he answered his cell phone. "Did you miss me or was it Jay that you missed?"

Jennifer laughed. "I miss you both, but I was relieved when I found the note of explanation on the computer screen. I nearly had a heart attack when Jay was gone. Where are you?"

At that moment, Jennifer's front doorbell rang. She was listening to Phil as she walked to the door to answer it. "We just left the office. Jay was great with my patient. You'll have to have him give you a report later tonight. I don't want to ruin it for him. We're on our way to the Tux Shop. Then we'll pick something up for dinner on our way home. Do you have any preferences about your dinner?"

"No, you can surprise me," she said as she opened the door. Before her stood two police officers dressed in uniform. "Hang on a minute," she said to Phil. "Can I help you with something?" she asked.

"We received a call from this residence regarding a lost nine-year-old child. We were checking things out to make sure he was all right."

"Oh, he's fine," Jennifer laughed. "He was gone with my fiancé to his office to help with a patient."

"Would you mind if we came in and asked a few questions?" the officer asked.

"Not at all," she said stepping back and waving them into the entrance of the house. "Phil, can I call you back in a few minutes?"

"Jennifer, did I hear correctly? Are they questioning you over the disappearance of Jay?" Phil asked.

"Yes, I'll call you back in a few minutes when I can, okay?"

"Put your phone on conference call and let me listen in and explain my side of the situation."

"Okay…this is my fiancé," she explained to the policemen as she put her phone on conference call. "He's the one who took my son to his office."

"Well, Ma'am, our dispatch operator said that the boy is nine years old?"

"Yes, he is," Jennifer answered.

"You said that he left you a note?"

"That's right."

"She also mentioned that you said he *can't write*. How do you explain that?"

Phil jumped into the conversation from the cell phone, "This is Doctor Phil Henson," he began, "Jay has no fingers on his hands. He was badly burned in a fire and all he has are two stubs, which are too short to hold a pencil. He uses Dragon Dictate to record his messages, and the computer program prints out his words. So it's true, he can't write, but he can speak and the computer writes for him."

"Would you like to see his computer screen where I finally found his note to me?" Jennifer offered the two police officers.

"Yes, we would." Jennifer took them to Jay's bedroom where they looked at the computer screen and verified that the message was actually showing up in Dragon Dictate as reported by Jennifer. With that verified, they asked when the boy would return home.

"We'll be home shortly after six o'clock," Phil answered.

"We may want to come back later this evening to make sure everything checks out okay," the officer said.

"Whatever you say, Officer," Jennifer answered trying not to sound too irritated.

The officers left and Phil said, "I'm so sorry, Jen. I had no idea it would cause this much trouble when I didn't call you first. I promise, it will never happen again—even if you are naked in a dressing room—I'll call!"

"I'm just glad Jay's okay. Once I knew he was safely with you I stopped worrying. Apparently, it didn't stop the police department's worries. I'm sorry I didn't think to look at the

246

computer before I dialed 911. Next time, I'll look there first. Meanwhile, back to my original reason for calling—how formal do you want to be dressed in our wedding pictures?"

"I hadn't given it much thought. I guess I was expecting you to give me marching orders and I was going to be an obedient servant."

"Terrific," she said sarcastically. "I can't make up my mind. I know we need to wear bright colors. Honestly Phil, I don't know what you have in red to choose from. You set the standard, and I'll dress to match."

"I tell you what," Phil said, "Jay and I will run past the apartment on our way home and I'll grab whatever looks remotely red, and then we can decide together after dinner—how does that sound?"

"Oooh, I'll look forward to having some of your clothes hanging in my closet," she said with a sultry lilt to her voice.

"Good. Maybe I should move all my clothes over there," he answered.

"I don't know about you, but I'm definitely looking forward to that," Jennifer said tenderly.

"So, any chance we can get married tomorrow?" he asked lightheartedly.

"I wish!" Jennifer responded. "I can't even get an appointment to try on a wedding gown until the day before we leave for California."

"You need an appointment?" Phil sounded astonished.

"Apparently. Alice and I thought we could walk in, try on a dress, buy one and leave. I'm afraid it's not such an easy task. No wonder couples have long engagements. If they don't elope, it takes them forever to get the proper wedding attire!"

"Are Jay and I going to have that much trouble ordering a tux?"

"I hope not, but I guess the only way you will know is to try. Good luck! I've got to go now—my first student is arriving. I love you and I'll see you later."

Chapter Forty-Nine

"Jay," Phil said, "We might have a problem on our hands—but we'll give it an honest try—are you up to a fast-paced shopping trip?"

"Sure. Where are we going?"

"Well, first we're going to the Tux Shop. Then we need to stop by the jewelers and pick up some rings for your mom. I'm hoping when we get through with those two stops we'll have time to hit Dillard's before they close. It appears I might need to buy a red shirt."

The Tux Shop was nothing like the Bridal shops had been. Phil and Jay were the only ones there and were immediately measured and fitted in formal wear. "It's not often we have a need for a child's white tux," the clerk explained. "We are able to get them in from one of our other stores, but I don't have any here in my store right now. We can use this black one to verify the fit and the measurements, but you will both need to come back the day before the wedding to check the fit. So if the boy's white suit doesn't fit exactly like this one, we should be able to get it right before the wedding."

Jay grinned from missing ear to missing ear. "I feel like some kind of royalty."

When they left the Tux Shop, Phil drove as fast as the law would permit to the jewelers. "I have both of your rings ready," the jeweler explained. "The company that sized the wedding band for me got it back sooner than I expected."

With both rings in his possession, Phil and Jay headed to the Fashion Place Mall. They arrived right at five o'clock. "We have exactly one hour to find a red shirt," Phil told Jay. "Let's see how fast we can meet that goal."

They went into Macy's first. Phil found a nice dress shirt in a deep burgundy, a light pink, a royal blue, but no bright red. They rushed off to Dillard's. Same story—shirts in teal, yellow, green, blue, pink, burgundy—no bright red. Phil hurried out of the store afraid he wouldn't be able to find anything before the stores closed.

When he realized Jay wasn't right by his side, he turned around to look for him. Jay was running ten feet behind him. Phil stopped, waited for Jay to catch up, then reached down and with a laborious grunt; he swung him up onto his shoulders. Jay squealed with delight.

"You'll find it's warmer up here than down where you live," Phil said as he took hold of his wrists and off they trotted to Nordstrom.

As they were entering the store, Phil hollered, "Duck! Giraffe's coming through!"

When they entered the men's department, Phil caught sight of a sales clerk. The gentleman had a measuring tape around his neck and reminded Phil of the man at the Tux Shop. "Excuse me, Sir; I'm looking for a bright red dress shirt. Do you have such shirt in your store?"

"What is l'occasion?" the man asked with a French accent.

"My wedding pictures," Phil explained. "We are going to be standing in front of a black and white winter scene and my fiancée wants us to be dressed in bright red."

"Aahhh, oui Monsieur. Will Madame also be wearing rouge?"

"Yes, I believe that is her plan."

"Then we must make le colours match," the clerk said. "Rouge is always diffee-cult to match."

Phil set Jay down in a chair where he could rest while Phil and the clerk worked on getting a red shirt. The clerk measured Phil's neck and arm length and then pulled a deep red shirt from the shelf in his size. It wasn't a bright red, but it definitely wasn't a burgundy either. Phil would have described it as blood red. It was a rich color and Phil knew he would feel comfortable wearing it.

"Now, Monsieur, we must find Madame a blouse to match, oui?" his dark eyes fairly danced with excitement.

"Oh, I'm not sure I can choose for the bride," Phil protested.

250

"Aahh, oui Monsieur. We must have Madame complee-ment Monsieur."

Phil motioned for Jay to follow them as the clerk took Phil over to the Ladies clothing department. The clerk was wildly waving the shirt past several other pieces of women's clothing. Suddenly he stopped waving the shirt by a flattering chiffon blouse. The blouse had a scoop neck with a lace inset down the center front. It had flutter sleeves and cascading ruffles down the front framing the lace inset. It was breathtakingly romantic and the color was the same hue as the shirt but with a lighter intensity. "Aahhh, oui Monsieur, ils vont bien ensemble!"

Phil had no idea what the clerk had said, but he knew exactly what he meant. Without any hesitation, Phil found a size he was sure would fit Jennifer and said, "I'll take them both!" Jay was grinning again. "What?" Phil asked.

"Mom's going to love that blouse. It's beautiful just like her!"

"Well, said, young man, well said," Phil beamed. "You don't think she'll be mad at me for choosing her clothes?"

"Not for choosing that one!" Jay said.

"Do you think I'll need to wear a tie with my shirt to be as dressed up as her in that blouse?"

"Non, Monsieur," the clerk said overhearing the question. "Madame will be le focal point! Monsieur must let her be le plus belle."

"Right. Why didn't I think of that?" Phil mumbled.

When they were finished shopping, Phil asked Jay, "What would you like for dinner tonight? I think you should get to pick."

"How about McDonald's?" Jay suggested.

Phil was sorry he had asked, but since he had, he agreed. "Okay. Do you know what your Mom would like?"

"Probably a filet sandwich. She likes that kind of stuff."

"Right." Maybe I should turn over all the decisions to other men. They seem to know her better than I do.

Phil quickly dropped by his apartment and grabbed whatever he could from his wardrobe that might be close to burgundy or red.

He had all of two burgundy shirts and one sweater. He needed to start moving sometime—now seemed as good as any—so he grabbed his tie-rack to mount in Jennifer's closet and all but three of his neckties that he would need over the next four weeks. For the fun of it, he threw in a pair of sweats and an extra pair of jeans and some polo shirts. As he was closing his closet door, he noticed his slippers. He laughed as he thought about wearing house slippers in Jennifer's…or *his* new house. It seemed ludicrous that he would ever need them since he loved to go barefoot—especially on her soft carpet. "But what the heck," he said, and threw them in so they could stay in Jennifer's closet. Each day, he was feeling more excited and anxious to be married and share everything with her.

"What's all this stuff for?" Jay asked.

"Well, I told your Mom I'd stop by and pick up some of my clothes for her to choose for our pictures tomorrow night. In case she doesn't like the new things we bought, I'd better keep my word."

"She'll like them all right. I've only seen her dress up fancy once before. That was the night you took her to the fancy place for dinner."

"La Caille? I thought you were asleep."

"Nope. I was pretending. I knew she wouldn't leave with you if she knew I was awake."

"WHAT? You impostor! Why did you even care?"

"I could tell you liked each other and I wanted you to marry her. When you told us you weren't a Mormon, Mom told me she wouldn't date you any more. I cried that night."

"So did I," Phil admitted. "It about tore my heart out."

"I wanted to have a Dad like you, and I knew having you marry Mom was my best chance."

"Well, thanks for the compliment. I guess it all worked out okay in the end."

"Did you *really* join the church because you knew it was true, or did you join to get Mom to marry you?"

"No, I joined because I knew it was true. Although I must admit it had crossed my mind a few times that I might want to find out about the church so your Mom would marry me. But after you had me read you the story of Ammon out of The Book of Mormon, I was so caught up in the book that even without you or your mom in my life, I had to have more. I might not be as good a missionary as you are, but I'm as convinced that it's true."

"That's good, because if you did it to get Mom to marry you, she'd be really mad when she found out the truth."

"I'm glad we don't have to worry about that, then," Phil said with a smile. "Have you ever really seen her mad?"

"Yeah... I remember one day in school one of the kids threw another boy down on the sidewalk and he got hurt really bad. Mom was on recess duty and she took care of the boy that got hurt first, but after she got him to the principal's office, she found the kid who did it and I'll never forget how she cussed him out. Then she hauled him off to the office and I don't know what happened there, but I didn't see that kid in school for a couple of days after that." Somehow that didn't surprise Phil.

When they reached the house, Phil and Jay entered quietly through the garage door so they wouldn't disturb Jennifer and her student. Phil started unloading his clothes out of the car and put them away in the walk-in closet in the master bedroom. He bolted his tie rack to the back of the closet door and draped his ties over the hooks. He purposely hung his new shirt next to his burgundy shirts, and hung Jennifer's new blouse with her red blouses to keep them color coordinated as she did with all of her other clothing. He put his slippers on the bottom shelf at the end of the closet where he planned to keep his shoes in a few weeks, and folded his sweats up and slipped them into one of the roll-out drawers and his burgundy sweater in another. He couldn't wait until all of his clothes were here.

He set out the sacks with the McDonald's dinner at the bar, rolled Jennifer's napkin up, and slid it through her diamond ring.

Then he went to find Jay in his bedroom. He was sitting in his bean bag and appeared to be asleep. "Are you faking it again?" Phil asked, now suspicious of Jay.

"Nope. Not faking it—just relaxing," Jay answered without opening his eyes. "My legs are tired. You walk fast, did you know that?"

"And did you know you're heavy? Besides, I have longer legs than you do. You were taking steps faster than me; you just didn't travel as far with each step."

"Do you think I'll ever be as tall as you?" Jay asked.

"Probably not. How tall was your daddy?"

"About six-foot I think."

"How tall was your momma?"

"About a head taller than Mom is," Jay said trying to measure by comparison.

"You might grow to be six feet tall. It's hard to say. You'll probably need more skin grafts as you grow."

"How tall are you?"

"Six-eight. How tall do you *want* to be?"

"Not as tall as you—I already stand out in a crowd. What will happen to my face as it grows?"

"You won't grow any ears if that's what you're thinking."

"I know *that*. Will the skin on my face stretch?"

"No. You'll need more surgeries," Phil said. They heard the front door close and knew that Jennifer's last student had left for the day. "Come on, Son, let's go eat dinner."

Jay smiled up at Phil. "Does that mean I can call you *Dad* now?"

"If you'd like to, I think I'd like that."

"Sure thing, Dad, let's go eat," Jay said as he rolled off the bean bag and stood up.

They were waiting for Jennifer in the kitchen when they heard the doorbell ring. The sound of Jennifer's footsteps retreated to the front door and they heard her voice.

"Hello again," she said. "Would you like to come in?"

254

"Is the young man at home?" a man's voice said.

"I haven't seen him yet, but I believe they returned a while ago," Jennifer answered.

Phil, overhearing the conversation at the front door, caught Jay's attention, and signaled him to be quiet. Phil quietly lifted Jay's mask from his head and slipped it into his pocket.

Jennifer led two policemen into the kitchen area where Phil and Jay were waiting.

"Hi," Phil said sheepishly. Ignoring the two officers, he added, "Jay requested McDonalds for dinner. If you want something different, I'll go out and get you something you'd rather have."

Jennifer looked at Jay and her heart melted when she saw his grin. "I think McDonalds sounds wonderful tonight." She turned to the police officers and introduced them to Jay and Phil.

"Good Lord! What happened to him?" one of the policemen asked.

"*God* didn't have anything to do with it!" Jay said indignantly. "My *mother* did this to me."

Both officers grabbed Jennifer by the arms and were ready to restrain her in hand cuffs when Jay screamed "Not *her*! My *real* mother did it! This is my *adopted* mother."

The officers released Jennifer from their grip.

Phil lifted Jay's arms revealing his hands with only two stubs on his right hand. "I believe this is what you were coming to verify, if I'm not mistaken," he said. "You see, this is why Jay couldn't write the note, but as you can see, he can speak very capably. With the aid of special computer software, he is able to dictate notes."

"That's right," Jay said. "And don't go blaming God for it!"

Phil stood and the two police officer's heads rose as they watched Phil's height reach his full stature.

"Sorry," the officer said. "We didn't mean to interrupt your dinner. If you'll excuse us, I think we are satisfied that the young man is safely home." With that, the officers left.

Chapter Fifty

Phil, who normally seated Jennifer first, quickly took the end barstool so Jennifer would choose the center one by him. He said nothing and waited for her to notice the diamond ring. She washed her hands at the sink and asked, "Why aren't we looking out the window at the lights in the back yard tonight?"

"I couldn't quite bring myself to serving dinner out of a paper bag at the dining room table," Phil explained.

"I see. Well then, maybe we'll have to wait until after we finish eating to hear Jay's explanation of his visit with the Guatemalan patient. I want to be able to look at his face when I hear the story. I can't do that if he is sitting right beside me at the bar."

Jennifer unknowingly sat in her assigned seat. "What are you two staring at me for?"

"I'm waiting to see the look on your face when you see that you're getting more than McDonalds for dinner," Jay said with a mischievous grin.

Phil watched as Jennifer looked at the counter to see what Jay meant. "Oh, my goodness!" she exclaimed. She removed the ring from the napkin and asked, "What have the two of you been up to? Did you *really* see the patient from Guatemala?"

"He really did," Phil laughed. "But us guys have to do more than work all the time, you know." Phil took the ring from her hand and slipped it onto her left ring finger. "Now I want you to keep that there until you have the wedding band to replace it. Then if you want to wear the wedding band alone, I won't mind." He leaned over and kissed her tenderly. "I want everyone in the world to know that you're taken!" he whispered.

"Fair enough," she whispered back.

"Hey, Dad! Can we have the blessing and eat now? My chicken nuggets are getting cold," Jay said.

"Dad?" Jennifer whispered to Phil.

"Yeah. He asked me if he could call me Dad and I didn't see why not. You're not upset are you?"

"Why would I be upset? I think it suits you well. As a matter of fact, I like it a lot."

<<<

When dinner was over and the counter washed off, they all sat in the great room with a fire going in the fireplace. "Okay," Jennifer said, anxious to hear his report, "Now you must tell me about the patient from Guatemala. What happened Jay?"

"Not much. Mr. Cardoza was sitting in the office with his interpreter when Dad took me in the office. We took my mask off so he could see my scars. When he looked up at me, he let out a loud scream—like he was scared of me. I told him not to be afraid, but every time I tried to talk, he screamed louder. I didn't know what to do, so I yelled at the interpreter so he could hear over the noise. I asked him why Mr. Cardoza was screaming, and he said he was afraid of me because I was cursed and evil. I laughed so hard, Mr. Cardoza stopped screaming and acted confused. I tried not to laugh, but I couldn't talk through my giggles. Then the interpreter started to laugh and finally Mr. Cardoza stopped screaming and started to laugh. That's when I explained to the interpreter that I was only cursed because I had a mother who did this to me. I told him I was not evil, but that my mother had tried to kill me and had lit me on fire because my father had killed himself and left her alone with four kids to take care of and no money.

"When the interpreter told Mr. Cardoza this story, he began to cry. His wailing was as loud as his screaming.

"I told the interpreter he would need to get Mr. Cardoza to stop so we could talk. They argued for a while, but then Mr. Cardoza settled down and I explained to them that I was not evil or wicked. I almost died, but Dr. Henson had saved my life and was going to operate on me some more to make me look better. I told him Jesus loved him as much as He loved all the other people who were born perfect.

258

When the interpreter got through explaining all this to Mr. Cardoza, he seemed quite happy and content. I told him I would come and see him in the hospital after Dr. Henson made him all better.

"Mr. Cardoza asked the interpreter if Dr. Henson was going to make him look like *me*?" Jay said with a laugh. "That's when Dad brought out the pictures of other people who had been born with cleft lip and he showed him the pictures after their surgeries. Mr. Cardoza cried again, but this time it was a happy cry—not a wail."

"My goodness! It sounds like an emotional day," Jennifer said. "How long will he be in the hospital, Phil?"

"Probably two weeks. With small children it's usually only two or three days, but with an adult who will be going back to an under-developed country, we want to make sure the incisions are not infected and are healed well enough to be safe."

"Will he be able to go home in time for Thanksgiving?" Jay asked.

"Guatemalans have never even heard of Thanksgiving. It is strictly an American Holiday," Phil explained to Jay. "It is possible, however, that he may be able to go back before we leave for California."

"Mom, do you have a Spanish Book of Mormon on the book shelf we could give him?"

"No, I don't. However, I'm sure I can get one." After a moments thought, she said, "I'll bet Mitzi and her husband, Denny, would love to visit with Mr. Cardoza. They both served missions in Venezuela so they both speak Spanish. They could visit without an interpreter and he might really enjoy that."

"That's a wonderful idea, Jen," Phil said, and Jennifer noted that he seemed as proud as if he'd thought of it himself. "Jay could introduce them to him, they could interpret for Jay, and then they could visit him on their own later."

"I'll check with Mitzi Wednesday night at choir practice," Jen said.

"Now, young man, I believe it's time for scriptures, prayers, and bedtime," Jennifer said.

"Could I wait until you and Dad decide what you're going to wear for your pictures tomorrow night?" Jay asked with a grin on his face.

"What have you guys got cooked up now?" Jennifer felt sure these two men in her life were plotting against her.

Phil began to stammer, "Well, I didn't have anything bright red to wear, so I decided to do some shopping after we got fitted for our tuxes. This French salesman insisted after selling me a red shirt, that Madame must have a blouse to match, oui?" Phil tried to mimic the French sales clerk. "We must have Madame complee-ment Monsieur and rouge is such a diff-eee-cult colour to match," he continued. Jennifer laughed at his imitation. "Jay decided the blouse the Frenchman chose was a perfect blouse for you and I had to admit it did look charming—otherwise I wouldn't have bought it. But the truth is, if you don't like it, I still have the receipt and the tags are still on the blouse if you want to return it."

"Well, where is it?" she asked.

"I took the liberty of hanging it in your closet while you were tutoring."

Jennifer practically ran to the bedroom closet with Phil and Jay right on her heels. She searched for the blouse and when she found it hanging next to her Sisters in Zion top, she squealed with delight. "Oh, it's beautiful! This must have cost a fortune." She looked at the price tag and gasped. "I have never paid that much for a blouse," she exclaimed.

"Other than the price, do you like it?" Phil asked.

"Like it? I love it!" Jennifer gushed.

"Are you going to try it on?" Jay asked. "I've been imagining you in it all afternoon."

Jennifer shooed Phil and Jay out of the room while she changed into her black slacks and the frilly red blouse. She let her ponytail down and fluffed her hair around her shoulders. She hurried into

260

the bathroom to look in the mirror. She gave a quiet squeal of delight and went to model for Phil and Jay.

After the cheering and the applause, she curtsied and turned to Phil, "Thank you. It's absolutely perfect for our pictures. But I have one question for you."

"Now what kind of trouble am I in?" Phil asked.

"What are *you* going to wear?"

"Oh, my shirt is hanging on *my* side of the closet," he said smugly.

Jennifer ran back into the bedroom closet and began to laugh with delight when she saw some of Phil's clothes hanging across from hers. "Are these here to stay?" she asked hopefully. "Or was this for effect?"

"They're here to stay if you'll allow it," Phil said as he took her into his arms and kissed her. "But I must admit I actually feel jealous of my slippers."

"How can you be jealous of an inanimate object?" she asked.

"I'm envious because they get to stay here with you for the next four weeks and I have to leave each night."

Jennifer laughed at the thought and leaned her head against his chest, "It will be a long four weeks, but at least it will be a happy four weeks. Waiting eight months to find out if Jay was still alive was pure torture."

Phil held her close, hugged her tightly, kissed the top of her head, and then whispered, "You are the most remarkable woman I know. Do you have any idea how fortunate I feel to have you in my life?"

"Ahh-hemm," Jay coughed, reminding them of his presence. "I guess it would be time for me to go to bed now," he said with a big grin and a sparkle in his eye.

They both turned to look at Jay. "This is all your fault, you know," Jennifer said to Jay accusingly. "If it hadn't been for you, we would never have met each other!"

"That's right," Phil added. "And just think—where would we all be if we weren't together as a family?"

"I'm *glad* my momma did this to me. If she hadn't, I'd still be living with her."

"So does this mean you have forgiven your mother?" Jennifer asked.

"I guess so."

<<<

"Julianne, what would it take to get a girl like you to consider marrying a guy like me?" Braxton asked over hummus and crackers in his apartment.

"Why do you ask?"

"Because I aim to do everything in my power, to get you to agree to be my wife. Any objections?"

"Not right now, but we've only known each other for a month."

"I know, but I can't believe how much we have in common. We even like the same foods." *I wanna gag on the hummus.*

Julianne smiled. "We'll see how I feel about it in another month or so."

Chapter Fifty-One

Wednesday evening when the Sisters in Zion showed up for choir practice, Kate handed IlaRae her black tuxedo jacket with tails and faux diamond buttons. IlaRae proudly modeled it and flipped her tails in the air as she sat at the piano. Kate also handed out a sleek jacket to Nadine, a simple shell to Mitzi, and a shell with a draped neckline in front to Alice.

The Sisters in Zion had perfected the familiar Christmas songs they were working on. IlaRae was up to her usual antics. She had her candelabra sitting out on the piano for the entire practice. When Alice got her flute out of her case to play the descant in "My Baby, Jesus," Mitzi pulled out a small candle holder that held three birthday candles. She walked over and clipped it onto Alice's flute so she could look as important as IlaRae.

"If this weren't such a serious song," IlaRae said, "I think we'd leave that in the show!"

"What if we use the flute in a lighter number and use the candle holder for that?" Mitzi asked.

"You name the song and we'll do it if Alice agrees to have the distraction on her flute," IlaRae said.

"I don't mind at all," Alice said. "I actually think it's pretty funny. Why don't we use it on 'Deck the Halls'—I mean 'Deck the flute'?"

"That will work great. We'll need to have that song early on in our performance. Then we'll need to remove the little candle holder for 'My Baby, Jesus'," IlaRae said. "We'll have our fun entertainment first and then settle into spiritual music toward the end. If we can get them to laugh, they'll enjoy the performance, but we need to leave them with a feeling of the Spirit."

<<<

Jennifer caught Mitzi on her way out after the practice and asked if she would stay for a few minutes. When everyone else was gone, Jennifer asked Phil and Jay to leave their chess game and join her and Mitzi in the great room. She explained to Mitzi their idea of visiting Mr. Cardoza in the hospital. When Jay explained his idea of a Spanish Book of Mormon, Mitzi's face lit up.

"In other words," she said, "You want us to teach him the Gospel."

"We want to offer him a 'Book of Mormon.' What Mr. Cardoza does with it is up to him," Jennifer said.

"We thought it might be a good idea for him to have a visitor that could speak to him in his native language," Phil explained. "What do you think?"

"I'm sure Denny wouldn't object, and I certainly think it's a great opportunity. When and where can we meet this Mr. Cardoza?"

"He had his surgery last Friday, so anytime now would be a good time to visit," Phil explained.

"If you'll let me know when you are going, Jay and I can meet you at the hospital, and Jay can be the connection between Mr. Cardoza and you. After that, you're on your own—you can visit or not whenever you want to," Jennifer added.

"I'll talk to Denny when I get home tonight and call you in the morning, Jennifer. I'll see if he and I can get off for our lunch breaks at the same time. Do you have the Spanish Book of Mormon already?"

"No," Jennifer said, "I was planning to get one at the book store, but I haven't gone there yet."

"Good! Don't bother to buy one. I still have a couple of extras with my testimony in the front of them in Spanish. I'll give Mr. Cardoza one of those."

"Awesome!" Jay said.

"We really appreciate your help on this," Phil said. "He's been a difficult patient to work with. His culture has made it impossible for him to believe that he isn't cursed and accept any help."

"Oh, yes. I know all about the curses. Did you know that there are actually sorcerers who put curses on people and Satan honors the curse? Several missionaries had to undergo multiple blessings to break the curses that the voodoo doctors put on them. It can be frightening at best."

"Really?" Jennifer asked. "I thought that stuff was a hoax."

"No, Satan can do a lot of damage to people's testimonies. If he thinks he can destroy someone through a curse, he'll make the curse a reality."

"Wow," Phil said. "How does that translate for Mr. Cardoza who thinks he's wicked because he was born with a cleft lip and palate?"

"That isn't actually a curse. That's one of the wives' tales they believe. Their society is full of them. Their technology and access to information is so antiquated they have no way of knowing fact from fiction. As a result, they maintain their traditional beliefs. In our own country, as recent as fifty years ago, we were told not to go swimming for an hour after we ate dinner. Now we realize it doesn't really make any difference, but they think they will surely die if they do, and so they don't swim after eating—ever! Another funny wives' tale they believe in is that you can't drink milk and orange juice together. They believe it causes some digestive problem that will kill you. I tried to explain to them that we have stores in our shopping malls that sell a drink with milk and orange juice mixed called an Orange Julius and *I'm* not dead after drinking it. Some people believed me, and some didn't. You never know how they will respond."

"I'm sure you will be a good visitor for Mr. Cardoza," Phil said. "Let us know when you can visit him. If I'm not in the office, I might join Jennifer and Jay for the visit myself."

"Sure thing, Dr. Henson," Mitzi said. "I'll call you in the morning Jennifer," she called out as she left the house.

Chapter Fifty-Two

Mitzi called Thursday morning and said Denny was excited for another missionary opportunity. He had arranged with one of his Glass Shop employees to cover for him while he took an extended lunch.

Jennifer called Phil to let him know the schedule and he said he might have time to drop over to the hospital long enough to be in on the visit.

When breakfast was over, she hurried to finish formatting the wedding invitations on the computer. They needed mailing within the week.

When she explained to Phil how much she enjoyed doing graphic designing and how much fun she had creating her bulletin boards in the classroom when she was teaching, he agreed to have her make the wedding invitations. She could have ordered them from a printing company, but knew she'd get a lot more enjoyment out of it doing them herself.

All the invitations looked the same on the outside. The beveled edge cut-out on the front, framed a photograph of Phil sitting on the edge of a large rock to bring his height closer to Jen's, his arms wrapped around her waist standing in front of him. The trees and stream in the background were heavy-laden with snow and ice.

The wording inside the invites to the ceremony was different from those to only the open house. Then there were the announcements they would send out to others to let them know they were married without an invitation to attend either the ceremony or the open house. When she had three piles of invitations, she began to merge the address files into her computer program for the mailing labels she would put on the matching cotton envelopes. Jay observed what she did and sometimes asked questions about the process.

Noon came quickly, and Jay and Jennifer left the office in disarray to meet up with Mitzi and Denny at the hospital.

Jennifer and Jay waited in the hall outside Mr. Cardoza's room. Phil arrived shortly after them and the three of them waited for Mitzi and Denny to arrive.

<<<

Mitzi and Denny were breathless from hurrying up the stairs when they tumbled out from the doorway and hurried over to Phil, Jay, and Jennifer. "I'm sorry we're late," Mitzi apologized. "We had to run back to our house because I forgot The Book of Mormon—then I had to go through several boxes to find it."

Jay's face lit up. "Mitzi, will you do me a huge favor?" he asked.

"Sure, Jay, what do you need?"

"Will you underline some scriptures for me?"

"What did you want me to underline?" she asked.

"*Third Nephi* chapter eleven—all of it—and chapter seventeen, verses six through seventeen," Jay said.

Mitzi used the counter at the nurse's desk to find the passages and underline them. When she had finished, she asked for an extra minute to regain her composure as she wiped her tears away and blew her nose.

"Are we all ready to go into the room now?" Jennifer asked.

Without answering, Phil opened the door to Mr. Cardoza's room and led the way with all the others following him.

Mr. Cardoza seemed nervous until his eyes rested on Jay. He smiled as best he could with his stitches in his lip and mouth.

"These are my friends," Jay began to introduce Mitzi and Denny.

When Mr. Cardoza looked puzzled, Denny introduced himself, Mitzi, and Jennifer in Spanish. He explained that Jennifer was Jay's mother and Dr. Henson's wife-to-be, and he and Mitzi were their friends.

Mr. Cardoza smiled and shook his head indicating he understood. He seemed pleased to have someone speak to him in his native language.

"Give him The Book of Mormon," Jay said to Mitzi.

268

Mitzi first explained to Mr. Cardoza that Jay wished to give him a special book. Since she had a copy in Spanish, she was giving this book to him for Jay—then she handed him The Book of Mormon.

He took the book and looked at it admiringly. After a long pause, he said that he didn't know how to read. He explained that his parents had kept him secluded from the public most of his life because they were ashamed of his curse and he never went to school with his brothers and sisters to learn how to read.

Denny explained the situation to Jay and asked him what he would like to do now?

"Can you read the underlined part to him so he can hear it?" Jay requested.

Mitzi interpreted Jay's request to Mr. Cardoza and he handed her the book so she could read it to him. She read all of chapter eleven explaining about the Savior's appearance to the Nephites.

When she finished that chapter, she turned to chapter seventeen and read.

"'And it came to pass that when he had thus spoken, all the multitude, with one accord, did go forth with their sick and their afflicted, and their lame, and with their blind, and with their dumb, and with all them that were afflicted in any manner; and he did heal them every one as they were brought forth unto him.

"'And they did all, both they who had been healed and they who were whole, bow down at his feet, and did worship him; and as many as could come for the multitude did kiss his feet, insomuch that they did bathe his feet with their tears... '"

Mitzi continued to read about the children being brought to the Savior to sit about his feet, and how Jesus prayed using words that could not be written because they were so marvelous.

Mr. Cardoza was wide-eyed. "Ask him to pray about what you read to him," Jay told Mitzi. "Tell him to ask Heavenly Father if it's true so he'll know!"

Denny and Mitzi both laughed at Jay's simple faith. Denny interpreted Jay's comments to Mr. Cardoza and he also laughed at the boy's exuberance. He told Denny to tell Jay he would pray about it.

Denny and Mitzi asked Mr. Cardoza about his family and explained a little bit about the Gospel plan for eternal families. They told him if he was interested in knowing more, they would send his name and address to the missionary department and when he returned home, two young men with white shirts would come to visit him and explain all about it.

Mr. Cardoza seemed genuinely interested and readily gave them his address. Mitzi asked if they could visit him again before he returned to Guatemala and he nodded his head.

Mitzi and Denny agreed to spend as much time with Mr. Cardoza as they could during the following week. Denny had spent a good share of his time teaching reading skills to the Venezuelans while on his mission. He was sure he knew how to teach Mr. Cardoza the basics at least.

Tears of gratitude ran down Mr. Cardoza's cheeks, manifesting how visibly touched he was by this serendipitous opportunity he was being given.

Chapter Fifty-Three

On the way home, Jay asked Jennifer if he could visit or at least call his sister, Emily. He hadn't talked to her since he gave her The Book of Mormon. Jennifer checked her cell phone to see if she'd saved Tonya's number, and when she found it, she pressed the call button.

When Tonya answered the phone, Jennifer asked her if it would be all right if she and Jay stopped in to visit Emily for a few minutes. "When were you thinking of coming?" she asked, drawing her words out to reveal her apprehension.

"We could be there within fifteen minutes," Jennifer explained.

"Well, I'm really busy this afternoon, but if you won't stay long, I guess it would be okay."

"Thanks, we'll see you in a few minutes, then," Jennifer said and ended the call. It seemed obvious to Jennifer that Tonya was not thrilled with the idea, but Jay was so excited Jennifer decided it was worth being considered a pest.

<<<

Emily answered the door and when she saw Jay, she politely invited them into the house, but didn't invite them to sit down in the living room so they stood in the entryway.

"Did you read The Book of Mormon?" Jay asked immediately.

Emily turned her head around to see if Tonya was listening, not sure if she could hear them or not. She pressed her index finger over her lips, "Shhh," she said. Seconds later, Tonya appeared and invited them to sit in the living room. As soon as they were seated, Emily asked Tonya if she could take Jay to her bedroom to show him something.

Tonya agreed but told her Jay could only stay a few minutes, "So make it quick," she demanded.

When the bedroom door closed, Emily whispered, "My mother doesn't know about the book. If she finds it, she will be mad at me, so I keep it hidden in my closet. When I'm alone sometimes, I get it out and read it, but I don't have much time when I'm by myself in the house."

"What do you think of the parts you have read?" Jay asked quietly.

"It's okay, I guess."

"*Okay?*" he repeated. "Are you sure you're *really* reading it?"

"I've read about five pages," she said defensively. "Look, Jay, just because you've gone off and joined the Mormon church doesn't mean the whole world will do it too." Jay's shoulders sagged and he looked down at his feet. Knowing she had caused him to feel bad, Emily tried to rewind and undo the discouragement she had caused, "But then it doesn't mean they won't either," she said perkily with a smile. "I promise, Jay, I'll try harder to read the book even if I do think it's boring."

"Don't start reading it from the beginning to the end. Start reading in the book of *Third Nephi*; especially read chapters eleven and seventeen."

Emily was sure Jay had lost his marbles. "What does the book of *Third Nephi* have to do with The Book of Mormon?" she asked.

Jay explained how The Book of Mormon was divided into smaller books with chapters and verses. "There are four books of Nephi—they are called that because they are written by men named *Nephi*. You need to read Third Nephi because it tells about Jesus coming to America right after He was resurrected."

"You mean Mormons believe in Jesus?" she asked in astonishment.

"Heck yeah! Didn't you know that?"

"Are you sure? Because Tonya...I mean my mother, said Mormons didn't believe in God and Momma and Daddy always said Mormons only believe in following some man who is president of their church."

"I know what Momma and Daddy always said, but they were wrong. They never really read The Book of Mormon to find out for themselves. I'm telling you Emily, if you read The Book of

Mormon and pray about it, you'll find out Daddy and Momma were wrong and so is Tonya...er...your mother."

Emily looked skeptical; nevertheless, she said she'd start reading in the third book of "*whatever*."

"Do you like living with your new mother?" Jay finally asked.

"It's okay. It's different than living at home with momma and daddy. Tonya and Trent don't fight like daddy and momma did, but sometimes I think they don't like each other any better. They don't talk to each other much, and Trent goes hunting and fishing instead of out drinking."

"Do they like *you*?"

"Trent doesn't ever look at me when he talks to me. Most of the time, he ignores me. Tonya talks to me, but I can tell she's irritated with me. She gets annoyed when I ask her questions."

"How is school?" Jay asked.

"I don't go to school. I study here at home because I don't want the kids to laugh at how ugly I am."

"You're *not ugly*!" he insisted. "You just have some burn scars!"

"What do the kids say to *you* at school?"

"I don't go to school either. Mostly because I have to keep having surgeries, and I can't be in the hospital and school at the same time. But my mom teaches me at home and she's a real good teacher too."

"My mother tells me to read some books, but she doesn't ever teach me anything herself." Emily said.

"Maybe *my* mom could teach you!" Jay volunteered. "She tutors kids all the time after school."

"I don't think my mother would like that too much," Emily said hopelessly.

<<<

Not sure what to say, Tonya waited nervously for Jay and Emily to return.

Jennifer asked, "How have things been going with Emily?"

"Not like I was expecting. I really wish she would agree to go to school so I could have my own life back. She put up such a stink at the school when I tried to enroll her, the school *refused* to accept her. They felt she should go to a behavioral modification school for children with special needs. I had no idea it was going to be this difficult when we agreed to adopt her. I wanted to have children badly enough I thought I could deal with her physical appearance, but maybe I was wrong."

"Has Emily explained why she put up such a fuss about going to school?"

"She says she doesn't want the other kids to laugh at her and poke fun of her because she's ugly."

"So are you home schooling her, or do you send her to a special needs school?" Jennifer asked.

"She home schools, but I'm not really qualified to teach her, so I have her read a lot hoping she'll get the information she needs."

"Have you considered sending her to a tutor?"

Tonya was hesitant to answer the question suspecting Jennifer's financial advantage over her own. "We can't afford to pay someone to teach her," she finally admitted.

"Tonya, I am a certified school teacher and I tutor students in the afternoons every day. I would be willing to have Emily come over three mornings a week and I could tutor her right along with Jay. I wouldn't charge you anything and I think it might be good for Emily and Jay to keep connected."

"I don't know. I'll have to think about it," she finally answered. The idea of sending Emily away for three mornings a week sounded too good to be true—especially if there was no financial burden. *But, they were Mormons*! She'd have to think about it.

"I could start in January. Right now I'm taking the next month off from tutoring because of my upcoming wedding," Jennifer explained.

"You're not married?" Tonya asked rather surprised.

"No. I'm getting married on the tenth of December. We will be mailing you and Trent an invitation sometime this week. Jay would really like Emily to be there if possible."

"How did you adopt without being married?"

"I didn't think it was possible either, but the State approached me and asked me to consider adopting Jay regardless of my marital status. Jay's disabilities were severe enough that his opportunities for adoption were limited. They knew we had a close relationship and thought it would be good for Jay. I was as surprised as you are. But after giving it some consideration, I decided to give up full-time teaching, go to part-time tutoring instead, and to adopt Jay. It's really been a wonderful experience for both of us, I think."

"So how long have you and your fiancé been living together?" Tonya asked.

"We haven't been living together!" Jennifer said emphatically.

"So were you dating this guy before you adopted Jay, or did this come up after you adopted him—because you looked like you knew each other pretty well on Halloween when Emily and I came over."

"Oh, that wasn't my fiancé! That was my best friend's husband, Dave. He had taken Jay trick-or-treating with their children and had agreed to video tape Jay's reunion with Emily for me that night. I thought it would be good to have it on record for Jay to refer back to later in life. No, I'm marrying Phil Henson. He's one of the surgeons that took care of Emily and Jay in the burn center at the hospital."

Tonya felt deflated. Here was this amazingly confident woman who appeared to have all her affairs in order, seemed to have adjusted to Jay's adoption rather well, and she was marrying a doctor. *Some people have all the luck!* "I'm not sure we'll be able to make it to the wedding," Tonya said. She was sure Trent would never agree to take Emily out in public, even to the wedding of her brother's adoptive mother. "If we do come, I'm sure it will only be Emily and me."

"Even if you are unable to come," Jennifer coaxed, "Let Emily come and we'll see she gets a ride back home after the Open House."

To Tonya's relief, Emily and Jay returned to the living room, and Jennifer and Jay excused themselves to leave. Jay and Emily gave each other a hug at the door, and Tonya closed the door, taking a deep breath, after Jay and Jennifer stepped outside.

<<<

Braxton slipped the diamond ring on Julianne's slender finger— luckily her finger was the same size as Jennifer's. "Now it's official," he told her, as he kissed her passionately.

"Yes, I suppose it is. I can't believe all this could be happening to me. After Dad died, I didn't think I'd ever find happiness, but you seemed to come along at just the right moment to rescue me from my loneliness."

"I suppose we should make some plans," he said. "How would you feel if I added you to my bank account, and you could use the money from my account to pay for the wedding?"

"I hardly think I'll need *your* money to pay for the wedding."

"Well, I want you to know that everything I have is yours. I'd still like to add you to my account." *My account that's almost dry, that is.* "Would that be okay?"

"I'll think about it."

Chapter Fifty-Four

The time to leave for California came quickly. Jennifer had all the wedding invitations mailed, Phil had all the Christmas lights set up outside in the yard, the tuxes were ordered, Jennifer's wedding gown was purchased, the rings were taken care of, the refreshments and wedding cake for the Open House were ordered, and the flowers had been arranged for. All that remained to be done, was the Christmas decorations inside the house that needed to be set up.

Wednesday morning, Phil arrived at the house to pick Jennifer and Jay up. Phil made sure Jay packed what he needed. When they verified they were ready, Phil pulled out Jay's plastic nose Bob had given him. "I fixed it for you," he said. "I cut some of the back off so it looks like a smaller nose, and I lined the edges with a soft pad so you won't have any skin irritation." Phil slipped it inside his elastic facemask and was impressed with the results.

With suitcases packed and ready, they loaded up in Phil's car and headed toward the airport.

"I've never been on an airplane before," Jay said with excitement.

"Well, you'd better get used to it," Phil said. "I'm sure this won't be the only time we fly."

When the three of them were finally boarding the plane, Phil had Jay sit by the window. Jennifer took the middle seat, and Phil took the seat by the aisle. When the plane started down the runway, Jay's plastic nose was pressed right against the window. "Cool!" he said when they lifted off the ground.

Jennifer offered him a book on the little tray she opened out in front of him, but he was too interested in seeing the ground far below.

Phil held Jennifer's hand and toyed with her engagement ring with his thumb. "You seem distracted," he said.

"I was thinking about my parents and about their plane crashing a few years ago. I was wondering what life would be like now if they were still alive. I wish they were here to get to know you."

He patted her hand reassuringly, "I would have loved to know them. They must've been wonderful people—they had you."

Almost immediately, after the trash was collected from their refreshments, they were told to prepare for landing. Jay had never removed his seat belt, so he sat back and relaxed as he again looked out the window to watch the plane fly into the San Jose airport.

Once they had their rental car, they headed straight to Bob and Mary's house. "Are we going to see the ocean?" Jay asked.

"Not today. We're going right to Grandma and Grandpa's house," Phil answered. "Maybe we'll take a trip up to San Francisco on Friday or Saturday. We'll have to see what your aunt and uncle have planned."

"I have aunts and uncles?" Jay asked. "Who are they?"

Phil told Jay about his brother Tim and his sister, Ruth. He talked about the nieces and nephew that Jay would be meeting and explained that they would soon be his cousins.

"I've never had cousins before," Jay said. "How many will I have?" he asked.

"Three," Phil answered.

"Cool," Jay said for the umpteenth time that day.

Bob was waiting at the front door when Phil, Jennifer, and Jay stepped onto the porch. Before he said hello to Phil or Jennifer, he swooped Jay up into his arms and said, "I see you have your nose on, young man."

Jay smiled, "My dad fixed it so it looks better and it doesn't even hurt."

"Hot diggety-dog! *Dad*, huh?" he said throwing a questioning look at Phil.

"Well, if he can call you *grandpa*... " Phil left his sentence unfinished.

"So you haven't eloped yet?" Bob asked.

278

"Not yet, but if you don't have separate bedrooms for us, we might have to," Phil threw in.

"I think Mother has everything all arranged. Phil, you and Jay can stay in your old bedroom. Jennifer can take Ruth's old room. I believe Ruth will be staying with Kenneth's parents."

Everyone got settled, then gathered in the kitchen for a light meal of homemade soup and rolls.

After dinner, Jennifer helped Mary as they prepared pies and salads for the big dinner the following day.

<<<

Bob dragged Phil and Jay off into his den to show them something *important*.

"I've been doing some research," Bob said. "I'm surprised you haven't thought of this yourself, Phil. There are companies out there that make props for plays and movies. Take a look at what I ordered for Jay." Bob pulled out a small pair of latex hobbit ears that looked like Frodo's. "See if these will work under your mask, Jay."

Phil and Jay both laughed. "Actually, that's about what we will be doing during our next surgery for Jay—only the ears we give him will look like mouse ears, not like Frodo's."

Chapter Fifty-Five

Jay was anticipating the arrival of his new cousins on Thanksgiving morning. When Ruth arrived, her son, Trevor, made fun of *the kid in the mask*. "Halloween is over," he taunted.

Jay smiled, explained the situation, and asked Jennifer to remove his mask so Trevor could see the reality for himself. He decided to keep it off the rest of the day. Before long, Trevor softened up to Jay and included him.

When Tim's family arrived from Alameda, everyone quickly gathered at the table for dinner. After Bob offered the blessing on the food, he formally introduced Jennifer and Jay to the family.

Tim, ever the attorney, had many questions about Phil's liabilities in adopting Jay, and complimented his good taste in women.

Ruth remained silent, but glared at Jennifer, and Jay during the meal.

<<<

After dinner, the children excused themselves from the table to go play, except for Jay who next to Jennifer.

Breaking her silence, Ruth said, "Phil, what are you thinking? First you run off and join the Mormon Church and then you marry a Mormon with a deform...a...handicapped kid. Don't you think this is a little extreme and rushed?"

Phil felt Jennifer's shaking hand under the table and he saw Jay's eyes open wide and look to him for an answer.

Being the outspoken child in the family, Ruth often drove Phil nuts with her opinions. Her ideas seemed to be an embodiment of the sensational media, which she was an integrated part of. She believed only people too weak or stupid to live their lives freely, believed in God, and perceived children as unnecessary burdens. The mere fact that Ruth had one child was amazing to Phil; he had expected her to have none.

He knew it made Ruth mad when he called her Ruthie. *"Ruthie,* I have never made a better decision or been happier in my life. I understand your family is planning to come to Utah for the wedding."

"I'm considering it. Although I'm not sure I can handle being around all those *Mormons,*" Ruth said.

"They don't all look like me," Jay offered. Bob and Phil chuckled but Jennifer appeared to be on the verge of tears.

"I've heard about the Mormons being abusive to their kids. I suppose you're a living example of it!" she said to Jay acidly.

"My parents were like *you*—they hated Mormons," Jay said. "Jennifer was my schoolteacher and she is the nicest person I know. If she's what Mormons are like, then I'm proud to be one."

"I'm afraid he's right," Bob said to Ruth. "We met quite a few of them when we were in Utah and they were nice people. Perhaps, Ruth, you have been given some wrong information about them."

"Any religion that practices polygamy is disgusting as far as I'm concerned," Ruth fumed.

"Bob was right, Ruth, you have been given some wrong information. The Church of Jesus Christ of Latter-Day Saints or *Mormons* as you call them, does *not* practice polygamy. As a matter of fact, anyone who *does,* gets excommunicated from the church. All of the polygamist groups you hear about in the news are break-off groups and are not affiliated with the L.D.S. church," Jennifer's voice was steadier than her shaking hands.

Tim defended Jennifer, "She's telling you the truth, Sis. Mormons have taken a bad rap for the polygamy, but they have nothing to do with it. I know because I've followed some of the legal processes with some of the polygamist groups."

"So you mean you don't intend to start a harem?" she asked Phil, her voice dripping with sarcasm.

"No, Ruthie, I don't intend to start a harem," Phil said with a tired sigh.

282

"Maybe you should find out the truth before you decide Mormons are all bad," Jay suggested. "Why don't you read The Book of Mormon and see what they *really* believe?"

"I'm not sure I care enough about them to waste my time reading their propaganda," Ruth huffed. "I've had a really hard time knowing that my own brother joined them!"

"I'm sorry you feel that way," Mary said. "We were so impressed with Jennifer and Jay that we have been reading The Book of Mormon ever since we got back from Utah. I highly doubt you could call it propaganda. It's really the word of God."

Phil looked at his parents with wonder, and when Bob winked at him, his face broke into a big grin.

"You WHAT?" Ruth asked. "Don't tell me *you're* thinking of joining their cult too?"

"Why does everyone think the Mormon religion is a cult?" Phil asked.

"Because they all live weird lives according to some code of behavior dictated by their president and written in one book!" Ruth answered.

"That's what my parents said. But they didn't know what they were talking about," Jay said. "They didn't understand that the Church is led by a Prophet. Most members are smart enough to realize that the Prophet tells the truth and so they *choose* to follow him. Some members don't do anything he says."

"It's like any other religion," Phil said. "There are good folks and bad folks. Being a newscaster, you only hear about the bad ones because they make sensational news. If you took the time to find out more, you'd find out that there are many outstanding Mormons."

"I suppose you mean like *Mitt Romney*?" Ruth said sardonically.

Knowing Ruth's political persuasions, Phil said, "Yeah, Mitt's a Mormon—just like Harry Reid. Orrin Hatch, and Jon Huntsman, the philanthropist who created the Huntsman Cancer Institute are too. The Osmonds are also L.D.S. I believe you liked them a lot when Donny and Marie were on TV. And what about Larry H. Miller, the guy who owned the Utah Jazz? You love to see the Lakers beat the Jazz. Did you know the owner of the Jazz was a Mormon?"

Ruth appeared stunned. "I *did* know the Osmonds were Mormon, but they seemed so young, I didn't think they were *practicing* Mormons anymore. I assumed they were brainwashed by their parents and would grow up and change their beliefs when they became independent."

"Not only are they practicing Mormons, but Donny has been a bishop in the L.D.S. Church," Jennifer said. "Jay's explanation that a Prophet leads our church, but the members choose for themselves what to believe or how to behave is evidenced by the fact that Mitt Romney and Harry Reid are both members of the same faith but have opposing political view points. If the L.D.S. Church was *really* a cult, wouldn't they both adhere to the exact same belief?"

Ruth's husband, Kenneth finally spoke. "It seems to me that perhaps we might need to research our facts a little bit more." Ruth glared at him, but kept silent.

Mary said, "It's Thanksgiving Day. Do you think we could find things to be thankful for instead of angry about?"

"I suggest we bring on the dessert. Where's the pumpkin pie?" Bob asked.

<<<

By the time everyone left that evening, Jennifer felt drained of energy and chose to go to bed early. She read scriptures with Jay and kissed him goodnight. She spent a few minutes with Phil who reassured her things would be fine. She went to her assigned bedroom and prepared for bed. She knelt by the bed to pray and cried to the Lord to help Phil's family—especially Ruth, to be more accepting of Phil's decision to join the church and to accept her and Jay and their religious beliefs. By the light of the lamp, she read her own scriptures until she faded off to sleep.

Chapter Fifty-Six

Jennifer was sleeping late when she faintly heard a tapping noise in her dream. The tapping eventually turned into loud knocking, and she heard Phil's voice, "Jen, are you awake?"

"I am now," she answered groggily. "What do you need?"

"I need my future wife to join me and my future son on an outing. Can I come in?"

"The door's unlocked," she moaned. The door slowly opened and she hid her face in the pillow.

"What's the matter—don't you want me to see you when you first wake up and have pillow wrinkles in your face and slobber on your chin?" Phil chided.

"What time is it?" she asked. "Is it really morning, yet?"

"It's almost seven o'clock—which means it would be eight o'clock if we were in Utah," he answered as he sat beside her on the bed. He pulled the pillow away from her and rolled her over to face him. "You're beautiful."

"You're crazy!"

"You're right—I'm crazy about you." He bent over and kissed her. "Would you like to go for a little drive?"

"What have you got in mind?"

"Well, I thought maybe we'd go up to San Francisco and show you the Golden Gate Bridge, and the Bay Bridge, and the ocean, and Fisherman's Wharf, and Muir Woods and... "

"All right, enough," Jennifer said. "Can we really do all that in one day?"

"Well, that all depends on how long you sleep and take to get ready to go."

"I can be ready in twenty minutes," she said and sat right up as perky as ever.

"That's my girl. I'll get Jay ready. Would you mind if I invite Dad and Mom to go with us? Or would you prefer to go it alone today?"

"I'd love to have your parents come along. I don't think I could handle Ruth and Kenneth, but your parents are more than welcome."

"Good. I'll see if I can get Mom to push Dad out of bed. I think she's in the kitchen making coffee."

"Where should I take my shower? Will your dad need the bathroom across the hall?"

"Nope. They have their own bathroom off their bedroom, so you should be fine. Give me five minutes to get Jay in and out and then you can have it all to yourself."

Jennifer was so used to taking care of Jay it took her a few minutes to remind herself that Phil took care of Jay for months before she did. Certainly *he* knew how to care for him. She relaxed and snuggled under the sheets until Phil knocked on her door saying, "Okay, the coast is clear—the bathroom is all yours."

She jumped up, quickly made the bed, grabbed her jeans, a sweater, and her toiletries and she was off to the shower. She was out of the bathroom in twenty minutes. *I'm getting slow. I used to be able to do this in ten minutes in gym class.* Back in her bedroom, she blew her hair dry, added a headband and dabbed on some mascara. "Enough," she said aloud and headed out to the kitchen.

Jay was sitting at the table drinking a cup of milk with a straw. The empty plate in front of him indicated he had finished eating something for breakfast with the plastic fork mounted to his stump with Velcro straps.

Jennifer gave him a hug and kiss. "You're the man," she said lovingly.

Phil walked into the kitchen, pulled her into his arms, and planted a huge kiss on her mouth. "Good morning, Sweetheart," he said. "What would you like for breakfast? We have eggs, toast, bacon, cereal, grapefruit, oranges, oatmeal, of course that can translate into French toast, waffles, pancakes… "

"Oh, I'm getting sick thinking of so much food," Jennifer said dramatically. "How about toast, half a grapefruit, and a bowl of cereal?"

Phil started to get things out and Jennifer took the grapefruit out of his hand. "I think I know how to prepare my own breakfast," she said. "Would you like the other half of my grapefruit?"

"I'm sure you know exactly how to prepare your breakfast, but we're in *my* parents' home and *I'm* hosting. Sit down and let me fix it for you," Phil said, snatching the grapefruit back from her.

"Are you two going to fight this early in the morning?" Bob said with a grin as he entered the kitchen in time to see the grapefruit exchange hands.

"Phil insists on taking care of me when I'm perfectly capable of taking care of myself!" Jennifer said defensively as Mary walked into the kitchen for the second time.

"I'm trying to be a good host," Phil explained.

"Enjoy the service while it lasts," Mary said. "Two years from now he will have forgotten how to find a knife in the drawer."

"I beg your pardon," Bob said. "Are you saying I can't take care of myself?"

"It's either you or your clone," Mary answered.

To prove her wrong, Bob ordered them all to sit down while he prepared breakfast for all of them.

Everyone took a seat at the table and watched with interest to see who would win this battle. It was only seconds after they all sat to watch when Bob asked Mary, "Now where's that little knife you cut the sections out of the grapefruit with, Mary?"

"I rest my case!" Mary said with finality. Laughter filled the room and Mary got up, found the knife in the drawer and took over with the grapefruit. "You go make the toast," she ordered Bob. "Phil, why don't you get the milk and cereal bowls out. Jennifer, you can make the orange juice. There is some in the freezer and the blender is in the appliance garage over there in the corner."

They set to work with their assignments while they bumped into each other in the jovial atmosphere. Soon they were finished washing the dishes and preparing to leave for the adventures of the day. "You'd better bring your jackets," Phil told Jay and Jennifer.

"I thought California was supposed to be warm," Jay said.

"Mark Twain said the coldest winter he ever saw was *summer* in *San Francisco*. You'll be cold when we get to the coast with the ocean breezes."

"Okay, Dad," Jay said and left to find a jacket.

"It does my heart good to hear him call you *Dad*," Bob said. "I *like* that boy—he's quite the young man." Jennifer's heart swelled with warmth. *If only Ruth could feel that way.*

Chapter Fifty-Seven

The day was sunny and balmy. Jay's fake nose was plastered to the window of the car with anticipation, as they drove through Oakland and across the Bay Bridge. He looked up at the cables suspending the bridge over the ocean with amazement.

"The Bay Bridge is the *longest* steel high-level bridge in the world. Its foundations extend to the greatest depth below water of any bridge ever built; one pier was sunk at 242 feet below water. It required more concrete than the Empire State Building in New York and is bigger than the largest of the Pyramids," Phil told them.

"Wow," was all Jay said.

They drove through China Town, then up to the Golden Gate Bridge.

"That's a baby bridge compared to the Bay Bridge," Jay said. "Why is *it* so famous?"

"Because they painted *it* orange," Bob answered sarcastically.

"Actually," Phil explained, "The Golden Gate Bridge has the longest span between its towers. This was an important area for ships coming into the bay from the Pacific Ocean. Nobody believed anyone could build a bridge high enough or wide enough for the ships to pass under.

"That's why they built it with the *long span* between the towers. It was designed so that if broadside winds coming in from the ocean blow at a speed of one hundred miles an hour, the bridge floor at mid span can swing as much as 27 feet without collapsing."

Once they crossed back over the bridge into San Francisco, Phil found a parking spot near Fisherman's Wharf. "Let's have lunch on the Wharf before riding the trolley car," he suggested.

"It sure stinks here," Jay said without diplomacy.

"That's why all the mermaids left," Bob said with a facetious grin.

Jay knew Bob was teasing because he knew all about mythical creatures like unicorns, mermaids, sea horses, and centaurs.

"I agree," Jennifer added. "Are we really going to *eat* here?"

"It's part of the culture," Phil said.

As they entered one of the restaurants, Jay looked at the fish swimming in an aquarium. Among some of the brightly colored creatures was a *sea horse*. "Are these real or fake?" he asked Jennifer.

"They're real, why?"

"I thought sea horses were *mythical* creatures."

"At one time they *were* considered mythical," Phil said. "They're difficult to find, but as you can see, they're real. The female sea horse lays her eggs in the pouch of the male sea horse. He then fertilizes the eggs and hatches them. They are the *only* male in the animal kingdom that has babies. They're interesting fish."

"Wow," Jay said again. "I can't wait to tell Emily they're real."

<<<

After lunch, they rode the trolley to the top of a hill, and then walked down Lombard Street. "In the summer, the beds between the zigzags of road are filled with flowers," Phil explained.

"Yeah," Bob chimed in, "that's where they buried all the people who got killed driving down the street."

"Remind me when we get back to Mom and Dad's to show you some pictures we took when we came here in July the year I was Jay's age."

"Exactly *when* were you my age?" Jay asked.

"Is this a trick question?" Phil asked back.

"No, I just wanna to know how old you are."

"It's none of your business!" Phil smirked.

"Mom's twenty-six. Are you older than her?"

"Yes, I'm older than her."

"How many years older?"

"Fifty—satisfied?"

"Not true! That would make you seventy-six, and Grandpa's only sixty-eight."

"How did you know that?"

"He said he retired when he turned sixty-five and that was three years ago—do the math."

"He's thirty-two years younger than I am if I remember correctly," Bob supplied.

"Oh, so you're *really* thirty-six," Jay rattled off at lightning speed. "Aren't you a little too old to marry Mom?"

"You want me to call it off?" Phil quipped back.

"No. I think we'll settle for an *older* man."

Bob laughed raucously, "You know, that's what I like about you Jay, you fit right in!"

"Jennifer, you may have your hands full with *those* two," Mary said.

"Perhaps I'll develop some appreciation for what you have endured for thirty-six years," she responded good-naturedly.

"If I didn't know better, I'd swear Jay was a blood relative of Phil and Bob!"

"Hmmm… perhaps that's why Phil had such an affinity for Jay from the beginning," Jennifer said thoughtfully.

"You could be right," Mary agreed. "Do you suppose there was some Divine Intervention that brought the three of you together?"

"Why do you ask, Mother?" Phil questioned.

"I'm beginning to think nothing in this life happens accidentally," Mary said. "We told you we'd been reading The Book of Mormon since we returned from Utah. After reading several chapters, Bob got a faraway look on his face and was silent for a long while. I waited for him to continue reading, but instead, he said, 'You know, I think there's something to this book I am supposed to know—there's something I feel when I read it.' We have both felt that Jennifer and Jay were a link to something important in our future—more than just future members of our family."

"Considering the thin threads that have connected us, I'm sure there's more to it than our mortal minds can understand," Jennifer said humbly. "Perhaps that's why Jay was sure he belonged in a different family all along. He said he was waiting for his *real* family to find him."

Mary hugged her and for a moment. The two women shared a deep kinship of love and appreciation.

They stopped at Muir Woods on the way back. It was beautiful. Jay and Jennifer were both impressed with the height and straightness of the redwood trees. The ferns and undergrowth were just as appealing.

Chapter Fifty-Eight

The trip to California ended far too soon for Jay. Spending time with his grandparents-to-be was the highlight of the vacation, but seeing so many new and exciting things was a close runner-up in importance to him. He loved seeing the seals at the ocean shoreline and watching the waves come crashing up to the rock cliffs. "Can we come back in the summer?" he asked Phil.

"*May* we," Jennifer corrected.

"*May* we come back in the summer?" he asked again.

"I'm sure we'll have many opportunities to come and visit Grandma and Grandpa," Phil said.

"Cool!" It seemed to be Jay's favorite new word. He was wearing his plastic nose and his hobbit ears when they hugged Bob and Mary goodbye.

"I guess we'll be roommates in a couple of weeks," Bob said to Jay. Then turning to Phil, he asked, "I guess you've shown me everything I need to know about how to take care of him?"

"He's getting pretty independent—as you have seen, but he still needs a little help with buttons on his shirt and showering. If you can handle that, he can tell you if he needs any other assistance. He still needs help with the seat belts in the car. He can get them off, but hooking them up is a bit of a challenge."

"Are you ever going to fix him so he can live a normal life?" Bob asked Phil.

"Next spring we'll be making some big decisions. We're either going to go with prosthetic hands or we'll need to make his stubs longer so he can actually use them like fingers. It will all depend on how much nerve tissue he is able to build up in his hands by then. We'll definitely be giving him a nose and some ears, but we're more concerned with making him functional than good looking."

Bob looked at Jay and said, "Is that possible?"

"To make him functional?"

"No… to make him good looking?"

"It's doubtful, but we'll do our best."

"I like him just like he is—don't mess him up too much. Besides, he looks good in Frodo ears." Jay was grinning over their banter and Jennifer shook her head and rolled her eyes at Mary who raised her eyebrows, shrugged her shoulders, and held her hands out with her palms up as if to say *don't ask me…I gave up on them years ago.*

<<<

The flight home was uneventful until they flew into the Salt Lake Valley and it was snowing. Jay exclaimed his excitement over the physical evidence of Christmas being right around the corner, and Phil felt butterflies of anticipation realizing Jennifer would be his wife in twelve more days.

On their way home from the airport, they stopped by the post office to pick up mail. The discussion in the car was primarily about the schedule the following two weeks. "We're going to need to make haste in getting the Christmas trees up and the inside of the house decorated this coming week," Jennifer stated. I won't have any more students coming so we'll be able to work a little longer each day except Wednesday when we have choir practice. The week after this, I will have a 'Sisters in Zion' practice on Tuesday, Wednesday is our performance, and Thursday and Friday will be busy with getting the house clean and picking up flowers and food for the wedding.

"Will Emily be coming to the wedding?" Jay asked.

"When I talked to Tonya, she seemed uncertain. I told her if she and Trent weren't going to come, they were welcome to drop Emily off and we would make sure she got home after."

Phil's ears perked up at the mention of a voluntary ride home, "I hope you had someone *else* in mind to take her home. I was planning to escape off into the sunset *alone* with my wife."

"Which reminds me," Jennifer said, "What should I pack— winter clothes or summer clothes? Am I allowed to know where we might be spending our honeymoon?"

294

"I would say plan for *cold* weather, but include a swimsuit," Phil said smugly. "Now about that ride home?"

"I'm sure Alice and Dave would be willing to drive Emily home, and if they can't, I don't think your parents would mind taking her—Jay can give them directions."

"Mom," Jay interrupted, "would it be okay for me to buy Emily a Christmas present?"

"What would you like to get her?"

"I don't know… I'd like to get her something to make her happy."

"I'm not sure that's possible," Phil said. "She's not easily pleased."

"I don't think her adopted parents like her much," Jay said.

"You could be right," Jennifer said, validating his instincts without confirming them.

After they unloaded their suitcases, Phil and Jay began to set up the Christmas tree in the formal sitting room while she started to fix some soup and sandwiches for dinner.

Before she began to fix dinner, she shuffled through the mail that had come while they were in California. There was a letter from the IRS. She quickly opened it and began to read the explanation.

Back taxes for three years were due and until they were satisfied, her account would be inaccessible.

Back taxes due? I've paid my taxes every year.

She looked at the copies of the 1040 forms they had included with the explanation. *BRAXTON!*

Three years in a row, he had failed to pay his taxes and last year, he filed "Married filing jointly." There was her name and her Social Security number right under his name. She looked at the signature line and gasped; as if she'd written it herself, the signature looked just like hers.

She threw the papers down on the counter and started fixing dinner, banging the pots and pans, slamming cupboard doors, and rattling the silverware in the drawers. She couldn't remember another time in her life that she had been this angry.

Picking up her cell phone, she started to dial Braxton's number. She intended to give him a piece of her wrath, but before she finished dialing, she envisioned him leaving the country as soon as he was alerted she knew. She flipped the phone closed.

Wanting to call the IRS, her attorney, or anyone who could help her, she remembered it was Sunday—they'd be closed.

The Police! There's a police investigation going on regarding my identity theft. A sickening thought hit her... was it Braxton who had run up the credit card debts? Would he really stoop to something that low?

Forgetting about the soup warming on the stove, she dialed the police investigation number.

"I have a lead on investigation number B5693541, regarding my identity theft," she said.

Just then, the soup boiled over. Jennifer dropped her phone, grabbed a hot pad, and lifted the pot off the burner.

<<<

Phil, hearing the ruckus with pots and pans banging in the kitchen, came to investigate. He rounded the corner of the kitchen as soup foamed over the top of the pot.

Jennifer jumped when she saw him, threw the phone down and lifted the pan off the stove.

The burning liquid smelled terrible, and was making black crusty residue on the burner.

"Jen, what's the matter? What's going on?"

"I forgot the soup," she said, as she reached for a rag and started to wipe up the mess.

Phil looked at the phone on the floor, broken into pieces. Then he looked at the papers scattered across the counter and the burned soup on the stove. Jennifer's reaction to him entering the kitchen, reminded him of a small child when caught with their hand in the cookie jar. *What was Jen doing that she didn't want me to know?*

He looked at the papers on the counter hoping to get a clue. When he saw the familiar 1040 tax forms, he examined them more closely. **Married filing jointly**: the words jumped out at him. Braxton's name was on the top line, and Jennifer's name was listed as spouse on the second line. Braxton... *the guy at the jewelry store! What was it he had said about who Jennifer was... she's my ex,"* he had said.

"Jen! Why didn't you tell me you'd been married?"

"I've never been married."

"These legal documents say differently," Phil said trying to control his anger. Her signature was recognizable. Everything started to add up. His dad had been right. Jennifer was in deep financial trouble. The betrayal facing him cut deeply into his soul. Plain and simple, Jennifer had deceived him.

Phil took her garage door opener out of his pocket, set it on the counter, and silently left the house.

<<<

Jennifer collapsed into tears at the bar.

Jay came into the kitchen, "Mom, where did Dad go?"

She couldn't answer with anything other than loud sobs.

Chapter Fifty-Nine

Jennifer went directly to the police station, taking the IRS papers Monday morning.

"Miss Heaps," the officer addressed her. "I was going to call you. I believe we have a good lead on your case."

"I believe I have one too," she said.

"Well let's sit down in my office and compare notes," he said as they went into a small room.

"We have received information from all the credit card companies regarding the initial charges," the officer informed her. "An interesting pattern occurred with each account after they were opened. There was a cash advance made, and they were all directly deposited into the same bank account. It's a local bank, and by this afternoon, we should have the name of the person owning the account."

"I might be able to save you some time," Jennifer said. She handed the officer the letter and tax forms from the IRS.

"Do you know this Braxton?"

"Yes. We were engaged. I broke it off a little over a year ago."

"Is this your signature on the tax form?"

"It looks like it, but I didn't sign that form."

"How did he have access to your Social Security number?"

"We had a joint checking account, but I closed it the day after I gave his ring back."

"My guess is… by then the damage had been done. He obviously kept your social security number, and copied your signature from the account application."

"Now what do I do?"

"Well, if we get the name from the bank account today and it turns out to be Braxton Thomas, I think we've got enough evidence to arrest him and lock him up for a long time. May I keep these papers from the IRS? I'll give you copies if you'd like, but I need the originals for evidence."

"Sure. I'd like copies for my records."

<<<

Phil had spent the night crying and praying. He had taken the month off work and it appeared it would be wasted time off, although he was glad he didn't have to go to work this morning in his present condition.

Jay. How will he react, knowing we aren't getting married? At least he has the last name of Heaps, and not Borky. What will happen to them when Jennifer looses the house from bankruptcy? I'm pretty sure all those millions of dollars was a lie too. Oh, I don't know anything anymore. I just know my life is a mess. Why, of all the women in the world, did I have to fall in love with a pathological liar? And why did she have to be the one who adopted Jay?

Phil called his parents at nine o'clock—which would have made it eight o'clock California time. He dreaded making this call, yet he needed their love and support.

"Hello," his mother answered.

"Mom, is Dad there with you?"

"He's just coming down the stairs, why?"

"I need you to put the phone on speaker. I need to be able to talk to you both at the same time."

"Phil, what is it?"

"Is Dad with you, yet?"

"I'm here, Son, what's going on?" Bob asked.

"Jennifer and I broke up last night," Phil said and he started to cry as the reality of his words were finally spoken aloud.

"Oh, no," Mary said. "What happened?"

Between heaving sobs, Phil explained that Jennifer was a fraud and a liar. She'd been married and he was pretty sure the credit card debt wasn't a case of identity theft, and she'd lied to him about having millions of dollars.

"I'm broken up inside, but grateful, Dad, that you brought this whole thing to my attention when you did, or I might have blindly

300

gone into a marriage that would have destroyed me worse than I am now."

"We have our plane tickets to come out for the wedding, would you like us to change them and come now?" Mary asked.

"It won't change anything, but a warm shoulder to cry on would sure feel good right now. If you're able to get the tickets changed, I'd really like to have you here for a while. I'll pay for the extra charges to change them."

"Let us call the airlines and see what we can do," Bob said.

<<<

Jennifer drove to the AT&T store to get a new cell phone. When she handed the representative the pieces of her phone, he laughed.

"What did you do, throw it across the room into a brick wall?"

"No, I dropped it on my kitchen floor. Granted, I was angry, but I had soup boiling over on my stove, and I was in a hurry to lessen the damage. I didn't realize I had thrown it with such force."

Fifteen minutes later, she was on her way to the attorney's office with a free replacement phone.

"Mr. Finch won't be in until tomorrow," the receptionist said. "He had court today."

"Could you copy these papers for me and give them to him in the morning?" Jennifer asked as she handed her the copies of the IRS letter and 1040 forms.

"Sure thing, Ms. Heaps," the receptionist said. She quickly made the copies, and put a sticky note on them for Mr. Finch.

Jennifer arrived at Alice's right before noon. "Are you hungry?" Alice asked. "I was just getting ready to fix lunch.

"I probably should eat, but I don't have much of an appetite."

"Jennifer, what's wrong. You look like you've been crying."

"I have. My whole life is in a mess right now, and I can't figure out a way to fix it."

Alice sat at the kitchen table across from Jennifer and listened to the entire story.

"Why haven't you said something about this until now?" Alice asked.

"I didn't think it was such a big deal, and I didn't want to burden anybody with my woes."

"Jennifer! You could lose your house, custody of Jay, and everything if this isn't resolved."

"I feel like I've already lost everything. Phil walked out last night in anger. I'm pretty sure he won't speak to me again except to take care of Jay's medical needs. Oh, Alice, what will Jay and I do without him?"

A tear trickled down Alice's cheek. "Oh, Jennifer, I'm so sorry. This is just awful. I'll bet Phil's parents will be disappointed too. They adored you."

A new flood of tears overtook Jennifer as she thought about losing Bob and Mary—the parents she was going to have. She remembered Mary saying she and Bob had felt a special kinship with her… and she was sure they would have joined the church eventually.

<<<

"We've changed our flights, Phil. We'll be arriving tomorrow morning at eleven-twenty, your time. The airlines charged us a hundred dollars for each ticket to change the departure date. We left the return date the same to save two hundred more dollars in charges. I hope you can put up with us for three weeks!" Bob said.

"Thanks, Dad. This means a lot to me. I'll see you in the morning."

<<<

"Miss Heaps, this is Lieutenant Garff. We got the information on the bank account. Just as we suspected, the account belongs to Braxton Thomas. The IRS has also frozen *his* account. I don't imagine he's too happy right now. Do you know if he's still at the address on the phony joint tax return?"

"As far as I know. That's where he was living when we broke up a year ago."

"Could you give me a description of him?"

302

"He's five-ten, blond hair, brown eyes, keeps his hair quite short, always wears tennis shoes—even with a suit."

"Does he have any unusual facial features, scars, or wear glasses?"

"No. He's usually quite tan, but he doesn't wear glasses, and his face is more or less square with no unusual facial features. There is one thing about him, though. He had a finger smashed in a door once, and the middle finger on his left hand has no fingernail."

"Thank you, Miss Heaps. I have two officers on the way with a warrant for his arrest. It shouldn't be too long before we notify you that we have him in our custody."

<<<

A middle-aged woman answered the door at the apartment.

"We have a warrant for Braxton Thomas," officer Brimley said.

"Who?" the woman asked.

"Braxton Thomas," he repeated.

"Don't know anybody by that name," she said.

"Do you live here, Ma'am?"

"Yep—I been here since January."

"Does anyone else live here with you?"

"Nope. Jest me."

"Could we get your name?"

"BobbyJo Binford."

"Okay. Thank you Ms. Binford," he said, as he and officer Longhurst turned to leave. Pulling his radio out, he called Lieutenant Garff.

"Bad address Lieutenant. A Lady by the name of BobbyJo Binford lives there alone—says she's been there since January."

"Damn. Okay. Go to the post office. Tell them you're dealing with a mail fraud case and you need Braxton's forwarding address. Show 'em the warrant."

"Will do, Lieutenant."

<<<

"We have a warrant for the arrest of Braxton Thomas," officer Longhurst told the postal inspector. "We're closing in on a mail fraud case, and we need the forwarding address of the man."

The postal inspector looked up Braxton's forwarding address and gave it to the officers. "I hope you get him," he said.

<<<

Officers Brimley and Longhurst looked at each other with chagrin when they reached the secure condominium complex. Knowing the best way to find Braxton included the element of surprise—they scratched their heads.

"Now what?" Brimley asked.

"Call the Lieutenant."

"Hey, Boss, we have a problem. Braxton Thomas lives in a secure high-rise condominium complex. If we push his buzzer, it'll tip him off we're coming for him. If we don't, we can't get past the front door. What do you suggest?"

"Take a walk for a couple of blocks until I get some back-up there. Then when your reinforcement arrives, push the buzzer for the manager. Ask him to meet you at the front door. Find out if there's a back fire escape and have two officers wait there. Send two more to the parking terrace to apprehend him if he comes outta the chute. I checked with the DMV—he drives a new silver colored Mercedes—vanity plate says Tango, November, Keelo, Uniform, Juliet, Echo, November. Keep one officer with the manager while you two go to the apartment. Let's make sure this snake doesn't get away."

<<<

Seven o'clock Tuesday morning, the phone woke Jennifer. She had slept very little all night, and groggily answered the phone by her bed, "Hello?"

"This is Lieutenant Garff. I thought you would like to know we apprehended Braxton. He confessed to everything."

"Now what?" Jennifer asked a little more awake.

"With a little luck, we can get the IRS to release your bank account, and the credit card companies to remove any negative reports."

"Will I have to pay any of it back to them?"

"I'm sure they'll sue Braxton for the money. Since there's evidence you didn't actually apply for the cards, you can only be held liable for fifty dollars on each card."

"That's over twelve hundred dollars!"

"Consider it a bargain, Miss Heaps. You could have been spending almost half-a-million."

Chapter Sixty

With all the craziness of the investigation going on, Jennifer realized on Wednesday morning that she hadn't dealt with calling anyone to cancel orders for the wedding. She dreaded calling all the people on *her* guest list to tell them the wedding was off. She wondered if Phil would remember to call his guests. If they showed up on the tenth... well, she guessed she'd just put a big sign on the front door and she and Jay would go to a movie or something.

She looked down at her left hand and saw the beautiful two-carat diamond Phil had given her. She knew she'd eventually have to give it back to him. "I'm sure good at giving diamond rings back," she muttered. "I wonder if I'll ever get to keep one."

"Mom," Jay interrupted her thoughts, "can I call Dad and see why he left without saying goodbye the other night?"

"No, Jay. He left because he was hurt and angry. I'm sorry, Honey, but Phil and I won't be getting married, and he won't be able to adopt you. Do you think you can live with being a Heaps?"

Huge tears spilled from Jay's eyes. He ran to his bedroom.

Jennifer found him lying on his bed crying. She pulled him into her arms. "I'm so sorry, Jay. I wish it could be different too."

"Why was he mad?"

"He thinks I lied to him."

"Did you?"

"No."

"Then why don't you tell him that?"

"Jay, it's a little more complicated than that. If he believes I am a liar, do you think he'd believe me if I told him I didn't lie to him?"

"I guess not," Jay said dejectedly.

"I have never lied to him. But unfortunately, I didn't tell him the whole truth before he found papers that made it look like I had lied. I should have talked to him about the problems I was having and then he wouldn't have been so surprised when he found the papers. Now it's too late. He'll never believe me again."

"Will he still be my doctor?"

"I hope so. I guess he could refer you to Dr. Halverson."

"I don't want another doctor. I want Dad!"

Jennifer broke down into heaving sobs.

<<<

Things had been pretty somber at Phil's apartment. Bob and Mary gave lots of hugs and encouragement, but all three of them were in the doldrums.

"Phil, have you called anyone on your guest list to tell them the wedding is off?" Mary asked.

"No. I guess I'd better call and cancel the tuxes too."

Bob sat at the kitchen table reading the Salt Lake Tribune. "It says here, there's a Festival of Trees going on until Saturday. Maybe we should go. It might cheer us up."

"Is that possible?" Mary asked.

"To go to the festival?" Bob questioned.

"No. To cheer us up."

"We *are* a pretty sad bunch," Bob admitted.

"Where is it?" Phil asked looking over his dad's shoulder at the paper.

"It says right here it's at the South Towne Center," Bob said.

Phil noticed a picture on the opposite page that looked very familiar… "Braxton!"

"What?" Bob asked.

"Let me see that paper for a minute, Dad."

Phil stared at the caption:

"Man Arrested for Identity Theft and IRS Fraud"

He scanned the rest of the article:

"Thirty-two-year-old male, Braxton Thomas, admits he stole his former girlfriend's identity to purchase credit cards, and filed his

tax returns with false information, claiming the former girlfriend was his wife to get better deductions on his 1040.

Police apprehended Mr. Thomas in his condominium late Monday evening, ending a two-month investigation.

He later confessed to police that he had spent the past year living "high on the hog" at his former girlfriend's expense. Police say he managed to go through half-a-million dollars in that time."

He threw the newspaper across the room. "That idiot!" he screamed. "He's ruined all of our lives!"

"Get hold of yourself, Son. What has gotten into you?" Bob asked.

Phil put his head in his folded arms on the table, and wept.

Mary stood next to him patiently rubbing his back and waiting for him to calm down.

"What is it, Phil? Tell us what you're so upset about," Bob encouraged.

Phil picked the newspaper up from the floor and handed it to his dad. He found the article about Braxton, and said, "Jennifer was engaged to him. Read the article—you can figure it out."

Bob read the article aloud so Mary could hear. When he finished, he set the paper down on the table and stared at Phil.

"Oh, my!" Mary said. "I guess Jennifer wasn't lying to you after all, was she?"

"Apparently not. I can't imagine what she must have been going through with the investigation and all—and then I'm sure I added immeasurable pain these last few days. Oh, Jennifer," he cried out, "and my sweet little Jay. How could I have been so wrong? What can I ever do to make it up to her, Mom?"

"Well, for starters, you might say a little prayer that she'll forgive you. Then you could go to her house on bended knee and *beg* for forgiveness. Chocolate and flowers might help."

Chapter Sixty-One

Jennifer and Jay had managed to finish putting up the Christmas tree in the great room but had done little else to decorate. The skies were gray and flakes of snow were beginning to float down from the skies. She turned the Christmas lights on in the back yard, hoping they would cheer her and Jay up. She had a sense of déjà vu. *Would every holiday season bring a bout of depression with it?*

She was putting the last dish from dinner in the dishwasher when the doorbell rang. "Who in the world can that be?" she asked. She was tired, depressed, and wanted nothing more than to hang out with a movie and big bowl of popcorn. She was definitely not in the mood for visitors.

When she opened the door, Phil stood before her with his hands in his pockets, looking down at his shoes. Her heart pounded. She wanted to slam the door shut before he looked up, but he looked up too quickly. "I suppose you want your tie rack back," she said.

"Jen, may I come in… I have something I need to tell you."

She stepped back allowing him to enter the house, closing the door behind him.

Jay walked around the piano and when he saw Phil, he screamed, "Dad!" Running to Phil, he wrapped his arms around his legs. "I *knew* you'd come home."

She watched Phil lift Jay into his arms and hold him tightly, tears streaming down his cheeks. "I need to talk to your mom for a little bit. Do you suppose you can find something to do in your room while we visit?"

"Promise you won't leave without saying 'goodbye' again?" Jay asked.

"I promise."

"Okay." After Phil set him back on the floor, he slowly walked toward his room.

Tears were so close to the surface, Jennifer couldn't speak. With the sweep of her arm, she motioned Phil into the formal sitting room.

"Jen, I owe you a huge apology. He pulled the newspaper article out of his coat pocket and handed it to her. "I can't believe I didn't trust you enough to believe everything you told me."

She read the article and her emotions took over. As the tears spilled from her eyes, she said, "Where did you get this?"

"It was in the Salt Lake Tribune. Jen, I feel terrible. Will you forgive me?"

Unable to say anything, she just cried. She felt Phil's arms embrace her and she leaned her head against his chest and felt him shake from crying too.

After several minutes, he lifted her face toward his, bent down, and kissed her gently.

"The past three days have been hell for me," he said. "And I wasn't the one being falsely accused. I can only imagine what you must have been going through. Please say you'll forgive me."

"I've missed you," she said. "But I hurt so badly inside knowing I had lost your trust. I should have told you about everything that was happening before you found those papers. I didn't know what was happening myself at first. I thought it was a little mistake that would blow over—certainly nothing I needed to worry you about. Then it turned into something ugly and it was too late—you found the papers from the IRS only minutes after *I* got them.

"I had the police to deal with, and Jay to console—which was nearly impossible, since I needed consoling myself. The thing that made me feel the worst, was knowing I had lost your trust and had no way to gain it back."

"You have it now—completely. I'm sorry for all the grief I have added to your trauma. At the time when you needed me most, I deserted you and left you to deal with it alone. I promise—it won't happen again."

"Where do we go from here?" she asked.

312

"If you'll still have me, I think we have a wedding coming up in a week-and-a-half."

Chapter Sixty-Two

The doorbell rang at ten o'clock in the morning. Jen made her way to the door and was greeted by the florist. "I have a delivery for Jennifer Heaps," the man said.

"I'm Jennifer Heaps."

"Okay, Ma'am. I have seventy poinsettias to bring in. Is it possible to park in your garage while I bring these into the house so they don't get too cold bringing them in? I'd hate to see them all go into temperature shock."

"How many?" Jen asked not believing her ears.

"Seventy—from Phil Henson."

No sooner had he parked the van in the garage, than the doorbell rang again. Phil, Bob, and Mary, were standing expectantly on the porch when Jen opened the door.

"We understand there's work to be done," Mary said with a broad grin on her face.

Jen burst into giggles, as she hugged Mary. "What kind of work did you have in mind?"

"Well, I, heard there's going to be a wedding and the house needs lots of flowers and trees set up." She hesitated for a minute before admitting, "Actually, I couldn't wait any longer to see you and tell you how much I love you. The past four days have been miserable thinking we had lost you!"

With all of them working together, they turned the house into a winter wonderland.

<<<

The "Sisters in Zion" debut was a smashing success. IlaRae's costume was a big hit—especially with the candelabrum on the piano. When Mitzi brought out the birthday candle holder and clipped it on Alice's flute, the audience responded with enjoyment. Then the choir sang IlaRae's rendition of "Deck the flute."

Deck the flute with lamination
Fa-la-la-la-la, la-la-la-la

Watch it burn with fascination
Fa-la-la-la-la, la-la-la-la
See the flautist flame and run,
Fa-la-la-la-la, la-la-la-la
Hurry, quick! call 911
Fa-la-la-la-la, la-la-la-la
Fire Departments on vacation
Fa-la-la-la-la, la-la-la-la
She's a victim of cremation
Fa-la-la-la-la, la-la-la-la
Hire new flautist wearing sandals
Fa-la-la-la-la, la-la-la-la
Light her flute with birthday candles (sung staccato while grinning
at the flautist to imply premeditated mischief)
Fa-la-la-la-la, la-la-la-la

The women in the audience roared with laughter.

Chapter Sixty-Three

The day of the wedding, Mary, Bob, and Tim's wife, Sheila, took the children to the Planetarium to keep them occupied while Phil and Tim helped Jennifer get things ready for the wedding that afternoon. At the last minute, Ruth had decided not to come. Jennifer was neither surprised nor disappointed.

When at last, everything appeared to be in its place, Jennifer sent the men off to Phil's apartment to get cleaned up and dressed.

Alice and IlaRae showed up in time to help Jennifer get into her wedding gown, and IlaRae started to play the piano when the guests began to arrive. Alice answered the door. Jennifer stayed out of sight in the guest bedroom.

<<<

Phil and Jay arrived in their white attire shortly before the rest of the family. Jay ran to greet Emily when she and Tonya walked in. They embraced each other. "I have a present for you for Christmas," he told her.

"What is it?" she asked with excitement.

"Come with me. I'll show you," he said. The two of them ran off to the garage.

Phil assumed the woman with Emily had to be Tonya, so he walked over to her and shook her hand, introduced himself as one of Emily's doctors, and then seated her one chair from the end of a row so Emily could sit by her at the last minute without disturbing the other guests.

Phil began pacing the floor and looking toward the glass patio doors.

"Are you thinking of escaping through those doors?" Bob asked.

"Yes. But I plan to take Jennifer with me, if you were thinking I was planning to stand her up."

"Well, I'm glad you're not going to run out on her. I'd have to disown you, you know. Your mother and I couldn't stand to lose Jennifer and Jay again."

Phil smiled. "Yeah, me too."

Suddenly voices hushed. IlaRae stopped playing the piano. The silence in the room turned into a wave of *oooh's* and *ahhh's* as a white horse-drawn carriage lined with red velvet and draped with green pine boughs pulled up onto the patio outside the great room. The driver was wearing a Santa suit, and Phil rushed out the door to talk to him.

Minutes later, he returned to the house with a satisfied grin on his face. "There," he said to Bob, "Now our ride is here, we can get down to the important stuff. I'll go get Jay and you go fetch me my bride, will you?"

Bob headed off to the guest bedroom, and Phil went to find Jay.

<<<

Jay and Emily were in the garage playing with a puppy. "I told you she'd like it," Jay said to Phil when he entered the garage.

"Jay! Look at yourself; you have paw prints all over your tuxedo."

Jay looked down at his clothes with chagrin. "I'm sorry."

"Put the puppy back in the box until later.

"Emily, you'd better get in by your mother, the wedding is about to begin.

"Come with me, Jay. Let's see what we can do to get you cleaned up."

Phil took Jay into the bathroom by his bedroom and began to sponge off the tux. It wasn't perfect, but most of the spots came out.

They were joining the crowd gathered in the great room when IlaRae gave them the signal that she was about to begin the wedding march. Phil and Jay walked up in front of the gathering and stood by Bishop Bowen. Jay carried the little pillow with the rings tied to it. Jennifer had sewn some elastic loops on the bottom for him to slip his hand through so he could hold it.

318

The march began.

The guests stood.

Phil watched as Jennifer, holding Bob's arm, walked slowly down the aisle between the chairs, and took her place at his side. Her eyes met his and he knew this was the beginning of forever.

<<<

When the reception was over, Phil swooped her into his arms and carried her to the carriage on the patio. He set her on the seat, wrapped a red velvet robe about her shoulders, and climbed in beside her.

As the carriage began to roll away, Jay was waving both arms wildly. "We're all Hensons *now!*" he called out.

Reading Group Questions

And Topics for Discussion

1. This story is a series of reactions to circumstances caused by decisions made by other people. What was the first decision that started this entire trail of events? How do your decisions affect others? Do we always know what affect our decisions make in the lives of others? What decisions do others make that impact your life?

2. Jennifer was hurt by Braxton and her reaction was to build a wall around herself to protect her from repeating the same situation again. What was the result of her reaction? What could she have done differently and what would the possible outcome have been? Where didn't she create a wall, and how did that impact her and others?

3. Jay went through a battery of emotions in his healing process. What events discouraged him and what encouraged him? What were his coping mechanisms? What are your coping mechanisms when overcoming hardships? How did humor help?

4. Jennifer made the decision to end the relationship with Phil because of her commitment to her religious beliefs. Do you think this was a selfish decision?

5. How did Phil's relationship with his family impact him? How did they affect Jay?

6. Which character would you like to emulate? Why?

7. Which character do you identify most with? Why?

About the Author

Coleen Mattingly Bay and her sweetheart, David are empty-nesters, after raising nine children, all girls except seven. Coleen has always loved writing from the time she was in grade school and won first place in the State-wide "Reflections" writing contest in high school. She attended Weber State University, where she studied English and creative writing. She has had articles published in the Ensign magazine and in the Salt Lake Tribune.

She began writing full-length books in earnest when she wrote life histories (her own and her mother's.) This was followed by a vigorous study of bookbinding. With the help of her husband, they hardbound the life histories for their posterity. She has authored *Silent World; Moving a Desk;* and *Life in the Trenches* in addition to *The Least.*

She and her husband reside in Brigham City, Utah in a home of continuous remodeling.

She volunteered on the Foster Care Citizens Review Board for two years and enjoys reading, writing, laughing at herself, and playing Pinochle.

You can email Coleen at baybuzz@yahoo.com